The
Garden
Club

The Garden Club

• • •

MURIEL RESNIK JACKSON

ST. MARTIN'S PRESS

New York

This novel is a work of fiction. The names, dialogue, and plot are products of the author's imagination or are used fictitiously. Any resemblance to actual persons, places, or events is purely coincidental.

Design by Judith A. Stagnitto

Library of Congress Cataloging-in-Publication Data
Jackson, Muriel Resnik.
      The garden club / Muriel Resnik Jackson.
          p. cm.
      "A Thomas Dunne book."
      ISBN 0-312-08196-0
      I. Title.
    PS3568.E7G37   1992
    813'.54—dc20   92-24155
                                                  CIP

First Edition: October 1992

10 9 8 7 6 5 4 3 2 1

Chapter 1

♦

♦ Everyone said Miss Emily's funeral was exactly the way Miss Emily would have wanted it. Jim Willis, eighty-two, and a pallbearer according to Miss Emily's will (he was said to have been courting her for years), fainted under the burden, and the coffin came crashing to the floor. That was on the way out, after young Mark's standard no-frills service. He tried to say something nice about Miss Emily, but settled for "much loved," sticking to The Book, and a stern glance at his parishioners to prevent any snickering.

Before Jim Willis fainted, the Joneses—Ruby, Towbin, Eldridge, Madison, and the twins—crowded into the pew the Davises liked to think of as their own. That was because the Jones boys, Towbin and Eldridge, were leading the way and hadn't noticed that the Davises—Taylor, Rose, Fanny, Styron, and Duncan—were already seated at the other end. Everyone in the church turned to see what would happen, as the Joneses and the Davises hadn't spoken since Smith Davis had got Effie Jones, now Davis, into trouble. That child, Jones Davis, was now sixteen and struggling with adolescence. Or as they say here, climbing Fools' Hill. Effie was there too, of course, sitting under the Davis stained-glass window.

All the black Davises were there and the black Duncans and

the black Joneses too. There's no race problem here as they're all kin. Grandpappy jumped the fence one night, the families liked to say. Well, from the looks of that crowd in the church, their grandpappies liked jumping so much they just kept on with it. And that's only the black Episcopalians. Most of Davis Landing's blacks are Baptists. They have their own church, which is the way all the Baptists, black and white, prefer it. Sitting listening to "Amazing Grace" rendered by a thin choir of thin seventy- and eighty-year-old voices (Miss Emily had specified only old Davis Landing singing over her, none of those new people), it was not for the first time I speculated as to how an extraordinarily healthy woman— never sick a day in her life other than a mild cold—a straight, fierce woman who could sit on her thick black hair, had all her own teeth, could read without glasses, and had lived in the house directly opposite mine for all the seventy-two years of her life—had managed to sprain her ankle on her way to the commode one night. She should have known where it was by then; yes, old people do fall a lot, but no one ever thought of Miss Emily as an old person. She was too vigorous and fierce and filled with malicious energy.

And then, after a week in bed with the ankle packed in ice and wrapped in an Ace bandage by Sammy Jo, her devoted younger half-sister, to die? Nobody dies from a sprained ankle! Not even in Davis Landing where the phones don't work if it rains, and the only fresh vegetable is collard greens. And according to Sammy Jo, to die writhing in pain? "It was terrible . . . just terrible," she said, between murmurs of "So good of you to come" to all the kin, and Warren and me. It just wasn't possible.

Miss Emily could have lived on to be a hundred, still running the town. And there wasn't a damn thing wrong with her except that ankle. I brought her some of my brownies just the day before, and she was trying out crutches to get around. Because, as she said, "There's too much here to be set right and no one but me to do it, and I'm not going to lie around this house while those trashy Tryons are selling moonshine not two miles from my nose! I've got to give Sam Pollock [chief of police] a piece of my mind again! And someone broke the chain fence around the school yard—Dubie's engine was taken out of his boat—I *can't* stay here!" And with that, she threw her crutch across the room like a javelin and broke one of her own mother's favorite cut-glass vases.

All her life, Miss Emily was known for her temper and was a troublemaker, I was told, with a fondness for stirring things up. She was mean and vindictive, stingy and autocratic, with her own brand of humor. She read Aristotle and Plato for diversion, as well as the Bible (and found the people in the Old Testament hilarious), and she could quote Shakespeare by the yard. She ran the town, and if anyone dared to cross her they'd better move on somewhere else. She chose the mayor. Well, of course, he was elected in a democratic process, but the local politicians always checked with Miss Emily to get her thoughts on prospective candidates before the names were mentioned above a whisper. She chose the new preacher and saw that he was got rid of if he didn't live up to her expectations. He *or* his wife. She'd run the Altar Guild for years. No one in Davis Landing liked her but me. Well, let's just say she had no real friends, and I'm including her court of mealy-mouthed, ever-smiling local ladies who came to call. They paid homage with flowers from their gardens and fresh baked cookies or a jar of pickled okra; they'd compliment her on the new dress Sammy Jo had sewn her. But before they even got themselves down the porch stairs they were exchanging glances, and once they were out of hearing they proceeded to do an enthusiastic hatchet job on her in that sweet, devious, southern way they have.

Miss Emily had liked Warren and me. Well, she liked Warren. She called him "that nice boy across the street." I think it tickled him, though it's hard to tell with Warren. I don't know if she ever really liked me. She tolerated me because I could make her laugh, and I think she found me interesting. A career woman. A *real* career woman. Girls growing up in Davis Landing knew they had a choice of being a teacher, a nurse, or working in a bank, but it was understood by everyone that they were just marking time until marriage. Or it was that way until the two-income family became a necessity. Now the goal is still marriage, but they go on working. The girls in the bank are *gorgeous*. Anywhere else they'd be models, actresses, dancers, or they'd break up marriages. They'd end up rich. But down here they all know they'd just better marry as well as they can, or at least someone with a good steady job and a chance for promotion. I never thought that much about geography in the short time I was in school, but it can really make a difference.

With Miss Emily safely interred in the Davis family plot in the old cemetery (listed on the National Register of Historic Places, what with the British soldier buried facing England in a standing salute to King George, and the little girl who sickened and died on the long voyage to a new country and was preserved in a keg of whiskey because her mama didn't want her to be alone in the cold, dark waters), everyone went back to Miss Emily's house for refreshments. Sammy Jo had done herself proud with the Davis cutwork linen cloth and the Fuller silver, the house scrubbed and the furniture polished, and the windows and mirrors gleaming. Miss Emily couldn't have passed on at a better time because Sammy Jo had been getting the house in perfect order and had had her hair permed at Miss Ophelia's for the ladies' annual New Year's Day nonalcoholic, made-from-scratch eggnog party.

The house really looked lovely with the Christmas candles lit in every window, the stairs festooned with garlands of pine and cedar, and huge bunches of mistletoe hanging in every doorway. Sammy Jo always went out to shoot down her mistletoe and hang it all over the house. (Sammy Jo was known to be one of the best shots in the county though she certainly didn't look it.) Some said it was to stir up her two rival suitors—Dr. Wilson and Judge Jones—into kissing her. There were others who were not so kind, referring to Sammy Jo's allegedly lurid, allegedly secret past and her shooting skills, which she was rumored to have learned from the trashy Tryons with whom she was allegedly closer than no decent person should be.

The table was covered with bowls of sweet potatoes in every form the South had ever dreamed of and a country ham and platters of fried chicken and mashed-potato salad and spoon bread and biscuits and all sorts of pickles and preserves and jellied salads with marshmallows in them and cakes and pies and cookies and pitchers of iced tea. There was a lot of murmuring about Sammy Jo's putting on airs and how she would just go wild now that Miss Emily was no longer there. Some people said she'd been devoted to Miss Emily all her life. Others whispered that she would have gotten rid of her long ago if she could have. (Davis Landing, like most small communities, is hard put to find a kind word for anyone.) I was listening to the murmurs and looking at Sammy Jo, who everyone knew had just turned fifty-seven—down here after they say hello they tell you their maiden name and their age—and remembering the ferocious look on her face as she knelt to clean up the broken glass and the flowers and the water after Miss Emily's crutch/javelin throw that day. I knelt to help her, but Miss Emily shouted at me, "You get up, Merrie Lee! Let her do it! Keep her busy!" And Sammy Jo's quiet response, "Thank you just the same," with her normal sweet, meek expression. I've often wondered what this town had against her.

For the funeral feast I brought some hot-and-sour Yankee pickles and my brownies. Davis Landing has gone quite mad about my brownies. Well, they're not really *my* brownies. It's a Connecticut (damyankee) recipe I got from my first husband's Aunt Rose, modified by Katherine Hepburn, who told me she had cut the flour from a heaping third of a cup to just barely a spoonful and urged me to try it her way, which I did, and have never gone back to the heaping third. Her way they're kissing cousins to chocolate truffles.

As I'd been married hastily in my early teens and was a mother before I could turn around, I hadn't had a chance to learn much about cooking or housework. I guess the groom's

Aunt Rose thought we could survive on the brownies, especially as you only use one pot.

You take a pot and throw everything into it—a cup of sugar, a stick of butter, and three squares of baking chocolate. Unsweetened, that is. Melt them all together. And while that's melting, you beat three eggs thoroughly, chop about a cupful of nuts, grease a brownie pan, and turn on the oven to 350. Then you fold the chocolate stuff into the eggs, throw in a third of a cup of flour (Aunt Rose's) or a tablespoon (Katherine Hepburn's), a teaspoon of vanilla and the nuts, pour it into the pan, and bake for about half an hour. Couldn't be simpler, and only the one pot to wash. I've never given it to any of these people down here in case I have to sell them. . . . If you really want to be decadent (Aunt Rose), you frost them, which is like gilding the lily. You could melt a square of unsweetened chocolate and a piece of butter the size of a walnut, add about a cup of confectioner's sugar, and mix. Then add a tablespoon or so of milk until it's spreadable and frost your brownies while they're still warm.

I *could* sell them here. And my English muffin loaf. But that's for when we really hit bottom. We can save almost all of any income that dribbles our way if we keep living here, where you don't need clothes, there's no theater, no movie, no place to go, no one entertains—and we've both stopped drinking. What's the point of feeling good if you're going to watch reruns of "Lassie" with Roddy MacDowall as a child? We're steadily pulling ourselves out of debt, which is very fine except my mind is turning to polenta.

But to get back to the funeral reception. Everyone was close to OD-ing on sweet potatoes spread all over Miss Emily's great-grandmother's beautiful Haviland china, and talking about the weather, which is de rigueur down here. It's safe and there's always something to say, our weather being extremely volatile. The locals like to say, If you don't like the weather just wait twenty minutes . . . everything from drought to floods, snow, hail, tornadoes, water spouts, and hurricanes. All agreed that it was very warm for Christmas, but there were many present who could remember warmer, when everyone went swimming Christmas afternoon. I sipped iced tea, waiting for *someone* to mention the shock of Miss Emily's death. To say at least that it was strange. But no, they segued right from Christmas swimming to the night the *Chrissie Wright* came ashore a hundred years ago. And they all stood there scarfing up calories and telling each other the same story they'd all known since childhood: How the *Chrissie Wright* blew on to the shoals in a blizzard and those poor people tried to build a fire so they wouldn't freeze, and they waved the ladies' petticoats for boats to come out and rescue them, but none of the local people, fishermen all, could get their boats launched against that terrible wind, and by the next morning all the passengers were dead—frozen stiff—including women and children.

When they finally finished with the weather, they got to the next topic, the church decorations: the yards of pine and cedar garlands the Garden Club had woven and hung on all the pews and the wonderful work the Altar Guild had done with Hattie Jones's Christmas roses and everyone stripping their yards of paper whites. And still no one had said a word about the deceased and how sudden it was and what *caused* it. The only mention of Miss Emily was the Garden Club decorations and that she would have approved. Or, as they were saying, *even* Miss Emily would have approved.

Miss Emily ran the Garden Club as she ran everything else in town—with a firm hand. She'd been president for as long as anyone could remember. Elections were held every four years, but Miss Emily refused to step down and poor Eulalee Merrill, who had been rightfully elected several times, and was certainly next in line for the top post, just went on being vice-president year after year without a word of complaint. But everyone said Eulalee was a saint. Putting up with Bubba, for one thing; Bubba Lee, that brother of hers. He was odd and that was about the best thing you could say about him. He hung out with the trashy Tryons and he'd been odd since he'd been a child. Never looked you in the eye. Getting stranger all the time. People said sometimes he lived in Eulalee's big black van instead of in the house. Sometimes people didn't see him for months and assumed Eulalee had him chained in the sewing room because he'd been bad again. Not anything really serious. Breaking and entering to take a can of beer and a pack of cigarettes. Simple-minded stuff. Getting his limit during the hunting season and then killing five or six more deer, or twenty more ducks, and offering them around the neighborhood as gifts. Sam Pollock, the chief of police, would bring him to his sister and she'd chain him in the sewing room.

Sometimes you'd see him on the side of the road weaving garlands of wildflowers to hang on people's doors, a tuft of white hair hanging in his eyes. . . . Not exactly the village idiot; a simple, generally kind soul. He'd actually had a driver's license before they revoked it for DWI twice, and he'd been through ninth grade. I'd never met him but I thought of him sort of as Heathcliff when he and Katherine were young. You could never ask Eulalee about him—if you ever wanted to— because she would just look away and tremble her lips.

Bubba was Eulalee's cross to bear and everyone agreed she was a living saint. But you only had to look at that patient face under the messy cloud of white hair to know that. The soft voice, the faded blue eyes. You didn't have to know about her work with Meals on Wheels and the church, calling on the sick, clothing and feeding the poor, always the first with the casseroles. Mark, our minister, said he didn't know what he'd ever do without Eulalee. And putting up with Bubba's strangeness and trying to help him. She said since their parents were gone Bubba was her responsibility. Mark said he prayed with her over Bubba: Bubba and the health of the community. She worked constantly to get Davis Landing people to learn healthy eating habits. Eulalee was a vegetarian herself but she didn't insist on other people's giving up meat. Just fats, sugar, salt, red meat, Twinkies, Moon Pies, and fried food. She even gave people little pots of herbs and Texas Pete hot sauce to use for seasoning instead of salt, but the herbs withered and died in most kitchens.

Anyway, Miss Emily's wake was just another in the round of Christmas festivities. No one even mentioned her. I had been watching Dr. Wilson circling the food table. He was now buttering the latest batch of hot biscuits with all the ladies hovering and urging him unnecessarily to "take two and butter 'em while they're hot" and slicing a bit more of the country ham with his surgeon's skill. Waiting until he'd arranged the ham slices on his plate and added some watermelon pickle and peach preserves beside the biscuits, I eased to his side. Dr. Wilson was the sexiest seventy-year-old I'd seen since old Henry Sell passed on. Henry was at one time or another editor of *Vanity Fair, Harper's Bazaar,* and *Town & Country. The New Yorker* had published a three-part profile of him. He was a direct descendant of Buffalo Bill or Wild Bill Hickock, one of those boys, and the consummate snob. I adored lunching with him and hearing his stories of how Elizabeth Arden got started and of New York in the thirties. The Great Depression. He said there were all the beautiful young creatures with the wonderful wardrobes and expensive tastes who suddenly found themselves unable to afford to go anywhere and literally starving, and the clubs they could no longer patronize empty. So he started a service and put them together. Said it worked very well, dressed up places like the Rainbow Room and gave the kids at least one decent meal a day. It might be time to start it up again. Dr. Wilson had the same white hair and the same sexy blue eyes as Henry Sell. They both looked at you and instantly recognized your potential in bed and I was sure, as I had been with Henry Sell, that he could still pleasure a woman.

Dr. Wilson had decided to munch on one of my brownies as a palate cleanser when I arrived at his side. He favored me with a pulse-raising blue twinkle. I actually had a small frisson, but I just said something pointless about how suddenly Miss Emily had left us. He swallowed the brownie, smiling at me, and allowed as how her time had come. I said she'd been lying there the day before, getting herself into a perfect snit (I've picked up some of these expressions and often, to my dismay, when I hear myself talk you can't tell me from a southerner) because her ankle was keeping her confined even though she was just as strong and healthy as ever, and people don't die of a sprained ankle.

He twinkled down at me and said at seventy-two we must assume the Lord had called her to him. I reminded him that Miss Emily had been a *young*, vigorous seventy-two and nowhere near ready to go. I allowed that the Lord might have a real problem there as we all knew that if Miss Emily didn't want to do something she didn't do it. I said I would have thought they'd do a postmortem and find out what actually took her. That was when his eyes cooled, the room hushed, and Sammy Jo appeared at my side with a soft rustle of her skirt. "Merrie Lee," she explained to Dr. Wilson, "is a Yankee." Like only Yankees have postmortems? And I wish they'd stop using both my names. My name is Merrie. Period. I only use the Lee when I'm signing contracts. It had been explained to me that down here everyone has two names, as southerners don't feel right about just one, but I don't feel right with two.

I persisted. "But what killed her?" I insisted. "What exactly did she die of?" Sarah Taylor Millet appeared at my side being protective and muttering, "Let it drop . . . Forget it . . ." Everyone was looking at me. Hostile looks. Dr. Wilson never answered, and everyone got on where the Garden Club's next bus trip would be going. Pretending I had never mentioned postmortems. The bus trip was always in May. This was still December. It wasn't exactly an urgent matter. More of an out than an outing. They were reminding each other it had to be a day trip somewhere and they'd already been all over the area within the distance of day trips and Miss Emily had always decided the destination. . . .

Of course I knew what Sammy Jo meant. She meant that I didn't mind my own business. That I was too outspoken. I didn't pussyfoot around and approach from an oblique angle. I came directly to it in my rude Yankee way. And I had to know why Miss Emily, a woman in perfect health, had died.

Writhing in pain. She had had a checkup just the month before and proudly announced that she had the heart, lungs, blood pressure, and cholesterol of a twenty-year-old, which she claimed to be due to clean living and a pure heart. Everyone said it was more like sheer mean-spiritedness that kept Miss Emily going. But she was extraordinarily healthy and had expected to live to at least a hundred like her mother and grandmother before her. I was just trying to find out what killed her. In my rude Yankee way.

I knew the Garden Club trip was just a smoke screen. I knew all about the importance of the day trip because I'd been a member practically since I'd stepped out of the BMW, exhausted after a twelve-hour drive, and put the key in the door of the old Davis house. The ladies arrived while I was still getting Jackie and Mathilda (my dogs) a bowl of water and before I'd even had a chance to find the bathroom. I don't know what it is down here—maybe jungle drums. They arrived with casseroles—my God, what a variety of sweet potatoes—welcoming me home—that was sweet—and said the Garden Club met the first Wednesday of the month and they hoped I'd attend meetings regularly. Especially because my grandmother Lavinia had founded their club in sixteen hundred something to save and exchange seeds and plants before garden clubs existed.

Chapter 2

◆

◆ I was part of Davis Landing before I arrived as a refugee from Manhattan after the 1987 crash to take shelter in Grandmother Lavinia Davis's house, which nobody in the family wanted. And why should they? It's a wreck. Oh, I suppose I'm kin to Miss Emily in a way because my Grandmother Lavinia, that is my great great whatever, was second cousin once removed to Miss Emily's great great whatever.

Warren and I are not exactly yuppies. That is, in age. We've both had children with other people and I am an incredibly young grandmother. But while we were in hog heaven along with the rest of Wall Street, we did manage to collect a few yuppie toys, among which were a forty-five-foot sloop, the *Merrily* (the love of my life), a really nice duplex penthouse in one of the best Park Avenue co-ops, a leased BMW, and the beginnings of an art collection. The normal yuppie mementos.

I loved the penthouse. I loved living in it, hosting European and West Coast house guests, and I loved working in the gardens. Roses on all four terraces. Antique, fragrant tea roses, and floribundas, roses climbing on arbors; wisteria and herbs, grapes, tomatos, a Paul Scarlett hawthorne, two flowering crabapples, and masses of bulbs—spring, summer, and winter. There was always something going on there.

My husband, the Stockbroker, enjoyed it because there were no close neighbors. He hails from the Dakotas originally, where his family had ranches until things went bad. How often have I heard his story of herding sheep when he was a boy? Nobody out there but him and the sheep and the horse and the dog. And then you'd see another rider on the horizon and stand in your stirrups and wave your hat and wave and wave and THEN . . . he'd see you and stand in his stirrups and wave back! *That* was communication, he'd tell me, during my frequent complaints about his lack of it. What do I have to do, get a horse to sit on so he'll *notice* me?

Anyway, I had this inspiration. New York rents were climbing to astronomical heights; we had an agreement with our co-op board that we could rent to approved people for a limited time. One year and then they were to be reviewed, and if they'd behaved they could stay another year. So why not rent our penthouse for a couple of months and go down to Davis Landing? Might be fun. Wall Street was in the doldrums, people were getting nervous and getting out, brokers were looking for something (anything) else to do, and I'd just accepted (reluctantly) early retirement at my advertising agency (they axed all the senior vice-presidents with the perks when we were taken over by smartass Brits); it would give us enough time to think and regroup, and most important, *cash flow!* Warren had already been the route of the head hunters and there wasn't much out there for a talented tennis player/ stockbroker/sheepherder edging past fifty, and he'd wanted to write a novel ever since I'd known him—said it was all in his head. What better place than Davis Landing? Of course I hadn't known then about the phones and what rain could do to them. Or that you had to import your garlic if you wanted to cook anything other than grits.

We did take the precaution of asking a local realtor to take a look at Lavinia's house to see if it was livable. He said he reckoned you could say that. You'll have some fixin' up to do, he said, and I said my husband was very handy. We arranged to have the water and electricity and telephone turned on and waited for a tenant for the penthouse. That's when we found out that there was no such thing as a short lease. Not with the sort of people who could afford the rent we needed to cover our mortgage *and* support us down here. So we rented for a year to some Brits with impeccable references, two angelic little boys who had been attending the nursery school Princess Diana had taught at, and a starchy nanny, and considered ourselves lucky. Cash flow!

Down here you can live well at the poverty level and no one even notices because everyone else is doing it too. When I say live well, you understand, it's relative. If there isn't a decent restaurant within miles and your social center is the Piggly Wiggly supermarket, you really don't *need* clothes. The tab for dinner at Le Cirque would feed and house a Davis Landing family of four for two months.

While we were sorting our clothes for packing, we got a letter from down here written on lined paper from some people we'd never heard of. Estabelle and Sonny. They said they'd been at the town hall paying their water bill and they heard that our water bill had not been paid (we'd never received one) and Erskine was about to turn off the water, which would have ruined our furnace and pipes. The furnace had been turned on by the kindly realtor to take the damp out of the walls. So they paid it and enclosed our bill stamped PAID. I just cried. (I was always very close to tears at that time at the thought of leaving my friends, my life, everything familiar, and New York. I loved New York with the passion of someone who is not a native.) But I mean where else today would you find some stranger paying your water bill for you, I said. It's Shangri-la, I told Warren.

"Have a drink."

"That is the dearest—"

"Merrie," he said, "go wash your face."

"We must have made the right decision. All those good people down there—"

"Here," he said, giving me a Scotch with a kiss on the cheek. "Pull yourself together."

So we resigned from the health club, the yacht club, and the country club; sold the *Merrily* for what we could get; said a very tearful farewell to Dolores, our Basque housekeeper for the last eleven years; took our two little Australian terriers; and left. To be precise, we left the furniture and the books (the Brits didn't want all those empty shelves) and the art. The Stockbroker drove his big old Ford pickup with the gun rack and the things that hang from the dashboard for his beer cans, his computer and all his software, his hats and guns, his Savile Row suits and Turnbull & Asser shirts and ties, his cashmere cable-knit sweaters and his Burberry trench coat and his Lobb shoes. I had my hair cut and colored, and a manicure and a pedicure, for the last time in the luxury and comfort of Kenneth's townhouse.

Mary Farr, who's been doing my hair since we were all wearing miniskirts the first time around, is originally from Columbia, South Carolina. She assured me I'd *hate* the South and I wouldn't stay there two minutes. I told her Davis Landing was different. I had some misgivings myself, but for a year it could be an adventure. This is what I had told Warren, and kept trying to convince myself of, as I drove the BMW, which was four years old and about to run out of its lease; and we headed south, a place I was accustomed to flying over on my way to winter vacations in the islands or houseguesting in Palm Beach.

I had been down here once when some relative died and the house came into our branch of the family and we all wanted to see what it was about; but that was a long time ago. I was a child then and my memory of it was a blur of small white houses with double verandas on a waterfront and lots of fishing boats along the main street. I didn't need the road signs to tell me I was finally emerging from Virginia (my God, that's a big state) into the real South. The car radio told me. Lots of hellfire preachers, although it wasn't Sunday, and some bizarre little swap shows: one previously owned studio couch to swap for a previously owned rowing machine and a previously owned size-sixteen wedding dress. That sort of thing.

And the farther we drove, the more I was made aware of God. Specifically Jesus. Or as He is known down here, His Son. Billboards advertised him. Bumper stickers: IF YOU KNOW JESUS HONK. JESUS PAID IT ALL. JESUS LOVES YOU. Everywhere you looked. On cars and trucks. IF GOD IS NOT A TARHEEL THEN WHY IS THE SKY CAROLINA BLUE? As a recently retired copywriter, I liked that one and wondered who had the God account. We were driving in a sort of convoy with pit stops for fuel, food, and restrooms. When we met at a MacDonald's—yes, the rest rooms *were* clean but the locks on the booth doors were broken and the only way to dry your hands was with those air blowers which lead to chapping—I asked the Stockbroker if this was the Bible Belt, and he said it was.

He knew more about these things than I did. I was raised without religion except at times of christenings, marriages, and funerals. He had a Norwegian mother who dragged him to any and all Lutheran goings-on. Not only church service on Sunday, but Sunday school, Friday night vespers, Wednesdays, Saturdays, all leading to his deep-rooted antipathy to any formal religion. We had no problem on that score. We just weren't religious. Although I remember one night at Elaine's—it was jammed with celebrities all shouting and table-hopping and making deals—when the Stockbroker entertained his Uncle Leon, a rancher from Montana who arrived in town unexpectedly with a bus load of Seventh-Day Adventists on an excursion to view the fall foliage in New England. Uncle Leon was a small man in a knitted cardigan, wearing a shirt with a tight, high collar and one of those shoe strings around his neck with an Indian silver slide and an extremely narrow-brimmed hat sitting high on his head. It was a brown cloth hat with a jaunty little green feather in the band. I had plenty of time to observe the hat during dinner as he never removed it. Warren asked him if he wouldn't like to, but he said he wouldn't. After Leon's first shock at finding himself about to eat *Eyetalian* food, neither of them paid any attention to me as they argued about the Garden of Eden and the casting out of its original occupants as if it had happened yesterday to people they knew well. I realized then that Warren would probably always remain a mystery to me.

Now you have to understand that Davis Landing is a typical small American town of three thousand inhabitants that happens to be in the South. There's a church on every corner and a flag outside every house except ours. Some houses fly the Confederate flag. Most people observe Confederate Independence Day in May along with the federal holiday on the fourth of July. Nobody locks their doors and many people leave the motor running when they stop at the post office or the bank. Cars stop to let pedestrians cross, and traffic is, to say the least, leisurely. Dogs sleep in the middle of the street without concern, born with the knowledge that people will drive around them. The shrimp boats go out every night and the natives speak a unique dialect, which is part Elizabethan English with an overlay of cockney mixed with a southern drawl. It is said that when the first settlers, English boat builders and fishermen, made their crossing in the seventeenth century, they stopped at the first land their boats hit, dragged the boats ashore, and built their houses right there vowing never to try *that* again. This land was an island and travel was by boat. Until the Roosevelt era when the WPA built the bridge to the mainland. Many of the islanders came down to the shore with their guns to protect their land and their privacy (this must be where the National Rifle Association started), but the Army and the Coast Guard arrived and there were more of them and their guns were bigger. People move slowly because there's nothing to hurry for. They speak slowly too. Our lawyer down here says he talks slow but he thinks fast. I wonder about the rest of them.

People take time for the manners and niceties of another era. They wave "hi" from their cars. When we meet on my morning dog walk everyone says "Good Moanin'." Sometimes they add "Howya doin'?" Mostly they say it's hot or it's cold or it's windy or the no seeums are really bitin' this moanin'. I am very careful to say good moanin' back and have made a diligent effort to drop all my *g*'s. This was a place I wanted to be a part of. At least for the length of our stay, primarily because it would be more comfortable to be part of it than an outsider. Of course, I had old Lavinia Davis going for me, but our family had been away for so long that she almost didn't count.

Not that this is all gentle sweetness and charm here. When I first arrived, it was the year when I was living in black Spandex tights and big sweaters and really good boots. It was a terrific look, easy to pack, you could ring all sorts of changes with different tops; I have good legs and, in fact, I didn't have much else in my closet. Our first day was really lovely with a nice breeze from the water, and after unpacking most of the things we'd brought with us, I washed my face, leashed up the dogs, and we went out to take a look at the waterfront. I was wearing black tights stuck into boots, and a huge black sweater almost to my knees. Strolling on the boardwalk I encountered two gray-haired ladies in black coats and sensible black oxfords wearing what appeared to be plastic bags on their heads. As we drew closer I saw they were indeed plastic bags. And as I continued to walk toward them they stopped, eyeing me from head to toe.

Smiling pleasantly, I said hello. They didn't notice the smile or hear the greeting. They stared. One said to the other, "There she walks in all her nakedness." I looked around. There was no one else. They walked on. My God, I thought, they're going to run us out of town on a rail before we've even had a chance to buy groceries. I raced back to the house and changed into an ancient pair of gray flannel slacks I'd brought down for painting or gardening, jumped into the car, drove to the nearest Rose's (glorified five-and-dime, like Lamston's), and bought myself several sets of sweats. In which I've lived ever since. Sweats for the winter, jeans for summer. It's not easy to be a southerner.

In the beginning, Warren protested (on rare occasions) that I didn't wear anything but those awful things and what happened to my pearls. My lack of makeup was never mentioned because he doesn't look at me that closely. The lack of pearls struck a note because he'd given them to me at various times. Birthdays, anniversaries, Christmas, Valentine's Day the year he'd peaked. I had masses of them and they were gorgeous, but pearls with sweats? Anyway, there was nothing, nowhere, and no one to dress for. The men in this town, old and young but mostly old, look at me like farmers looking at a cow after they've sold the farm: without interest or regret. I was beginning to feel less of a woman although I am a tall, slim blond (getting blonder by the minute) with regular features. I'm slim and I've been careful about keeping my shape. I mean, I'm not Ava Gardner at her best, but on the streets of New York, Paris, Rome, London, I'm worth a second look, a smile, a wink, a murmured compliment, a touch of the chapeau. Down here I've got one of the few waistlines in town, but I might just as well be a piece of old mooring line. And I miss talking to a man who appreciates women. I like to flirt and I miss it.

We've been here almost five years now though it seems like fifty. After the crash of 1987 came the tumble of Drexel Burnham Lambert and our original tenants returned to London poorer, perhaps wiser. We still hadn't paid off all of our yuppie debts and couldn't hang on to the New York place without renting it, nor could we live down here without that income. Or anywhere for that matter. New York rents were no longer astronomical, becoming almost reasonable due to all the Drexel Burnham people abandoning their leases and their townhouses. It was now a buyers' market, we were told. Our broker said we were lucky to get the Japanese couple. They adored the place. But the gardens . . . She kept asking in a tiny, high, sweet voice if I didn't like rocks? Rocks?

Big rocks, little rocks?

Ah, yes. A Zen garden.

I suggested she find a place for the rocks—there was plenty of space—and please water my plants when necessary. The new rent was a third less than we'd grown accustomed to, meaning we'd be southerners a lot longer than we'd planned. But the co-op board approved, thank God, we put a three-month cancellation clause in the new lease, and we lingered in Davis Landing. In fact, we became residents of the state, changed the licenses on the car and truck, and voted here. Democrat. As Miss Emily had told us, "We're all registered Democrats here, but we haven't voted that way for years!"

And we adjusted. The rest of my family was kind enough (and rich enough) to say that since we'd been making so many improvements, and Warren had been working so hard on the house, that we might as well have it in our name. And we were able to pay off the BMW lease by selling one of my pearl necklaces. Warren objected, but we had to do something. Either pay it off or refinance, and the rates were godawful. I told him I could do it because I knew he'd be buying me more pearls any day now. Warren is very clever and when he wasn't repairing the house he was working on possible investments at his computer as well as at his novel. He'd make it back. I told him not to forget he owed me thirty inches of ten and a half millimeter pearls. So it was all neat and tidy. And there was a certain comfort in paying off debts and living within one's income.

Davis Landing is a friendly place and we were accepted. Warren was immediately. As soon as he slung his shotgun in the gun rack and put on his old Stetson (the filthy one with the band of sweat and the holes, coveted by every waiter/actor in New York), jeans, and broken boat shoes. They did find the dogs curious. The Davis Landing dog is a black Lab and the only variation is two black Labs. I was known not by name, but as the lady with the two little dogs.

Even before we moved into the house the parade of casseroles started. I didn't know then that it's a southern custom. If Miss Emily had sprained her ankle *then*, I would have known instead of acting like a foreigner and saying dumb things like "You shouldn't have" and "Oh, but I couldn't't"— dumb damyankee things—instead of "Thank you so much, won't you come in and have some tea." When Miss Emily was down with her ankle, as soon as one car moved off the next one would pull up. And always the ancient drivers would emerge from their cars holding their casseroles carefully and climb the porch steps to pay their respects. When I brought her my own offering of the famous damyankee brownies I asked her what they were going to do with all that food, just the two of them. She said the refrigerator was full and the freezer was full and she just didn't know what she was going to do with all those sweet potato pies and sweet potato biscuits and just plain sweet potato casseroles. Maybe give them to the church. She said she never had liked sweet things. Always preferred pickles. Sour and hot like me, she said, without smiling.

I developed a genuine affection for Miss Emily, and so did Warren. No one else in Davis Landing seemed to like her. Except Jim Willis (the pallbearer who fainted), and he hardly counted. No one was sure at eighty-two what state his mind was in. And Sammy Jo—her attitude was more dutiful than loving. And I never forgot that look that flickered over Sammy Jo's face when Miss Emily broke her mother's cut-glass vase. There certainly was no love there, or even liking. Sammy Jo's usual attitude was that of a curator for a national treasure. She seemed to be awed, to feel privileged to live in the same house and wait on Miss Emily hand and foot, to shampoo that luxuriant hair and brush it dry in the sun, to clean up the kitchen after one of Miss Emily's cooking bouts—or temper bouts.

Did I tell you that Sammy Jo was a beauty? The whitest, palest woman I've ever seen. With her blond hair going white, eyes liquid and pale as water, skin exquisitely white and wrinkle-free, and the carriage of a ballet dancer, she had an aura of magic and mystery. Probably because she rarely spoke. Slim and graceful, with long, slender legs and arms and small, high breasts, she had the body of a girl; she was a head turner. At fifty-seven she looked thirty-five. Drifting like a slender ghost in her soft, white dresses, head high, she seemed unreal, enhanced by her silence. She had a way of looking at a man, gazing into his eyes, then lowering hers and looking away, and slowly raising her eyes to his again, the corners of her soft pink mouth curling in a Mona Lisa smile. . . . I practiced that look in front of the bathroom mirror, but when I did it it was the look of a bar girl trying to connect with a live one. Sammy Jo's was an invitation, but subtle, mysterious. Only her little dog, Pepper, an ancient dachshund, seemed to arouse any real emotion in that woman. Except for that look I'd caught when Miss Emily broke the cut-glass vase. She walked Pepper three times a day, on a leash, the only other dog walker in town. She told me in her whispery voice that he didn't need the leash for running away or anything, but since he'd gone blind and deaf he tended to not know where he was. He'd just stand there and shiver from not knowing where he was, she said.

To get back to Miss Emily's wake, we left soon after the little contretemps with Dr. Wilson. I felt a definite chill in the air of Miss Emily's parlor that day, and although the mouths were smiling once again, the eyes were not. Sarah Taylor Millet gave us a wink, and Warren and I walked across the street to our house in silence.

Chapter 3

•

• Once safely inside our own door I said, "You don't have a sprained ankle and not a damn thing wrong with you and suddenly in the middle of the night start writhing in pain and frothing at the mouth and boom you're dead! You don't!"

"How do you know she was writhing in pain and foaming at the mouth?"

"Sammy Jo told me. First thing that morning. I was walking the dogs just as Beau Johnson was leaving."

"You didn't tell me."

"I did. You were reading the paper."

"You did not—"

"She just blurted it out—sort of fell on me sobbing and blurted that out."

"You never told me—"

When he gets into his stubborn mode the only thing to do is distract. "Will you be hungry tonight?"

"God, no!"

"Me too."

"Who's Johnson?"

"Beauregard Johnson. The undertaker."

Along about five-thirty—since we don't drink anymore we eat early—we decided to call No Name Pizza for a couple of their Greek salads, the only ethnic food around here. Unless you call fried ethnic. The idea of crisp lettuce and shredded cabbage and sweet onion and salty feta cheese and little salty black olives after all that sweet stuff was appealing. You get a crisp little garlic bread with it and it's almost like being back home. And much cheaper. Four-fifty for that good food? With an olive oil and wine vinegar dressing with lots of oregano? It's not Lutèce, but what can you get at Lutèce for four-fifty? A glass of Fiuggi water and a book of matches.

Once we settled down in front of the television for the "MacNeil/Lehrer News Hour," which comes on at six down here, I was watching Charlayne Hunter-Gault who was growing her hair out after trying blond and wishing she'd go back to her old look and trying to think of who would want Miss Emily dead and there were so many candidates. . . .

Warren said, "There is no real reason for suspicion."

You know, that happens when two people spend too much time together for too long. "Well, aren't you? Suspicious?" I said.

"Certainly not! It was probably a heart attack or a cerebral hemmorhage or a stroke or . . . any one of those sudden things. Nobody in this town is about to kill anyone," he said with conviction. "They believe in hell."

"I wonder who inherited her estate—the house and car and everything? That would be a clue, wouldn't it?"

"Merrie, why don't you think of a nice, tax-deductible reason to go to New York and see your friends—"

"Don't you think it might have crossed Sammy Jo's mind once or twice? To be free? She didn't like Miss Emily—"

"Nothing crosses Sammy Jo's mind—"

"If you have a heart attack do you turn blue and froth at the mouth? I never heard of anyone doing that—"

"Merrie! Forget it! If you're so bored you have to dream up a murder maybe you should look for a job."

"What could I do down here? Open a bakery? That takes money."

"Anything! Good works! You're driving me crazy with this obsession."

Just then the dogs started such a racket we couldn't hear Charlayne or ourselves. Our doorbell was broken and we'd been thinking of repairing it or even getting a new one until we realized it wasn't necessary. The dogs were more than adequate. When I went to answer it no one was there. Someone had inserted a white envelope between the screen and the front door. It wasn't addressed to anyone. A plain white envelope with a Christmas seal on the back. Inside was a white slip of paper. Printed in block letters with a purple marking pen, it read simply, MIND YOUR OWN BUSINESS.

"Heart attack, huh!" I said triumphantly, tossing the paper on to his tray. "How about *that?*"

His eyes passed back and forth over the page. No comment.

"If it's nothing then why are they getting their ass in a sling? Tell me that!"

He stared at the page.

"I consider this a definite proof that poor Miss Emily did *not* die of natural causes!"

He returned the note to me.

"I'm going to find out who killed Miss Emily!" I said.

He got that look, that tolerant, amused look, that, oh well, if it keeps her busy and out of trouble—the little woman look.

"I will, Warren! Even if no one else cares, I do!"

He smiled. The same smile he has for Mathilda when she brings him a bone.

A couple of days later I arranged to have lunch with Dr. Wilson's nurse, a very friendly, very blond woman who, with her husband, goes around the South winning shag contests. (If you didn't know, the shag is a southern dance that originated around Wrightsville Beach about the time of World War Two and the lindy. Or maybe the shag was the lindy!) I felt around the circumstances of Miss Emily's death. She became very guarded. So I asked if you died of a heart attack would you writhe in pain and froth at the mouth? Her answer was that the Lord worked in strange ways. Thanks.

One of the neighbors who worked as a therapist at the hospital told me that a heart attack could be very painful, but if it was the kind that killed, you were gone before you knew it. I asked the pharmacist in the next town. He looked at me strangely and suggested I ask my doctor. Then I received another note. Just two words in heavy black marking pen: STOP MEDDLING.

Warren's only comment: "Merrie, obviously you're boring the whole town!"

The little library next to the town hall was no help. It never was. There were a number of books on the history of the South, the history of Davis Landing, the Civil War, and southern cooking. There was no medical encyclopedia. I know because when I first arrived here I went to the library to take out a card. I looked in the file cards for Styron (who hails from here), Updike, Mailer, Beattie . . . anybody! Nothing. I was told that the books were selected for the library. (Probably by friends of Senator Helms.) But right up front there were shelf after shelf of Japanese books. By that, I mean books written and printed in Japanese. I asked if there was a large Japanese population and was told there wasn't. Then I asked who read the Japanese books to decide if they were suitable for Davis Landing reading. The poor woman didn't know. I asked if she was aware that the Japanese were known for their exquisite erotica and that these books might be d-i-r-t-y? The poor woman. Anyway, there was no medical encyclopedia. And I had begun to make an unfortunate name for myself.

The two doctors down here wouldn't be of any help, being kin to all the families, so I decided I'd go to New York and ask my doctor there a few questions. I was determined to get the answers. Of course, it could have been just "old age," or a heart attack, or a cerebral hemmorhage, or a stroke. . . . All I wanted was for someone to *tell* me!

Well, I hadn't been to New York for quite some time. I'd forgotten. The noise. The dirt. The excitement. The energy. Stepping off the plane at La Guardia, I thrilled to the security guards having a jolly conversation in Spanish. My own steps quickened to the pace of the other arrivals, hurrying to beat each other to a taxi. So many languages. So many different skin colors, so many kinds of people. And then the wonderful taxi ride into town behind the fiercely moustachioed Egyptian driver who spoke no English; the short stops, the fast sprints, the near accidents—I was *home!*

When we left New York so precipitously, my friends advised me not to stay down there wherever it was. Whenever they phoned to invite us to a little dinner, a big party, a cocktail, whatever, I'd think of the cost of two air fares. Impossible. Then they'd urge me to come by myself. One airfare plus Warren eating out plus the tips and doormen plus the taxis and the thank-you gifts. Protecting Warren's pride (I had none) I made excuses, never mentioning lack of money. They wouldn't have understood. My friends urged an arrangement with my husband. That is, *ahrahngemant*, as in the French. And always, they offered me their guest rooms. But when push came to shove their guest rooms were filled with children on school holiday, or with European or West Coast houseguests who always stayed for three weeks, or they'd just had a new and complicated alarm system installed which their third-world maids could understand, but somehow would be beyond my limited comprehension. Any kind of a hotel is two hundred a night, but fortunately I have a ninety-three-year-old Aunt May who has one of those huge old Park Avenue apartments and she has given me shelter when necessary. Although there are certain disadvantages.

Aunt May doesn't like to drink alone. It's dangerous to sit down anywhere. Sitting for even a minute is to Aunt May a natural time to have a friendly drink. Like ten-thirty in the morning. I protested that it was too early, she said it's never too early. Perfect Bloody Mary time. I don't mean to imply she's anywhere near being a dipsomaniac. Aunt May is just a lonely, energetic, tireless, and sociable lady.

When the Egyptian cast me out on the street and sat calmly picking his teeth while I struggled to get my baggage out of the front seat where he'd wedged it, I was rescued by the kindly

Irish and Spanish white-gloved doormen who remembered me as a good tipper from my previous visits. And upstairs, there was Aunt May peering into a magnifying glass and seriously concerned because she thought she'd found a new wrinkle on her cheek. With the tray ready with the glasses and the ice bucket. In my bathroom there was cologne and bubble bath and bath oil and several packages of condoms in assorted colors. Aunt May is a truly thoughtful hostess. And out the window of my room, there it was. The towers and the lights and the penthouses and the gardens and the roar of the traffic and the police sirens and the fire trucks. . . . And the restaurants! Within walking distance there was a choice of French, Turkish, German, northern Italian, southern Italian, Sicilian, Japanese, Szechuan, Hunan, Cantonese, Mexican, Tex-Mex, Spanish, Afghanistan, Pakistani, Indian, fish, beef, vegetarian.

That very first night Aunt May and I walked to a favorite restaurant of hers. Cantonese. She ordered Dewar's on the rocks. I asked about the condoms. She said I wasn't her only guest and I wondered if she'd bought them herself. She'd had two Dewar's on the rocks before we left her apartment. After our dinner she linked my arm, refused to take a cab, and we staggered up Park Avenue together. I know everyone who saw us thought I was the drunk.

The next morning I walked down Madison Avenue to my appointment at Kenneth's. I had the works and listened to all the current gossip—my God, I was out of touch—and left fully groomed. Kenneth mentioned that I was talking funny. He meant southern, but I can't help it. It crept over me like a kudzu vine. I got a beautiful manicure and that always makes me feel better. Nobody seeing my hands these days with their unpolished nails filed down as far as it's decent, hangnails and cuticles hung like ornaments on a Christmas tree, would ever believe I was asked to be a hand and foot model before I blundered into advertising after my first divorce.

Walking to my doctor's—my darling friendly doctor who would always work me in—and walking in the Davis Landing style, leisurely, friendly, smiling, making eye contact. I was pushed and battered and, making eye contact with an angry young black man in a stocking cap, was told, "What's the matter, lady, you wanna fuck?" And then when I got to my darling doctor's office I found his nurse clearing out the files, my darling doctor having expired ten days before.

"I didn't even know he was ill!"

"He wasn't. It was very sudden."

"Heart?"

"Stroke."

I invited her to lunch at a very good French restaurant around the corner and she accepted. (I have always felt that nurses know more than doctors, and I was sure Nurse Anderson could tell me what I wanted to know.) I said it was so we could talk about my darling doctor. She had been devoted to him, seeming to have no other life. Well, as the lunch progressed and the waiter kept pouring the wine, a particularly nice Côte du Rhône, it evolved that she did not, in fact, have any other life because she had been the doctor's mistress for the last twenty-seven years. She sobbed into her salad and I shed a few tears for them into my omelet, and we talked about sex and its role in women's lives. I told her the man who'd meant the most to me of all of my men—and I'd had three husbands and so many lovers I'd forgotten many of them (her tears were drying), and I'd slept white, black, red, and yellow (she was fascinated)—and that this man who had meant the most to me had had a sprained ankle and then suddenly started writhing in pain and foaming at the mouth, and everyone said it was a heart attack, and then he was dead.

"Oh, no," she said. "It couldn't have been the heart."

"Really?"

"No, no, that was something he ingested."

"Ingested?"

"Swallowed. Could have been a reaction to a new medication."

"But he never took anything, not even aspirin," quoting Sammy Jo about Miss Emily.

"A violent reaction to a new food then—something that

might be harmless to anyone else but acted like a poison on him."

"Ah-ha," I said.

That little lunch with two bottles of wine, mostly consumed by Nurse Anderson, cost me over a hundred dollars including tax and tip, but it was worth it. I'd been thinking poison all along.

Now I couldn't wait to get back to Davis Landing to continue my investigation. Warren was calling me Agatha Marple and thinking it was all rather amusing, but Miss Emily was my friend and I was determined to see justice done. And all that afternoon while I visited my eye doctor to find out why my eyes were so itchy, even when he tweezed out two lashes which I sorely need and even when he announced, after a microscopic examination of the lashes, that I seemed to be breeding mites in them possibly due to the environment in which I was living, even then, although I was momentarily taken aback by the grossness of *anything* breeding in my lashes, I felt good about Miss Emily and the cause of death. I was convinced that I was right. I was sure Dr. Wilson had written natural causes on the death certificate—and who would question it at her age? Who would question Dr. Wilson?

Impatient to get back to Davis Landing, I had to wait because I had one of those cheapie tickets—you could only come and go on the dates you'd already selected, stay over a Saturday, that sort of thing. So I stayed and went to dinner with my friends and to lunch with them and amused them all with Aunt May's colored condoms which I kept in my purse. Aunt May was a legend with my friends. I marveled at how young everyone was. In Davis Landing people are old. Oh God, but they're old. There isn't a lift in the whole town and only two tinted heads, mine being one of them. And now here I was surrounded by lovely, young, unlined faces with perfect, white teeth, long, smooth necks, beautiful streaky blond and brown and red hair, and old hands. They all asked me what we *did* down there and how were the parties. How were the *parties?* "Garden Club is big," I said. They laughed.

I believe that these coastal people are born with the gardening gene that says to the fetus in the first second: You are a gardener. And keeps nagging it during the whole nine months so when they come out with their little fists waving around what they're really looking for is a trowel. It's the genes and the Gulf Stream but I've never understood the Gulf Stream. Anyway, Davis Landing is in zone eight, which means we're living in a Mediterranean climate here, surrounded by gardenias and camellias and crape myrtle and magnolias and wisteria and paper whites grow outside and bloom at Christmas and oxalis is like a weed and gaillardia is a wild flower, and the air is thick with fleas and mosquitos and ticks, and the roaches grow large enough to saddle and are called water bugs. And if you throw some seeds in the ground, you'd better step back fast.

I looked around at the lunch ladies, thinking of the Garden Club. These ladies would as soon have walked past their doormen without clothes as without a manicure. The Garden Club hands looked the way mine usually did. Unkept and uncared for. Gardeners' hands. The kind of gardeners who don't wear gloves, preferring to scrabble in the dirt.

Chapter 4

◆

◆ That first meeting, which I was absolutely *dragged* to, was such a new experience for me that I fell in love with Garden Club right then. Before the actual meeting started we prayed! All the white-haired ladies and me. Aloud! I couldn't believe it. The prayer was called the Garden Collect and I have long since memorized it. It goes like this:

> Help us, O Lord, to grasp the meaning of happy, growing things, the mystery of opening bud and floating seed, that we may weave it into the tissue of our faith of life eternal. Give us wisdom to cultivate our minds diligently as we nurture tender seedlings, and patience to weed out envy and malice as we uproot troublesome weeds. Teach us to seek steady root growth, rather than a fleeting culture, and to cultivate those traits which brighten under adversity with the perennial loveliness of hardy borders. Thank God for gardens and their message today and always.
>
> Amen.

We all hold hands when we say that. Actually. Picture me holding hands and praying aloud with my New York group!

That part was purely spiritual. The rest was adorable. We discussed the dues, which were being raised from five dollars annually. There was a great difference of opinion as to whether they should go to ten dollars. Many members felt that doubling the dues was untenable. Others felt that ten dollars today was not a lot of money. The final decision was that if you wanted to pay ten you could, but if you wanted to pay seven-fifty you could do that too. Adorable. Then there was talk about perennials and shrubs and the news that a landscape gardener was coming to town—Davis Landing is growing—and although he was out of county and in fact out of state, being from Savannah, he was a Jones and kin to our Joneses and therefore qualified. Miss Emily had already spoken to him about coming to be a guest at one of our meetings although the consensus was that there was nothing he could teach us; and then everyone applauded the ladies who had contributed the cookies and the lemonade and then we asked for a blessing and the meeting was concluded. I went home to Warren, who was in his usual surly mood, which comes over him whenever the sink gets stopped up, and in the middle of telling him about the prayers and how darling they all were, I started to cry.

"Oh for godsake, Merrie, *now* what?"

"It's them! Their innocence! This place! There's nothing like it any more. This is going back a hundred years when there was morality and standards and *innocence*—"

"I wish to hell there was a fucking decent plumber!"

I had plenty of time to think on the way back from New York to Davis Landing, and decided it was time to take Sarah Taylor Millet to lunch. Sarah Taylor lived in one of the large waterfront houses with a plaque—Taylor House 1690—and she was not only kin to everyone, but she kept up with all the goings on, overt and covert. I knew I'd need her knowledge, for a misdeed once done down here, is buried deep in the local mix of clay and oyster shells. By the time they've added grass clippings and time and dimming memories and let it sit for a while, no matter how criminal it started out to be, when they dig it up it's been transformed into the sweetest smelling compost you'd ever want to spread on your flower beds.

Sarah had a favorite restaurant, the Harbor View, which was, not surprisingly, on the harbor. Although the food was inedible, the view was unsurpassed. Sarah Taylor sailed in like the dowager she is and was given a window table as her due. We settled down to our three-ninety-five specials: oysterburgers and iced tea. An oysterburger at the Harbor View, by the way, is a few heavily battered and deeply fried (no longer hot or even warm) oysters inserted between the halves of a soft, cold hamburger bun with a light sprinkling of cabbage slaw, all of it anointed with bottled tartar sauce. The only tea they know down here is iced tea. If you say "tea," that's what you get. If you want *tea* you have to *say* "hot" tea. Iced tea comes heavily sweetened unless you ask for unsweetened. I usually pick the oysters out of my bun because I like oysters no matter what's happened to them, and washed down with the tea . . . well, it's not great, but I've had to lower my standards. What do you want for three ninety-five? *La Côte Basque?*

Sarah Taylor and I met when I first arrived, and I liked her the best of anyone. She was eighty-something and I was forty-something, but we got along very well. Sarah Taylor was class anywhere in the world. I used to see her when I walked my dogs early in the morning, and she'd come out to let Shenandoah into her yard. Shenandoah was a large golden retriever and Sarah Taylor was a tall wisp of a white-haired woman in a robe. Red flannel in the winter, navy blue silk in the summer. I was accustomed to seeing all of Davis Landing in their night things because Jobie Pruett took a fiendish delight in delivering his papers as far as possible from the front door or even the porch. I met almost everyone in Davis Landing that way. They'd stand there in pink satin robes and striped pajamas and chat about the weather and wave at their friends in passing cars in no hurry to get under cover. One day I was standing behind a fragile white-haired woman at the post office who was berating the postmaster because she had a package notice in her box that was meant for some other box, apparently not for the first time. She finished with a heartfelt, "Call this a post office?!"

When she turned away from the window and saw me she gasped and apologized for her temper. Then she realized who I was and said a very proper southern-lady-style hello. And I said, "This is the first time I've seen you dressed." And we both laughed. After that, when she saw me in the morning she'd ask me in for coffee and although I was dying to see the house, I had to get back and fix our own coffee. If I didn't get to it first, Warren'd make a huge pot of cowboy boiled coffee, with the eggshell, so strong and bitter that I couldn't drink it and if I didn't drink it his feelings were hurt and the day was ruined. This was his only culinary accomplishment except for eggs over easy, which the way he did it was just tough, greasy, overcooked eggs fried in bacon fat.

I'd watched the fishermen cook their lunch down on the docks—fried fish and something with cornmeal. What they did was to get some white Blue Ribbon cornmeal and mix it up with a little salt, put a pan of any kind of oil (they used Wesson) on the fire and heat it up, then add enough cold water to the cornmeal to make it wet, pat it out like mud pies, and fry it up. They gave me some and it was great—like potato chips made of cornmeal. They called it fried bread. (*Froid* bread.) I suggested this to Warren to enlarge his repertoire, but he said, "You make them."

Eventually, Sarah Taylor and I drifted into lunching together once in a while. She liked to pick me up at eleven-thirty, driving her huge old black Cadillac convertible with the fins and twenty-three thousand miles on it, and after lunch we cruised the town and the waterfront at fifteen miles an hour, driving around sleeping dogs, while she told me the histories of the houses and the families. It was fascinating. I enjoyed every minute of it. I could never explain this to any of my international friends, but I really enjoyed it.

Anyway, once we settled down to our oysterburgers, and I had given her a carefully edited account of what I did in New

York, I asked how Sammy Jo was getting on without Miss Emily.

"That one," Sarah Taylor said.

"What's going to happen to Miss Emily's house?"

"That's a little murky," she said.

"Wasn't there a will?"

"Oh, yes. The judge saw to that. And it's been probated. She left the house and the contents to Sammy Jo so she'd have a place to live. But nothing's ever simple in Davis Landing."

"Come on, Sarah Taylor!"

"Sammy Jo's family is what got it all started."

"What family?"

"All those Tryons."

"What Tryons? Not *the trashy* Tryons!"

"Sammy Jo's family."

"My Lord, Sarah Taylor, you can be hard." That's the way I talk down here.

"Well," Sarah Taylor said, "I suppose . . . you are kin . . . but you must promise never to breathe a word of this."

"I promise, I promise. Tell me about the trashy Tryons."

"They are. Just plain white trash. Used to be a fine family when the first Tryons came down from Virginia. Said they were getting to feel a bit crowded up there. That was some time in the seventeen hundreds, and it was gettin' right settled. They were all right in the beginning, farming their land and riding their horses and fishing and hunting and tending their boats and their nets like everyone down here, but after a while . . . hundred years or so . . . they started moonshining . . . shooting at sheriffs . . . that whole family got *mummocked* up. (Translation: messed up.) Took Indian girls to live with, and those little Indians got themselves a taste for moonshine. You know what happened then?"

"I've heard about Indians and moonshine, but what happened then?"

"Let's see, where was I?"

"Indian girls and moonshine."

"Well, I'll have to go back to the girls' father. . . ."

"The Indian girls."

"No! Sammy Jo and Emily."

"Oh! Those girls."

"All right. Well you have to understand how badly Judge Davis wanted a son. He married a girl he met at Chapel Hill when he was young. Lilith. A very nice Charleston family. Well Lilith had a lot of miscarriages and then finally, Emily. The judge said they'd just keep on working at it. Working at it," she snorted. "And all their work paid off because Lilith produced another baby, but it was born dead and it was another girl and poor Lilith died having it. Lilith was a sweet little thing, but no match for the judge. He could stomp the life out of any woman. And it didn't take him too long to start courtin' again. This time it was a local product, his clerk, Ruby Tryon. Those Tryon women were all good-looking and strong and healthy. Maybe it was their Indian blood. The women were hard workers but the men . . . ! Ruby Tryon was the only one to make anything of herself. She went all the way through school to high school and graduated. Ruby was all right. Not quality like Lilith . . . but all right. And he married her. Thirty-three years older, but he was a catch. Still good-looking, had all his hair, took to combing that stuff through it Reagan used to take his gray out. The judge forgot about his eyebrows though. Dark hair and thick white eyebrows. Judge Davis was quite a man and didn't he know it. Well, in the proper time and without a minute to spare, Ruby had Sammy Jo. But the judge was still hell-bent to have himself a son and wouldn't you know, about one year later, *Ruby* dies in childbirth! Both times Ruby wanted to have a midwife, one of her own kin. But the judge wasn't taking any chances. He wanted his son to be born *right*. Well the doctor we all used drank a lot and people say that's why those two Davis wives died the way they did. It wasn't a boy anyway. But the judge was not to be stopped. He was determined to have that boy to carry on his name. Started looking for another woman to court before Ruby was cold, and he figured he'd found her in a visitor from Raleigh, kin to Effie Fuller. He was out sailing and showing off the way he did so she could watch him from Effie's porch on the shore. Well, the local class boats had just organized a race, and there was the judge carrying on like a fool . . . he managed to capsize his boat and that was the end of the judge."

"He drowned?"

"Sure did. Just disappeared. Probably hit by the boom. Everyone said the body should have washed up *somewhere* sometime. But it didn't."

"Do you have great white sharks around here?"

"Nothing more threatening than dogfish."

"It's like a Greek tragedy."

"Not really. He was such a selfish man! Perfectly willing to kill those women off, one after another, because he was so crazy to carry on the name! As if we didn't have enough Davises down here. But the judge was making a hobby of breeding."

"I declare!" I use that sort of expression a lot because you cannot say "fuck" down here.

"So poor Emily who wasn't that much older—well, Emily must have been about fifteen—when she had to become the mother to that new baby, and she was a good one, I'll say that for her. She did the best she could."

"She must have been terribly strict. Poor Sammy Jo."

"Poor Sammy Jo my foot. Poor Emily."

"And Sammy Jo's other family? The Tryons?"

"Oh, Emily would never let them near that child. Any of them. She was enough of a handful without the Tryons."

She sat, staring out at the water, remembering.

"And now that Miss Emily's gone, the Tryons are bothering Sammy Jo?" I prompted. "Is that it?"

"No, that's not it," she said irritably. "Of course, the Tryon men are hanging around and not a good one in the lot. And *handsome?* They are the best-looking people. But she's always had men hanging around."

"Then what is it?"

"The problem is with the Davises, the judge's family. They want to take the house away from Sammy Jo."

"But how can they do that? It's hers, isn't it? Legally?"

"Yes, it is."

Penny came along and asked if everything was all right. We said it was. She asked if we'd like some more tea. We said we would. Sarah Taylor takes her time. It's a thirsty business.

"But the Davises are saying Sammy Jo isn't the judge's daughter at all."

I almost choked on an oyster.

"They're saying she was born to one of the Tryon women the same night Ruby was having her child, and the babies were switched. The Tryon baby was healthy and lived, and the Davis baby was sickly and died."

"That's impossible. In a hospital?!"

"Anything can happen in this hospital, my dear. It's third world."

"What is Sammy Jo doing about it?"

"What *would* Sammy Jo do? Gave it all to a man to straighten out. She's gettin' on to sixty though she doesn't look it. She gave the whole mess to the judge's younger partner because he's very good-looking. I swear that woman will never act her age."

"She doesn't look the least bit Indian—"

"She'd have a right to look Indian because of Ruby. But Ruby was the whitest woman you ever saw. Pale blond, pale blue eyes, pale. That's where Sammy Jo gets her looks."

Penny poured us some more iced tea. They never rush you down here. So much more relaxed than Mortimer's, if only they had Mortimer's food. You can linger all afternoon if you want. Of course, there isn't exactly a line into the street of people waiting to have lunch. But even so. It is pleasant.

"You see," Sarah Taylor continued, "it was the Tryons that got the Davises all fired up." (Fired pronounced *fard*.) "All those Tryon men hanging around the Davis house and it's the family house with the Davis plaque, 1693, and the Davises don't approve of a porch full of great big dark and handsome men in jeans sitting on their spines and drinking their moonshine out of jelly jars right out in front of the Lord and everyone. Well, you must have seen them—they're right across the street from you."

"We never noticed. We don't look out the windows at night, and I don't think that sort of thing happens until dark."

"Probably they wouldn't dare in the light of day, tryin' to stay out of sight of the Davises. The Davis men have always been highly educated and run to judges and doctors. But they could have expected the Tryons to come throngin' up on that porch once Emily was gone because Emily was the only thing that kept them off it when she was alive. She didn't exactly take a broom to them, but they knew it was coming. And it was only to be expected once Emily was gone. . . ." She looked around to see if anyone could possibly overhear her.

"Because Sammy Jo's such a flirt."

"If I tell you something do you swear you'll never tell another soul?"

"Who would I tell? Warren? He never hears a word I say."

"You promise?"

"I promise."

"Well, poor Emily told me when she came down with her ankle and I carried some of Lula's fried chicken up to her—it was the week before she was taken so suddenly—Emily said would I please keep an eye on Sammy Jo for her while she was housebound. 'Follow her,' Emily said. I said, 'Emily, you know I'd do anything to help you out, but following a grown woman to the Piggly Wiggly just doesn't make any sense! After all, I have a life of my own.' And that's when she told me." She glanced over her shoulder and lowering her voice said, "Poor Emily was worried sick about Sammy Jo and one of her Tryon cousins carrying on. Luther. The best-looking of them all. Real dark hair and eyes and skin. Looks like a movie star. Like that Presley boy. And Luther has a wife and five children and everyone in town knows how jealous his wife is. She took his shotgun and went into the woods after some woman who came over from Charlotte to buy moonshine from Luther and kept coming back almost on a daily basis, and you know that's a two hundred and fifty mile drive one way, and his wife tried to kill that silly woman! Poor Emily had visions of Sammy Jo splattered all over the Davis plaque."

I sat there thinking that this town was like an onion. You could keep peeling the layers of a pretty yellow onion and when you got to the heart of it, it could be rotten.

"Of course Sammy Jo's pretty good with a gun too," she added.

"Couldn't Luther get a divorce?"

"Couldn't and wouldn't. No man in this town would divorce over Sammy Jo. Poor Emily. That girl was a worrisome burden since she was a child. It started with lying and stealing and she never got over it. Then when she reached puberty— oh before—she was about eleven—it was men." She sighed. "Poor Emily did her best."

"And I always thought Miss Emily was so cruel to Sammy Jo, keeping her on such a tight rein. I actually thought that she had some kind of unhealthy hold over Sammy Jo—"

"You see, my dear, nothing is as it seems. I've been having some silly thoughts myself that I could never tell any of the kin. They'd just say, 'We always thought Sarah Taylor was out of her head.' But I've been thinking," she said, and laughed in an embarrassed way, "putting two and two together: Luther and Sammy Jo, that is—neither one of them any better than they should be—and Luther having all those gardening supplies, sprays and things for when he gets off his backside to actually do some work, and the two of them having to meet in the woods or on the beach because of Emily, it must have occurred to them at some time that life would be more comfortable if they were under a shelter. And they could only arrange that if Emily were gone. . . . I must be out of my head. . . ."

"And Miss Emily dying violently from a sprained ankle."

"Exactly."

Chapter 5

♦

♦ I couldn't wait to get home and tell Warren that Sarah Taylor didn't think I was crazy or obsessed, and I burst into the house meaning to, but I found him in the kitchen enjoying a cup of his coffee and crying over the comics. Crying from laughing. He's always liked "Calvin & Hobbes" and "The Far Side" and fortunately the local paper carries them both. Sundays are the best day in the week for Warren. Most of the time, if he's building shelves or repairing a bathroom leak or painting, he puts the comics away for a time when he's clean and relaxed and quiet. There's always something with this house. Fix one thing and something else breaks. Stop up one leak and another pipe breaks. But this was one of the rest periods for the house and for Warren. I said, "Warren!" and he said, "Merrie!" and proceeded to shove the paper under my eyes.

Admittedly, we are rather an odd couple. Some people would say mismatched. But we've been together for longer than I've been with any of my other husbands or lovers and it seems to work. Even so, he does adore the comics and he'll be doubled up over them while I'm frowning and sighing over the editorials. In one way, it's good because we don't want the same part of the paper at the same time. On the other hand,

I don't really understand the comics and this annoys him out of all proportion. He insists that I understand and laugh and takes great pains to explain them to me in an extremely pedantic way. Sometimes I think I should fake it. Like an orgasm.

Warren has a B.A. and an M.A., more than I ever managed; and when he first got his M.A. taught English at the college level. So when I ran in, filled with my new theory *and* confirmation of same by no less than Sarah Taylor, I was stopped cold. His glasses down at the end of his nose, he looked at me over them, and with great patience explained each frame and the meaning of the whole. It was sort of nice having the comics read to you. Like being a child again. And then he told me that he always loved to listen to La Guardia read the funnies over the radio.

"La Guardia!?"

"Mayor La Guardia. From New York City. We could get him in North Dakota. He was great."

"I wonder if he ever knew that people in North Dakota were listening to him."

"On a ranch. In a blizzard."

"I bet he never knew. He thought he was doing something nice for the people of New York. Keeping the kids busy so the parents could sleep late or fuck or something. . . . North Dakota! . . ."

I had forgotten all about Miss Emily and Sammy Jo and Sarah Taylor, getting sort of fascinated, and not for the first time, with our differences, Warren's and mine. It's like being married to a gentleman from Calcutta, if they have cowboys there, but they must. Who takes care of the sacred cows if they don't? And then our dog doorbell went off.

When I got to the front door there was no one there. Just a white envelope stuck in the screen. While I was taking it out I looked across the street and there was what could only be a Tryon car parked in front of Sammy Jo's house. Some General Motors vehicle from the sixties with Coors stickers, rust spots, and JESUS LOVES YOU on the bumper. When I slit the envelope, there was a single sheet of white paper. The heavy green magic marker printing jumped off the page: WE WARNED YOU. I quickly stepped out on the porch and looked up and down the street. You never saw a prettier piece of Americana. All the houses with their Christmas decorations and every window on the street with its Christmas candles (they don't take them down for a long time, but not as long as the Russian Tea Room on Fifty-seventh Street in New York where they never take them down) and at the end of the block the boats rocking in the water with their masts wound with tiny white lights like little stars. Not a sound but the wind in the live oaks. So quiet. So peaceful. No one to be seen. The street was empty except for me standing there with a handful of threat.

Racing back to the kitchen, I thrust the latest between the Stockbroker and the comics. He kept staring at it while I was telling him about my lunch with Sarah Taylor. "So you see, it's Sammy Jo who poisoned Miss Emily! She had a motive and she did it with Luther with some spray or insect poison he's got."

He was still examining the note. Warren is nothing if not deliberate. "Luther?" he said vaguely.

"Luther Tryon! I told you about Luther!"

"I never heard of—"

"You weren't listening—"

"You never mentioned him."

Oh God! "Warren, that's Luther's car across the street! The car that's been there every night since Miss Emily's funeral! We've talked about the car and Luther—"

"Never. I thought the car was abandoned. Why do you think he has insect spray?"

"Because that's his business! When he's not doing sex he's doing lawns and gardens!"

"Anyone can buy insect spray—or ant poison—or roach powder—I bet there isn't one house in Davis Landing that doesn't have some kind of poison—We've got some ourselves."

"I think we should go to the police!"

"For what?"

"To warn them—before they kill someone else!"

"Now Merrie," he said calmly and quietly and with a great deal of obvious patience. "We don't know if anyone killed anyone—"

"Well if we don't go about the murder—"

"You don't know it's a murder—"

"Then shouldn't we tell them about the threats I'm getting—"

"Kid stuff."

"—before they kill me too?"

"Nobody's going to kill you! You're no danger to anybody even if you tried!"

I glared at him. "You seem to have forgotten the first night we had dinner?"

His eyes got paler and went opaque. Blue-eyed people really can't disguise their emotions. Not from me anyway. When I saw that blankness I knew he'd forgotten.

He said, "How could I forget?"

"All right, tell me about it." Such a liar.

"You give me your version. It's always better than what actually happened."

Isn't that devious? What actually happened was first we went for a sail on his boat (this was in Connecticut on the Sound where I was visiting my mother and he was a renter with his children and their nanny). We sailed out to a small, uninhabited, and very rocky island. "Let's take a walk," he said, ignoring the fact that walking was impossible as there wasn't a single inch of that island that was level enough to take a step. Nothing but rocks. So we leaped from rock to rock until we'd circled the island. "Now let's do some shooting," he said. He'd come prepared with a cooler of beer, two rifles, and a pistol. My God, I thought, he's going to kill me. And I didn't really care, having just gone through a second bloody divorce. We sat on a rock, drank some beer, and shot at the empty cans. I used the pistol and he was deeply impressed. Or I thought he was.

"We did some shooting," I reminded him.

"Oh yes," he said.

"I think we should tell the police."

"Merrie, this is all in your head."

I waved the threat at him. "This isn't. I think we'd better send off for a pair of bulletproof vests."

"Why two? They only want you."

"I'm going to see Miss Pearl if she'll see me."

"Who's Miss Pearl?"

"Warren, please!" Obviously, he lives in a vacuum, but it gets to be really irritating. I'm always walking out of rooms.

Davis Landing boasts a witch, a woman of 105 years who never comes downstairs. Naturally, or maybe not, the locals have given her supernatural powers. Miss Pearl. And I have told him about Miss Pearl *so* many times. I've always been interested in the occult. I have my astrological chart drawn every year (and always forget where I put it). Now Miss Pearl might just be a 105-year-old woman living down here in this remarkably unstressful place. But then again she might just be a witch. She is also Sarah Taylor's kin.

Miss Pearl's longevity is due in part to their French fore-bears (The Millets were very laid back pirates who came to Davis Landing to light fires on the shore to attract ships that thought it was a lighthouse and then sit and wait for those same ships to break up on the shoals and then go out and scavenge. They lived to be very old men.) and in part to a fifth of Bourbon every day. She didn't eat much but that Wild Turkey was like a tonic. Her cheeks were unlined though somewhat florid, and she looked in fine condition, her hearing and eyesight were excellent. Downstairs was a chronic state of chaos, children and in-laws and grandchildren and great-grandchildren constantly surging through the house like a perigee tide. Upstairs, Miss Pearl sat in her rocking chair, silently rocking through the day, calm as could be. Even when the children were roller-skating or fighting or riding their bicycles through the rooms or setting fires, upstairs all was calm. Nothing bothered Miss Pearl. The family had put a color television set in her room, which she never watched. She never even looked out the window. She was not interested in reading anything, even the Bible, said very little, and seemed to live within herself with great ease and contentment. It was said that if you could get her attention, she could tell you things. If she wanted.

Chapter 6

♦

♦ Sarah Taylor and I went to call on Miss Pearl, armed with Sarah Taylor's beautifully wrapped gift, a pretty shawl woven by Sarah Taylor's mountain kin, and my brownies on a foil-coated paper plate covered with plastic wrap. Wading through toddlers, dogs, and cats we mounted the stairs to Miss Pearl's room. Some of the children downstairs wanted to know what we'd brought them.

Sarah Taylor said we hadn't brought them anything at all and why should we bring dirty children like them anything, such dirty faces she never had seen, and we were going upstairs to visit with Miss Pearl. They watched us mount the stairs in silence. Miss Pearl's door was closed. We knocked. And waited. And knocked again. And waited. Then one of the older ones, a little girl, came clattering up the stairs and flung the door open for us. Miss Pearl didn't even look around.

Besides the four-poster and the marble-topped chest of drawers, the room was furnished with three Victorian rocking chairs upholstered in red plush, a large pot of bamboo palms, and a hanging Boston fern. Miss Pearl rocked in the largest chair beside a small table holding a half-filled glass, an open bottle of Wild Turkey, and her teeth.

"Howya doin', Miss Pearl?" Sarah Taylor said. "This is my

friend Merrie Lee Spencer. She's a transplant from New York."

"Connecticut," I corrected.

"Don't say that," she hissed. "Then you're branded as a damyankee. New York is obnoxious, but damyankees are the ones we hate."

"Sorry."

"It's been real warm for Christmas, hasn't it, Miss Pearl?" She was speaking in an unnaturally high, loud voice, enunciating each word with great care. "We brought you a little something." She proffered the gifts.

Miss Pearl waved them away with a languid backhand. Miss Pearl didn't look 105. Don't expect a shrunken, mummified creature confined to bed. What you get is a seemingly vigorous old woman in a kilt and sweater. Her white hair was neatly held on top of her head with pearlized combs and golden hairpins. Her legs were still shapely and her feet in little brown pumps showed no signs of swelling. Her expression was pleasant, half-smiling as she stared at the blank television screen. Sarah Taylor said, "Put your brownies on the table."

I did, careful not to crowd the teeth.

She placed her gift on the bed. "We might as well sit down," she said, taking one of the rockers. I took the other.

Now there's not much you can do in a rocker except rock. Miss Pearl had a nice rhythm going, slow and steady. When I started I was too fast, a little on the jerky side. Sarah Taylor caught Miss Pearl's beat instantly. I got it after a bit. Then we all rocked in unison. Sarah Taylor got on the weather. Swimming at Christmas. The *Chrissie Wright*. Mark, the young preacher. The red tide killing the fish. Garden Club bus tour. Miss Pearl's smile remained fixed.

I said, "Get to the point."

Sarah Taylor said, "I'm warming up to it." Then she started on gardening, how big everyone's paper whites were this year, some of the camellias were opening due to this heat—I sensed she was almost at Miss Emily and how she died. The three of us didn't miss a beat while Sarah Taylor started on the Joneses' Christmas roses.

Miss Pearl's rocker stopped. She twisted slightly, still smiling, picked up her teeth, and dipped them in the glass of Bourbon.

"She's going to talk to us," Sarah Taylor said, very hushed.

Miss Pearl inserted her teeth in her mouth and took a good swallow of Wild Turkey. Then, still looking at the television screen, she said, rapidly as a machine gun, "Yack-yack-yack-yack-yack," replaced her teeth on the table, and went back to rocking.

Sarah Taylor and I picked up her beat. "I have the feeling she's not going to be very helpful," I said. "Maybe we should go."

Miss Pearl never looked at us but she passed wind, long and loud and musical, continuing to rock.

"I think we better had," Sarah Taylor agreed.

As if to make her point, Miss Pearl lifted one arm and with a steady hand pointed to the door.

"She must be tired," Sarah Taylor said. (Pronounced *tard*.) As we left, she raised her voice to our hostess, "Miss Pearl? Now you take care, you heah? And we'll be back to see you again."

As we passed out the door Miss Pearl picked up her glass.

Sarah Taylor managed some polite chitchat with one of the adults downstairs, and we went out to the car. This time it was my BMW. That day I was just too tense to face Sarah Taylor's driving. I was parked on the south side of Queen Charlotte Street facing east, and after helping Sarah Taylor into the passenger seat and having to fasten her seat belt as she didn't believe in them, I walked behind the car to get into the driver's seat. As I opened the door, a pickup truck came from nowhere and hit the door and me with such force that I was thrown into the street. The door was ripped off. Lying in the street, stunned, I looked up at Miss Pearl's window. I remember she had pulled the curtain aside and was looking down at me, smiling. That was the last thing I saw before I passed out.

The next thing was Warren's face looking down at me. He seemed worried. I said, "Miss Pearl was standing at the window looking down at me and smiling."

Warren said, "Don't talk," and held my hand tight.

Sarah Taylor told him I must be delirious. "Miss Pearl never looks out her window. Not in the last ten or fifteen years."

We seemed to be in an emergency room. A quiet one. And then a young doctor in one of those pukey green hospital shirts—couldn't they have picked a color that would be becoming to some people?—said, "Mrs. Spencer, you have a mild concussion, sprained shoulder, and bruised arm."

Warren said, "You should see the car door."

That's Dakota humor. "What happened?"

Sarah Taylor said, "Some idiot drove by in a pickup truck and hit you and the door. You never let go of it."

"Bloody hell, we paid off the lease!"

"Mrs. Spencer," the doctor interrupted, "we'd like to keep you here for observation."

I caught Sarah Taylor's eye. "No way," I said, trying to sit up. "No way!"

"I'm afraid I'll have to insist—"

"You insist. I'm going home."

"But Mrs. Spencer—"

"My husband is right here. He can drive me home and I'll go right to bed."

"But there may be a delayed reaction—we don't move concussions."

Warren and Sarah Taylor were whispering. I heard her say "third world," and then she took charge. "Now you get Mrs. Spencer a wheelchair to take her out to Mr. Spencer's truck, and once she's home she'll be very quiet. Trust me. I happen to know that Mr. Spencer is an excellent caregiver." She was bustling around collecting my clothes. "And once she's settled, I'll get the word out and the ladies with the casseroles will be on her doorstep! Now where's that wheelchair?"

Warren, for once, had his hands hanging at his sides. And

no corny jokes either. He tried to lift me off the gurney, but I said we'd better wait for the wheelchair. And then he grabbed my hands again and hung on tight. "Warren," I said, "you got a real scare, didn't you? Thought you'd lost your cook!"

"I'd like to kill that sumbitch," he said.

"Did you report the damage to the police? For the insurance?"

"I told them."

"But did they see it? So they could write a report?"

"They saw it. They got the emergency rescue squad and—"

"And carried you right off to the hospital. I tell you those men were so gentle the way they handled you. Watermen, all of them. Three shrimpers and one oyster opener, and the way they handled you, you might have been made of glass," Sarah Taylor said.

Warren had gone out to see about charges. I pulled her close. "Do you think this had anything to do with—"

"Probably everything."

I shivered. "We'd better get out of here, Warren and me. I'm scared. They're not just kidding around."

"I didn't think for a minute you were the kind that would run."

"I don't run. But I'm scared shitless—excuse me—I mean I'm scared out of my wits."

The doctor insisted I be brought home in the ambulance and we let him win that small victory to save face. Of course all we had to do was drive up Queen Charlotte Street to the house in the white Emergency Rescue Squad van with the siren blaring—God knows *that* wasn't necessary—and it served notice to everyone who could see and hear and hadn't already heard that I'd been hurt and was now at home. And then the watermen insisted on carrying me up the stairs to the bedroom, on a stretcher, saying it was their responsibility and no sooner had the door closed on the last waterman than it reopened with the first casserole bearer. Warren was in no mood for pleasantries, simply accepting the bowls with a curt thank you and closing the door on those expectant faces eager for the whole story.

He came upstairs and announced that he wasn't going to open the door anymore. "Let them leave the damn stuff on the porch."

I was feeling too shaky to argue, and my head ached.

"What do they do?" he grumbled, "Cook the damn things ahead of time so they'll have them on hand for the next disaster?"

"Who was here?"

"You know I can't tell those ladies one from another—"

A thought hit me right between the eyes. "Sammy Jo?"

"She was the first."

"Warren—"

"Followed by hundreds of others. Damn things are all over the kitchen table . . . the dining table . . . the hall table . . . the porch table . . ."

"Warren!" I sat up. My brains hit the inside of my forehead just above my eyes. "Warren! Which one is Sammy Jo's?"

"How do I know?"

"It's important! We mustn't eat it! Could be . . . poisoned."

"Are you crazy? I wouldn't touch any of that stuff if I was starving—marshmallows and jello and sweet potato and—"

"Is Luther's car across the street?"

"Who's Luther?"

"Look across the street. Tell me what you see." The pain forced me to close my eyes. "What's happening out there?"

"Sammy Jo's standing outside talking to some guy in that car."

"Very handsome?"

"I can't see his face."

"It's Luther's car so it has to be Luther."

"You can see right through her dress. . . . That woman's got damn good legs!"

He hovered. Even with my eyes closed I could tell. I asked for a cold wet cloth to put on my forehead. He went away and came back with a plastic bag of ice cubes, which he placed with a minimum of crashing on my aching head, and asked if I could sleep awhile. I said I could. As soon as he'd tiptoed out, I staggered into the bathroom and got myself the cold wet cloth I'd asked for. I do love that man.

During the few days I remained in bed, we suddenly had three inches of snow accompanied by thunderstorms. I'd bought a flat of pansies the day before the truck hit. It was worrisome, knowing they were out there under all that, still unplanted, and I was too shaky to explain to Warren where they might be buried. I suspected they might still be in the trunk of the car but I was too weak to cope. *Tant pis.*

Sarah Taylor came to pay a sick call and said Sammy Jo's little dog had died. Natural causes. Said she (Sammy Jo) just took a fit. Hadn't stopped crying since. Luther made a little coffin out of heart pine and Sammy Jo lined it with padded silk and laid him on a down pillow of Miss Emily's in a silk cover. He was buried in the family plot behind the church beside her mother and Miss Emily. Young Mark said it was all right if that's what she wanted. They had a funeral if you please. None of the Davises came probably because all the trashy Tryons did. Young Mark said the prayer for animals over that poor creature and Sammy Jo practically collapsed over his little grave. Sarah Taylor said she was still in mourning.

"Black?"

"No no, she has no black. She told me white was the color of mourning in China. Or maybe it was India. One of those places. She's crying. Looks absolutely dreadful." Sarah Taylor looked terribly pleased at the thought of Sammy Jo looking absolutely dreadful. I remembered someone telling me that Sarah Taylor's late husband had been quite a ladies' man and wondered if Sammy Jo had been one of the ladies. Possible. "You had a real mess of food here, didn't you? Casseroles lined up in front of the door? Whatever did you do with all that stuff?"

"I haven't been down to the kitchen so I really wouldn't know. I imagine Warren's been living off it." Remembering Warren during one of his hovers remarking that the garbage disposal he'd just reinstalled was a great invention and a really good investment. Even our "previously owned" one.

Sarah Taylor went on about how ghastly Sammy Jo was looking and how Miss Emily would never have permitted her to carry on this way. "I'm convinced . . . you know . . ." she said, nodding and winking. "It may not be all grief over her dog," she said.

"Guilt? You mean . . . Miss Emily?"

"I'm not saying."

But when I saw Sammy Jo for the first time after ten days I wasn't so sure. I was setting out my pansies, which had survived the snow jubilantly. Always slender, she was now a skeleton, her head a skull wrapped with disheveled white hair, no longer gleaming. The beautiful, limpid colorless eyes were hidden behind red and swollen lids. Her lips were dry, chapped, bleeding; the Mona Lisa smile had vanished. She was putting a bale of pine straw in handfuls around the base of her beautiful mahonias and nandinas, but when she saw me with my terriers, her gloved hands dropped to her sides and huge tears slid down her sunken cheeks. She stumbled across the street and fell on my shoulder.

"I'm so sorry, Miss Sammy Jo. . . . It's very hard to lose a pet."

Tears running down her chin, she said that her baby was not a pet, he was her baby and most of all her very best and only friend.

I remembered that there hadn't been any tears for Miss Emily. None that I'd seen. But I was truly sorry for her even though she might have tried to kill me, and I was ready to think that she'd been unduly influenced by Luther Tryon. After all, Sammy Jo had never had a plan for anything, no less committing a murder. Seemed to me that would take extra careful planning and a great deal of organization and Miss Emily wasn't around to do it for her. Sammy Jo had never seemed very bright to me and I was sure the perpetrator of a successful and undetected murder wouldn't tell you how agonizing the death was. . . . Would she? . . .

The next time I saw Sammy Jo was when I was taking the dogs out for their morning walk and she was coming out to retrieve her paper. If possible, she looked worse. Coming slowly down the porch stairs, holding carefully to the hand-rail, she took a few steps to the live oak and clung to it to steady herself. The woman was wasted. I crossed the street and picked up her paper. She looked at me without seeing me and murmured what sounded like "appreciate." That's what everyone says down here. Her eyes didn't seem to focus.

"Sammy Jo? Have you seen a doctor?"

But she didn't answer, concentrating on getting up the stairs.

The next time Sarah Taylor and I were lunching at the Harbor View I mentioned that I thought Sammy Jo's condition was deteriorating.

"Pity," she said, enjoying the thought.

"Don't you think she should see a doctor?"

"I believe she prefers her mother's medicine man. Another one of those trashy Tryons."

"But wouldn't Dr. Wilson—I mean, it would be just natural for him to take an interest—Isn't he supposed to be in love with her? For years?"

Sarah Taylor twinkled. "I wouldn't be at all surprised if Dr. Wilson's nose was a bit out of joint with Luther's car always being parked outside the house and Luther always being parked inside the house. I don't believe he or the judge have been able to get to see that stupid woman since Luther Tryon moved in."

Penny, who was waiting on us, remarked that she'd heard that Miss Sammy Jo had gotten worse. She'd had to take to her bed. Young Mark had been to see her.

After she'd poured us more iced tea and left, Sarah Taylor said, "Do you suppose it's serious?"

"If she's having the preacher—Sarah Taylor, if you'd seen her, you'd know it was serious. The woman's on her way out."

"My goodness, we can't have that. She's got to be able to stand trial!"

"It's more than grief. She's sick. Barely able to stay on her feet."

"I'll have to have Lula fry up some chicken and bring it over. Lula's fried chicken is good enough to bring back the dead just to gnaw on a drumstick."

These people have no idea of a proper diet, invalid or not.

After our lunch and our leisurely cruise along the main drag to see the sights—there weren't any, the town was empty—Sarah Taylor brought me home. We both automatically looked across the street at Sammy Jo's house. Something had been added. A garland of dried wildflowers around the door.

"Bubba's been there," Sarah Taylor said. "He always did like Sammy Jo. Along with every other male in town."

Something was missing. Luther's horrible car.

"Looks like Luther's gone," she said. "That wife of his probably dragged him off. She's real jealous."

"I've heard." From Sarah Taylor herself, actually. "I think I'll make Sammy Jo some of my brownies. That should fatten her up."

"And I'll have Lula make some of her mashed potateos and gravy along with her fried chicken. And we'll throw in a can of three-bean salad for greens." (Just the thing for a dying woman. Brownies wouldn't help much either.)

That afternoon I went into a baking frenzy. It wasn't just for Sammy Jo. There were all those empty casseroles, which Warren had washed so neatly, and which could not be returned empty. That's the unwritten law down here. I made dozens of brownies, hoping all the time that Sarah Taylor would be able to identify the casserole owners and thankful for the modest souls who had used foil-covered paper plates.

That was my own method. I brought a dozen brownies on one of them to Sammy Jo's door and knocked. Without waiting for an answer I entered. Luther was just coming down the stairs. I almost dropped the brownies.

"She's sleeping," he said in hushed tones, taking the plate. " 'Preciate."

"Is she any better?"

He shook his head. "Don' look like she be better."

"Shouldn't she see a doctor or—"

"She don' wan' no doctor—"

"Or go to the hospital where someone can look after her?"

"I look after her."

I couldn't wait to get out of there and into my own house and on the telephone to Sarah Taylor. "We have a new neighbor across the street," I said.

"Where? Which house?"

"Sammy Jo's."

"Now Merrie Lee, don't you tease me like that—I'm an old woman."

"Luther seems to be in residence. Says, 'She don' wan' no doctor. She don' wan' no hospital.' He's taking care of her."

"I wouldn't trust him—I wouldn't trust any of those trashy Tryons—"

"I think it's rather sweet—"

"Don't be stupid, girl. He could be killing her."

"I don't think he is. He's got his car parked on the lawn in back of the house, and if he were killing her wouldn't he want to disappear and not be connected with her death at all?"

"You've been seeing too many old movies on television. The person he's got to be scared of isn't the sheriff, it's his wife!" The parade of casseroles for Sammy Jo was steady. Luther seemed to be far more gracious about it than Warren. We could see the ladies leaving the house empty-handed and smiling. Occasionally we'd hear scraps of chatter as they passed each other on the porch steps.

"Is he still there?"

"I swear, he's just about the handsomest man I ever did see."

"Isn't it romantic?"

"He must love her—"

"My husband would just leave me to rot. . . ."

Nobody ever got to see Sammy Jo. She was always sleeping. According to Luther.

And then one dark and stormy night—there'd been a tornado warning all night creeping across the bottom of the television screen—shots rang out across the street. Warren and I jumped out of bed and ran to the window in time to see Luther's car come careening around Sammy Jo's house, across the lawn, and off toward the water. Someone must have called 911 because before we were dressed Chief Samuel Pollock was there in his patrol car. The door was open, and we all went in together.

From upstairs, Sammy Jo's voice was weak. "Luther?"

I ran up to her bedroom. She was in bed, lying there calmly with about four pillows plumped up behind her. The bed was smooth, the hospital corners precisely squared, the linens clean, Miss Sammy Jo's hair was brushed smooth and neatly braided on either side of her face, and she was wearing a dainty white cotton Victorian nightgown. On her head she wore a crown of paper whites. Unmistakably Bubba's work. Although still wasted, she was no longer distraught and her pretty eyes were clear and untroubled. All in all, the product of expert nursing care. She smiled. Her eyes drifted to a bowl of wildflowers and fern. "Luther has been . . . so kind. . . ." Her voice was whispery but no more so than usual. "Where is Luther?"

Chief Samuel Pollock appeared at the doorway. "Good evening, Miss Sammy Jo," he said, removing his cap. She had that effect on all men, besides driving them mad with lust. "Mis' Spencer," he said, "there's no one else in the house."

I offered to stay the night. Warren said he'd be downstairs waiting for Luther. Chief Samuel Pollock took our testimony on what we'd seen and heard. We were careful to give him the facts and only the facts. While he was talking to us he received some reports on the two-way radio clipped to his belt from people on Queen Charlotte Street who could see Miss Emily's house from the rear. They'd seen a man and woman run out of the house after the first shots. They seemed to be struggling for possession of a gun. They heard two shots and then the man had picked up the woman and thrown her into his car and driven off.

Eventually both patrol cars left. I went down to the kitchen for a glass of ice water for Sammy Jo. Warren and I engaged in a murmured discussion mostly about my not staying there more than the night. "That woman belongs in a hospital," he said. "You are not a nurse."

"I'm calling Doctor Wilson first thing in the morning."

"Right," said Warren.

I couldn't help noticing that the kitchen was immaculate. Luther'd been caring for Miss Emily's Boston ferns and they looked better than ever. And now there was a row of little pots with Eulalee's herbs, bright green and flourishing.

But I didn't have to phone Dr. Wilson or do anything more for Sammy Jo. Warren had gone home, and I was dozing in the old rocker next to Sammy Jo's bed when I felt a hand on my shoulder. I looked up into the handsomest face I'd ever seen off the screen. My lord, that man was good-looking. "You go now," he said, and escorted me to the front door. " 'Preciate," he said, and closed it with me standing on the porch in the first light of day with the breeze that always comes along with the tide change. I heard the lock snap. And that was that.

Chapter 7

◆

• Of course, the talk went on for days. Especially because Luther's wife had never returned and there were all those motherless children having to make do while Luther stayed with Miss Sammy Jo doing God knows what. Samuel Pollock started investigating the disappearance of Mary Tryon, and Social Services started investigating the alleged neglect of the children, and the whole town was firmly convinced that Luther Tryon had murdered his wife. I heard it at Town Meeting and Piggly Wiggly and Garden Club, although Eulalee, who had finally become our president with Miss Emily's demise, made a very dignified little speech about people abusing other people when they didn't *really* know what they were talking about. I was told that young Mark preached a whole sermon about false witness, but I was also told that Chief Samuel Pollock was getting ready to book Luther on suspicion of murder.

Sammy Jo, of course, knew nothing of the hot winds of gossip and suspicion that blew around her house. Emmy Lou Willis, who had more balls than anyone, and had run upstairs to see for herself before Luther could pick her up and set her out on the porch—well, Emmy Lou reported that Miss Sammy Jo's room had been so clean and the bed looked so clean and the room smelled so nice from Eulalee's herbs scattered on the floor near the bed and the patient herself had looked clean and well cared for, and that she looked happier and more peaceful than Emmy Lou had ever seen her, wearing her crown of paper whites that looked like Bubba's work, and someone had tied pink satin ribbon in bows on her braids and who else could that have been but Luther and she thought that was real sweet.

Although I believed more firmly than ever that Luther and Sammy Jo had done away with Miss Emily, I was convinced that it was Luther and not Sammy Jo who had thought of, planned, and executed the deed. Sammy Jo was simply incapable of thinking, planning, and carrying out anything, even the day's shopping at Piggly Wiggly, without having it all spelled out for her in great detail and simple language. I'm not implying that her mind was subnormal, or anything like that, but to quote Sarah Taylor, "Sammy Jo's mind is between her legs. It always has been and will be until the day she dies. And it's real hard to get her to focus on anything else."

Warren was skeptical over his glasses. "You're writing your own scenario," he said, "the way you'd like it to be. If that's the case, Luther and Sammy Jo being the murderers, then who arranged your accident with the pickup truck? You think they did?"

Now Warren had argued with me long and hard that the driver of the truck had not been aware that he'd hit me. And I had countered just as vigorously with the tearing sound of metal against metal, loud enough to bring Miss Pearl to her window for the first time in twenty years or whatever. Then he dared to suggest that the truck driver might have been deaf. I made short shrift of that. Then he said maybe the driver had been a hit-and-run person and that was what the police and the insurance company were assuming and the police were still looking for the truck. And I had stopped arguing because my head hurt. And *now* he says, "Who arranged your accident with the truck?" Who *arranged?* Obviously, having forgotten everything he'd already said on the subject and all our previous arguments. He's a very bad liar because he can never remember what he said. I felt a chill knowing he'd been lying just to make me feel better.

"Oh? Now it was deliberate?" I said.

"What? What was deliberate?"

"After working so hard to convince me that it was an accident and I had nothing to worry about except to get well and that *no one* was out to kill me—"

"Shit!" He'd remembered.

"Now I'm scared again."

He held me close. "I'm taking care of you. Nobody's going to hurt you, Merrie, I promise. . . . No one's going to hurt you. . . . No one's going to hurt you. . . ." His sweater needed washing. "I'll kill them if they do, whoever it is . . . I'll kill them. . . ."

"That's not going to help me."

"Nobody's going to get anywhere near you," he promised. "From now on I'm your personal bodyguard."

Oh God. Constant hovering. But he'd probably forget he'd said that.

This was the time of the seed catalogs, always a joy, and good for hours and hours of browsing and cautious decisions. Warren and I were now arguing about compost rather than killers. I'd always wanted a compost pile. He said if we put food scraps in it, it would attract rats, which was easy enough since we're so close to the water and everyone has seen water rats scampering in the marshes at one time or another. And what did I think he'd installed that garbage disposal for? Not to collect garbage and rats in the yard.

Grass clippings, I said. Weeds. Plants that have been thrown out or thinned—that's what makes compost.

But then someone dug up Sammy Jo's little dog's grave. There was nothing left but a hole. The little coffin and its contents were gone. And the whole town erupted. Except Sammy Jo, who was spending more and more time sleeping with a peaceful smile on her face and a crown of flowers on her head. There were those who said it was a disgrace. A blot on Davis Landing. A prosecutable offense. They implored Sam Pollock to find the culprit and hang him by the balls. That last was me. Warren and I had been truly shocked and grieved to find this kind of mean-spiritedness in Davis Landing. Of course, privately, we wondered why the poor little thing hadn't been buried in the Davis perennial border or beneath the dogwood or under the trellis with the white Lady Banksia climbing rose. I have had dogs all my life and have always buried them close to me on my own property, wherever it happened to be at that moment in my life.

Admittedly, I often wondered, after I moved on, how many of those poor little skeletons wrapped in deteriorating baby blankets would turn up to puzzle the next owners. Sammy Jo could easily have done that and no need to worry about the next owners as that house hadn't gone out of the family since it was built three hundred years ago. A little marker could have been put in any of those places and it being family property no one could have objected. Although, this being Davis Landing, there's always someone to object to anything no matter how harmless.

Warren and I are dog people and possibly biased on the subject. But the other side was making a fuss out of all proportion to the facts. Those who objected to sharing the same hallowed ground as poor little Pepper didn't give a thought to old General Latimore being buried in *his* family plot with his favorite hunter, Ranger, as well as his favorite hunting dog, Ralph, beside him like some Egyptian pharaoh. And young Mark *had* said the prayer for animals over Pepper's grave. There were some who said they wouldn't rest knowing that a dog was lying at their heads. They were from the families in the neighboring plots. But then there were others who said they'd a lot rather have their heads beside little old Pepper than Miss Emily. Or even Sammy Jo. And then there were those who said what with General Latimore's horse and dog (of course that dog was a black Lab and therefore more acceptable than a dachshund) and the British soldier buried in the standing salute to King George and the little girl in the whis-

key keg, who were they to object to another dog? That ceme-
tery was a pretty kinky place *before* Pepper'd been laid to rest.
The only thing that almost everyone agreed upon was that it
had been a particularly mean-spirited episode in the history of
Davis Landing. Of which there were many. We all knew that
Miss Sammy Jo had taken great pains with the marker. It was
Italian marble, with a baby angel smiling down at a wreath of
hearts and flowers and the inscription FAREWELL MY HEART'S
DELIGHT. Many thought that was a slap in the face for Luther
Tryon, but the town never really got a chance to get into it, as
the grave was desecrated and the coffin gone and not even one
little bone left before the design had even been carved.

We were watching the "MacNeil/Lehrer News Hour" and
I was thinking how familiar their experts had become, when
Warren said, "It's about time they got some new faces on that
program. Same old experts and same old opinions. The only
one I don't mind is Lee Cullum from Dallas." I told him that's
because she's pretty and I was getting myself into a depression
thinking of the two of us never getting out of that place and
finishing each other's sentences or thinking the same things at
the same time until we died probably in the same hour and
that's what's known as a successful marriage! God! Which is
about when we became aware of flashing lights outside. Our
television is in the downstairs room at the front of the house,
which at one time had been a bedroom, and in which several
family members had breathed their last, but we called it the
library in deference to the bookshelves Warren had installed.
The flashing lights were joined by angry shouts. That was
enough to get us out of our seats, abandoning our dinner, my
pasta Amitriciana, and on to the front porch. Chief Samuel
Pollock was dragging Luther Tryon in handcuffs across Miss
Emily's lawn toward the patrol car flashing its red light. Both
men were shouting and struggling, sweating and disheveled.
Samuel Pollock's face was bruised. He threw Luther Tryon
headfirst in the rear of the car, the part fenced off with heavy
chicken wire.

"What happened?"

"Mis' Spencer, I'm bookin' that no good sonofabitch if you'll excuse the language for suspicion of murder."

"Sammy Jo? Is she dead?"

"No ma'am, Miss Sammy Jo's condition is unchanged. I'm bookin' that trash for suspicion of murderin' his wife."

I wondered, and not for the first time, exactly what Sammy Jo had to drive men mad. Okay, she was beautiful in her ethereal, unsubstantial way. When we were back within our own walls I asked Warren.

"How do I know? Ask Luther Tryon."

"Couldn't you guess?"

"No."

"Would you like to do sex with Sammy Jo?"

"What kind of a trick question is that?"

"I mean, she's so unreal. White hair, white face, white clothes, little white voice—"

"Great legs—"

"And sort of all bones—I mean, there's not much there for the guys who want something to hold on to on a cold night, is there?"

"Great legs . . ."

"Can't we even have an intelligent discussion?"

"No we cannot have an intelligent discussion about the sex appeal of a woman who is dying."

"She could recover."

"When your approach to the subject is undiluted jealousy—"

"I am *not* jealous of Sammy Jo—oh God, she's alone in that house now with no one to look after her—What if—" I went slamming out to the front porch and stopped short. The doctor's car was there, the judge's car was there, and we were going to need a traffic cop soon to keep things moving what with all the cars stopping in the middle of the street and ladies moving eagerly up the steps of Miss Emily's house with their casseroles. More going in than coming out and cars left with motors running—I tell you it was a mess! I could see this happening in the east seventies: I could hear the horns blaring and the swearing drivers—I could hear the obscenities all the way down here in Davis Landing just like I'd heard it for years on any rainy day.

Chapter 8

♦

• The local weekly said that Luther Tryon was being held
without bail on suspicion of murdering his wife—Miss Emily
wasn't even mentioned—due to the disappearance of Mary
Tryon, his wife. And in a separate article it said Miss Samantha Jo Davis was confined to bed and not receiving her friends.
She was resting comfortably and all her friends in Davis Landing were hoping for a swift recovery.

"What friends!" Sarah Taylor and I were having shrimp-
burgers at the Harbor View just for the hell of it. Shrimpburg-
ers are like oysterburgers except they're made with lukewarm
shrimp boiled to the consistency of wood. She was reading the
Davis Landing Weekly. "Miss Eulalee Merrill has moved into
the Davis house to look after Miss Samantha Jo Davis—"

Penny was pouring iced tea. "Miss Eulalee loves to take
care of the sick and the dying. I mean, she'll get on her hands
and knees and scrub floors and stay up all night and make her
herb teas and collard purees. . . . My husband says Miss
Eulalee is a saint. Lots of people say that."

Sarah Taylor said she'd have some of Susie Bell's key lime
pie. "I seem to have developed a craving for that damn pie,"
she said. "Woke up this morning and that's what I was thinking. Key lime pie."

"You're not the only one, Miss Sarah," Penny said. "How about you, Miss Merrie?"

I declined. That pie was so sweet it'd set your teeth on edge. We watched Penny's retreat to the kitchen, switching her hips all the way.

"You know, I haven't seen Eulalee over there—just once with a casserole—"

"If it says so in the *Weekly* then she's there."

"I didn't know that Sammy Jo and Eulalee were friends!"

"They're not."

"I didn't know they were the least bit close."

"They're not."

"Then what—"

"You don't have to be a friend of Eulalee's. You heard Penny. She's a saint. Eulalee is stricken with the necessity to Do Good. You know . . . Meals on Wheels, the church, the poor, the hungry, the homeless—"

"Maybe I should go over and help her—"

"Don't."

"But she's just a little white-haired lady! It's not easy to change sheets and turn patients and—"

"Let Eulalee do it her own way. Stay out of it. She likes to be Chief Do-Gooder. There's more than a bit of the martyr in that woman. Buried two husbands, you know. No children with either of them though she wanted young 'uns both times, but she said the Lord had other things for her to do like mothering other people's young 'uns—helping people—feeding them that terrible vegetarian slop of hers—herb teas . . ."

You know in this place people really do say "young 'uns." And critters. I'm thinking of trying it myself. But it would probably sound too phony. So I just said, "Sammy Jo is used to herb teas. Luther's got a lot of Indian remedies for things— Sarah Taylor! Can they just hold that man indefinitely on *suspicion?*"

"In Davis Landing—"

"I know. But there's the law. The law of the land."

"Here it's who you are, not what the law says. You should

know that by now, Merrie Lee—After all, you're one of us."

"But doesn't he have to have some representation? Doesn't he get a chance to defend himself? Have they told him what the charges are—"

"He knows it's suspicion of murder. He stands there big as life and says he didn't murder anyone and he doesn't know where his wife is. Says he's innocent. Frankly, I don't think anyone that good-looking is ever innocent."

Penny set Sarah Taylor's key lime pie before her. "Isn't he just the best-looking thing you ever saw?"

I thought of that dawn when I'd awakened in the rocker to look up into his face. "For sure," I said. "The best."

Penny told us he had women outside the jail every day. They sent him notes and food and sat outside his window singing sad songs and knitting sweaters for him. The teenagers knitted mufflers as they hadn't learned sweaters.

And then Davis Landing received another shock and the phones were ringing so hard you couldn't talk to anyone you wanted to talk to. Chief Samuel Pollock had received an indignant letter from Luther Tryon's *wife!* And Darleen in the sheriff's office had seen it and made an illegal copy of it on her machine and was kind enough to circulate it all over town. People were having their own copies made. Poor illiterate thing, I won't even try to reproduce it for you, but the gist of it was that she was sick and tired of taking care of the young 'uns while Luther took his pleasure wherever he wanted and she was in Florida to take her pleasure wherever *she* wanted and he and that skinny old white woman of his could take care of the young 'uns from now on. She said this was an official document serving notice that she was giving her children to their father, Luther Tryon of Davis Landing, and to let that man out of jail so he could look after those poor little critters. Well! Davis Landing just about went crazy! The word got out to the women outside the jail and they started marching and carrying banners and shouting to release Luther Tryon. And since Luther was being held on suspicion of murdering his wife and that very same wife had just written a letter saying to let him go because she was never coming back to housework and children. . . . Well, there didn't seem to be any case. Even Judge Davis said to let him go.

Luther came out of jail to the sound of drums and bugles—the girls from the high school band and a serenade by the Love Pats, our local country group, playing their guitars and shaking their curls. He went home, he said later, to get rid of that damn jail smell and fix himself nice to go see Miss Sammy Jo, but when he appeared a couple of hours later, all slicked up and so gorgeous I had to keep from running across the street to throw my arms around him, with a bouquet of flowers, he met Dr. Wilson at the door. Dr. Wilson was wiping tears. There was no need for words. He said Sammy Jo had died with a smile on her face.

It was very sad. Eulalee said Luther had just rushed upstairs and picked up that dead Sammy Jo and sat in the rocker holding her and just rocked her and rocked her singing little Indian lullabies to her like she was a little girl that could hear, with the tears streaming down his face. Eulalee said it was a very romantic death and Eulalee should know. She's seen most of the dying around here.

The funeral was subdued compared to Miss Emily's. Luther Tryon wasn't there. One of Bubba's best and prettiest wreaths was on the coffin. Eulalee said Luther had said goodbye in that rocker upstairs. The town got quiet and started talking about the weather, and the preservationists and the environmentalists joined forces against the developers, and things pretty much settled down to normal. Or what's considered normal around here.

Until the news of Sammy Jo's will leaked out. It was a handwritten will, but it was legal and she'd gotten two witnesses out of those trashy Tryons and they signed and there it was. All legal. She'd left the old house to Luther Tryon. And her 1987 Subaru and all the money in her bank account. I tell you tongues were wagging from both ends. Not helped by Luther Tryon moving in to the old Davis house with that historic plaque and all the years of history and Miss Emily's reign over the town from that very house, which now had trashy Tryons sittin' on their backsides drinkin' their moonshine out of Miss Emily's best old Waterford goblets and Luther's five kids all over town in Luther's old car now that he had inherited Sammy Jo's. (Oh God, I've started thinking in southern.)

Now I am a grandmother, although I don't publicize that fact, but I have raised two of my own and seen their little ones. For a while I was den mother of a Cub Scout troop when I was married to my first husband in Connecticut until the scout master and the Congregational minister came to call and asked me to please wear a bra for scout meetings. And here I'd been thinking the troop's unusual attendance record was because I always made them my brownies to have with their milk. Of course, I told those men that it was perfectly normal for little boys to want to look at tits (I said breasts), especially if they were as good as mine, and that they both had really dirty minds, and I resigned right there.

But I have never seen such an undisciplined and wild bunch as Luther Tryon's kids. Boys and girls alike. Dirty, driving up and down the streets and none of them old enough to have a license—you couldn't see them behind the steering wheel— and shooting off their rifles and pistols like they were a posse. They went up and down this town and shot holes in the historic plaques, and I tell you that didn't go down very well.

A lot of people spoke to Judge Davis, who was plenty upset about his ancestral home anyway, and a lot of people spoke to Sam Pollock, and others went to the sheriff, but there was nothing anyone could do because Luther Tryon had a perfect right to live in the old Davis house as it was legally his. They tried to nail him on his kids driving without a license, but they never could catch any of them behind the wheel of that car. Once those kids caught sight of state troopers or Sam Pollock or any official, they just jumped out of the car and ran, and they were *fast*, those little Indians.

Some people even went to the governor, but he was researching the Caribbean. And then there was the group that started up that rumor again that Sammy Jo wasn't a Davis really and therefore had no right to the house when she was alive and none at all after she was dead. But that sort of thing requires documentation and solid proof and nobody'd come up with any of that yet. But it wasn't the least bit amusing living on our street anymore, or even very pleasant. And our tenants in New York were very much ensconced and paying their rent promptly on the first of every month so there was nothing we could do except close the windows against the noise and draw the curtains against the sight of those trashy Tryons milling around. A number of people stopped me at the Piggly Wiggly or walking with my dogs along the waterfront and commiserated on the horrors of living right across the street from that mess and how I must feel being a Davis myself.

Chapter 9

♦

♦ We were living in a constant state of gloom and dusk. It was so depressing that I found myself calling Dolores, our darling Dolores, in New York and asking her how things were up there. It was snowing, she said. Everything was getting more and more expensive. The subway was more dangerous than ever. People killed in the street every day. *Every* day! Shopping, even on Ninth Avenue, even on Fourteenth Street, was more and more expensive. Everyone in New York hated the mayor (but then they always do no matter who he is). No police anywhere to be seen.

The more she castigated New York the more nostalgic I became. Dolores has always had a wide streak of *La Passionara* in her. And the more I heard the more choked up I got. When she'd worked for us she'd always come in at eight-thirty promptly after stopping at Saint Ann's for her soul, given us the *New York Times* (for the world news) and the *New York Post* and the *New York Daily News* (for the news of our friends in the gossip columns) and orated about the state of the world. When she finished by saying that she was thinking of going back to Spain, I said "No, Dolores, please, we'll be back." But she insisted that life in the city was just getting too hard. She and her husband (a retired merchant seaman) had been talking about it a lot. I started to cry. Immediately, her strident tone changed to one of soft, crooning sympathy. She wanted to know what was the matter. I was beyond speech. Then she said she was coming down to see for herself. She said I needed her.

Oh, just the thought of it was soothing as a massage. Dolores on her hands and knees, scrubbing behind toilet bowls, baseboards, corners where the dust had been undisturbed for a hundred years . . . making her wonderful tortillas (Spanish tortilla is a frittata made of eggs, onions, and potatoes, and Dolores's are the best I ever tasted). . . . I moaned that I'd send her a plane ticket in the next mail, but she reminded me somewhat indignantly that she was a rich woman, probably having more money than I did. She mentioned the apartment in New York, the apartment in Madrid, the house in Salamanca, the two mink coats down to her shoes, and announced that she would buy her own ticket and not to argue. I blew my nose and we arranged a date for her visit. It was so comforting to know that Dolores was coming and would take care of everything. As was her wont. It cheered me enough to open the curtains and look across the street. Five Tryon men had added three slutty women from God knows where.

That porch was really crowded. I mean they were hanging from the rail. Noisy. Rowdy. I closed the curtains and found Warren on the back porch tinkering with the previously owned garbage disposal, which was once again no longer working. But when I told him about Dolores's visit in a tone of great jubilation, he just grunted. And he was really very fond of Dolores. . . . It can get pretty lonely down here. I'm so isolated.

Thank God for Jackie and Mathilda. They had provided introductions to lots of people I might not otherwise have gotten to know—"Those little dogs terr'rs?" I'd explain what breed they were and how Australians were the result of a Norwich-Cairn-Yorkshire blend that originated in Australia and they were used to herd sheep and also as ratters. Then the talk inevitably turned to the prevalence of fleas down here, flea remedies, and the ferociousness of the native colonies.

But they weren't just conversation pieces, they were my constant companions. Jackie in particular. Now I've had dogs all my life—Boston bulls, wirehaired terriers, Irish terriers, cocker spaniels, springer spaniels, dachshunds, Yorkshires, and then Jackie and Mathilda, the best dogs I'd ever owned. Undemanding. There was never any whining or unnecessary barking. No trouble. They'd sit quietly tuned in to you and your moods. Ready for a walk, a run, a ride, or a nap. If I ate, they ate. If I slept, they slept. They were not only the smartest, they were definitely the most considerate. And that little Jackie sensed every time I was down. He'd come over to me and just rest his chin on the seat of my chair (they weren't permitted to get on the furniture) and look into my eyes with understanding and sympathy. I couldn't have survived in Davis Landing without Jackie. Mathilda too, of course, but Jackie was special. Dolores loved them too. Our babies, she said.

There was a lot to do before she got here. I was very busy putting things away, emptying boxes, throwing out trash, rearranging closets and drawers. . . . She'd look into everything. Vacuuming. Bleaching towels and bed linens, which had an unfortunate tendency to yellow in Davis Landing water. I even did a little weeding in the dooryard garden. First impressions are important.

And I cooked. Cinnamon buns I thought she'd like for breakfast. The recipe was one given me by a fellow traveler on USAir when we'd been held up by missed connections. It seemed that the more the fares rose the worse the service got. Unfortunately there isn't a direct flight from here to any-where, so it's most important that planes be on time, which they never are. To fly six hundred miles it is necessary to plan on spending a full day to reach your destination. Forty-five minutes to drive to the airport and then sit and wait. The plane is usually coming from Charlotte, but it might just as well be Cairo. Of course when it comes in you are already an hour late for your connection in Charlotte, Baltimore, or wherever. I have spent three hours waiting in the Baltimore airport, which was not great. They gave me free long-distance calls to cancel all my afternoon appointments in New York and a ten-dollar chit for MacDonald's! Can you believe *anyone* eating ten dollars' worth of food at *MacDonald's*? Anyway, this very attractive man and I started talking about food and he'd taken a course in baking when he got divorced. He gave me the recipe for cinnamon buns, which I had never tried and had wanted to ever since.

And then there was a recipe in *Esquire* for souse. It said that this was a southern tradition eaten during the holidays, and that the recipe would feed a crowd and last from Christmas to New Years. Okay, it was well past that time but I thought I'd try it anyway. It was always good to have something in the refrigerator. And something different to serve and eat. I am so *bored* with my own cooking. Now that we've eliminated red meat, butter, cream, salt, sugar, pastries, and anything good, we're left with fish and chicken, pork once a week, everything simply grilled or poached, vegetables with fake butter flavor, and fruit such as it is down here. There is a great scarcity of doctors and a third-world hospital so we don't dare get sick. We're healthy but oh my God there's not much pleasure in living.

A couple of days passed while I shopped for ingredients and cooked pork neck bones and pig's feet according to *Esquire's* recipe. Then, one whole day picking the meat off the bones, shredding the meat . . . I won't go into the whole procedure, but I was pleased with the result. It was sort of a super-deluxe, sophisticated-palate head cheese with a hot pepper flavor. The recipe said serve it sliced with vinegar. Warren said it was okay, but he'd never cared for jellied anything. I decided to share some of it with the neighbors and carried little portions to the various houses. It was presented prettily, resting in bright green parsley, but the reaction was, to say the least, disappointing. They'd look at it dubiously and say, "What is it?"

They were supposed to know! "Souse!" I'd declare with the air of one dispensing gifts of myrrh and frankincense.

"Souse?"

They'd heard of it but never eaten any. And when they obliged me by tasting it they really didn't care if they *never* ate any. Great disappointment for me after all that work. I was still scraping pig's feet out from under my fingernails, but there was a lot of souse for Dolores.

Then the cinnamon buns. I was rather pleased with my first attempt at the recipe. They smelled wonderful while baking, good enough to rouse the Stockbroker from his bed. "Cinnamon buns," he said when he came into the kitchen. Okay, they weren't quite brown enough. More of a beige. And I hadn't frosted them because we were on this healthy no-sugar kick. He took one bite and pronounced them doughy. He did eat one, though. I spent the next week before Dolores's arrival baking cinnamon buns. She and I had baked bread together, huge loaves of coarse, chewy country bread, which, when baked, she held against her bosom, slicing toward her. That knife could have been lethal in anyone else's hand, resulting at the very least in a mastectomy, but Dolores knew what she was doing. I wanted to display my cinnamon bun prowess to her. Every morning Warren came down to a new batch of cinnamon buns. Every morning he pronounced them doughy. I couldn't believe it. I had been trying various oven temperatures and baking times, but he was never satisfied. I took to passing them out to the neighbors up and down the street, asking for their opinions. Standing over them while they tasted. They all said my cinnamon buns were delicious. Great. Best they ever tasted. I'd run home to Warren and triumphantly repeat their praises. They asked for the recipe!

"Merrie," he said, "these people are lying to you. You know how they are down here. Two-faced."

One of the women said my husband was probably jealous. "Jealous of what?"

"Of you gettin' that recipe from that man in the airport. Sugar, he's jealous of you talkin' to that man!"

She didn't know Warren. Warren ignored me except in times of crisis like when I'd been hurt by that truck. Years ago Halston had made me a short, flame-red raw-silk caftan, which I adored and kept dragging out to wear when we entertained at home or when we went to a small dinner at someone else's house. I wore it with all my pearls, and it was a really great dress because you didn't have to hold your stomach in all the time. It was so comfortable and never wrinkled and of course, it was madly becoming. I'd been wearing that dress steadily for at least ten years when I put it on one night in New York and he looked at me and said, "New dress?"

He'd have a long wait for cinnamon buns down here. I'd bake them for Dolores and that would be the last cinnamon buns he'd ever smell in this house.

Cleaning and baking and making souse had taken up so much of my time that I hadn't paid much attention to what was going on in town, if anything. Whenever I went out of the house to walk the dogs or get in the car and do my shopping I was unavoidably aware of the porch directly across the street teeming with Tryons, but I tried to ignore them. Warren brought home the local paper, which he'd bought to find out if there was anything happening with the environmentalists versus the developers and I glanced at it while I was waiting for the cinnamon buns to come out of the oven. Elvira Lewis was confined to her bed unable to have visitors. Miss Eulalee Duncan had moved in to the Lewis house to tend to her friend.

"That Eulalee Duncan has got to be the Mother Theresa of Davis Landing. She doesn't seem to have any life of her own."

Warren grunted. He was chuckling over "Calvin & Hobbes."

"I bet her mail and her phone messages really pile up. I know since I don't have a secretary if I'm away one week it takes two weeks to catch up with myself." Just babbling. Suddenly I felt I *had* to communicate with another human being. I phoned Sarah Taylor and luckily she was free for lunch and would be delighted to pick me up at eleven-thirty.

There was hardly anyone at the Harbor View. Sarah Taylor said she'd heard they were thinking of closing for the three winter months. Nobody came to Davis Landing in the winter. Harbor View did business with summer tourists and boat people traveling the Inland Waterway in October and November on their way to Florida and the Caribbean and in April and May when it was time for them to show their faces around Bar Harbor and Newport. I said if the Harbor View had better food they probably could attract people from all over the state all year round. God knows they had the best view in Davis Landing.

Sarah Taylor didn't comment on the food. She was fiercely loyal and the Harbor View was her favorite place to eat. She asked if I knew what was wrong with Elvira Lewis. I told her I didn't. "I didn't even know she was ill until Warren brought home the *Weekly*."

"She's your kin."

"She's your kin, too. I can't keep track of the state of health of all my kin! The whole damn *town* is kin!"

"There's no need to get testy, Merrie Lee. This lunch was your idea."

"Can I get you something to drink," Penny interrupted in her brightest, chirpiest voice.

"Not iced tea," I told her. "It's too damn cold in here. Have you got the air conditioning on or something?"

"No ma'am, we just don't have any heat on," she said. "Business (pronounced *bidniz*) hasn't been too good lately. But"—and back to chirping—"our special today is a cup of Down East chowder and a half of an oysterburger."

Sarah Taylor and I looked at each other questioningly. Then she turned to Penny and said, "How much?"

"Two ninety-five on the special, Miss Sarah, and it's real gu-u-ud."

"We'll have two specials."

When she'd disappeared into the kitchen, Sarah Taylor said that Elvira Lewis had never had a sick day in her life. Until now.

"That's what they said about Miss Emily."

"Well, dear, there is such a thing as old age. We're all vigorous but no one is immortal."

"True."

"Still. I would like to know what Elvira Lewis has got."

"I'd like to know what Sammy Jo had to make my husband who never sees me notice her legs. Anytime you said Sammy Jo, he said great legs. Like pushing a button. Sammy Jo—great legs."

"I hear Luther Tryon is completely broken up. He's telling people his life is over without her."

"Not from what I see across the street."

"Lord knows where all those people are sleeping!"

"Those scruffy men—"

"I believe they're Luther's brothers—"

"And I see three women who seem to be living there—"

"Trash."

"That house used to be so quiet and beautifully kept—"

"Merrie Lee, I've had one of those crazy ideas, but I got it in my head and I can't get it out. . . ."

"Tell me—"

"Well, you know how Sammy Jo was—always in white, with that hair—like a ghost—"

"And that little white voice—"

"And just sort of floating along instead of walking like other people—"

"Like a human hydrofoil on slow—unreal."

"My thoughts exactly. Like a creature from another world. I think she had powers. To keep herself attractive to men—all sorts of powers—I think that using all her Indian lore she put a spell on poor Luther!"

I thought about that.

"She was a witch. Maybe. Indian witchcraft!"

I considered *that*. "But Luther is Indian too. He could have fought her spell with his own spell."

"If he wanted to. But hers was so strong that he lost the will to fight against it."

We were silent for a while. Then I said, "Come on, Sarah Taylor! You don't really believe that, do you?"

"I don't know if I do or I don't."

Penny served the Down East chowder. It was gray and watery and full of potatoes. Tasted, it was a hot liquid with a slight taste of clams. But at least it was hot.

Penny asked us if we'd heard about Miss Elvira Lewis. She'd been working in her garden digging in some old horse manure that her son had brought her from Texas for Christmas, diggin' it in around the roses and she just fell over. She'd been feeling fine and it was a real nice day to work in the garden, a lot better than one of those terrible hot and humid days, but there she was. Just fell over. Miss Eulalee happened to see it when she was passing and went right into Miss Elvira's house and dialed 9-1-1 for Emergency Rescue. But they couldn't find anything wrong and the Emergency Room at the hospital couldn't find anything wrong and so they just sent her on home with Miss Eulalee.

"As a matter of fact, I had just had a cup of coffee with Elvira. Must have been a couple of hours before. Said she wasn't feeling all that good. She'd been trying some of Eulalee's herbs and seaweed sticks and vitamins and she said she didn't know what was doing it. She was going to stop the seaweed."

"You do get around, don't you?"

"Merrie Lee, you forget I've spent my whole life here. This is my *home*."

"Unlike mine?"

"Merrie Lee, what *is* the matter with you today!"

"Sorry. I really don't know. I think—maybe—well, when we came down here it was for a limited length of time and it was sort of an adventure—like going to live in China for a year. Or India. You know, totally foreign. Different language, different customs, different food, different way of dressing..."

"I wasn't aware that we were all that different from the rest of the country, Merrie Lee. Although we certainly have better manners than you people up there—"

"Damyankees—you might as well say it."

"All right! But I don't feel I'm offending *you* because you're one of us—"

"But that's just it! I am and I'm not! You know, in the beginning I was very curious about *everything*. It was all research. Living with history. My attitude was mostly sociological, really. But we've been here too long for it to be an adventure—or foreign. I'm more comfortable with Davis Landing—although I still can't go along with shooting swans and then frying them. And now I want—I need—I need to feel I belong here—that I'm not just that lady with the two little dogs. I need to be accepted—to be one of you—"

"But you are, my dear. You were born to Davis Landing."

"And at the same time I miss New York—I miss my friends—I miss my work—I'm so torn—"

"Of course you are. Being a transplant is painful. But you have to put down your roots somewhere, child."

"I guess I'm just lonely. Warren and I spend so much time together and he doesn't talk very much. Or listen."

"Warren is a lovely man." She was firm about that.

"I know. . . . He probably misses things too. Of course he'd never say—All he's said about it is that he misses his tennis game. . . ."

"That's one of the things on the town agenda, you know. Cleaning up that old court out on the point."

"Needs more than cleaning. That court needs a whole new surface. The clay doesn't drain at all. Warren went out to look at it and he says we need a totally new court constructed over some good drainage."

"Then we do. Warren is a lovely man and you are a lucky woman. Every woman in this town envies you—and he never looks at anyone but you."

"He doesn't look at *me* . . . and who the hell is there to cast an eye on in this swamphole? Name me one young, attractive woman—just one—"

"Well I'd have to say you're about the only one, Merrie Lee. And lucky not to have any competition."

I remembered what I'd heard about Sarah Taylor's husband, that she'd spent many a night alone while he was "working." And then there was some sort of hushed-up scandal. Something about his dying of a heart attack in the saddle so to speak. Some one else's saddle so to speak. I said, "I know I'm lucky . . . maybe it's just loneliness. . . . It's damn lonely being married to Warren, but then my second husband was a compulsive talker and there was never any getting away from the sound of his voice. Even when he was sleeping."

"Maybe next time you'll hit it right. Cheer up. Garden Club is tomorrow and they're having a guest speaker—that new landscape architect. That's what he calls himself. Can't imagine how he's going to make a living around here. Everybody's gardens have been all set for a hundred years or more and if we want anything new we'd just do what we've always done and ask for a cutting. That's how Miss Emily got her old-fashioned petunias many years ago. And we all got ours from hers. Yours too. But you might find Garden Club interesting tomorrow. I hear he's been all over the world and knows all about everything."

"Just so he can tell me what the hell is eating the insides out of my hibiscus buds before they can open."

Chapter 10

♦

♦ The next morning we sat waiting for the stragglers. The talk was of the weather interspersed with the news of Elvira Lewis who was said to be failing. I looked around the room. All the ladies had obviously been to Miss Ophelia's. They sat quietly with their freshly done hair and their walkers and their canes, looking very pastel, all of them with those glasses that have the ear pieces that are at the base of the lens, very elaborate frames that wind into curlicues and double back on themselves. There was a flag on a stanchion in the corner of the room. That was new. Probably bought with part of the fought-over dues was my guess. And there was a very young, very good-looking guy over in the corner. *That* was new. He was looking at me, somewhat bemused. I flashed him a welcoming smile. He looked startled for a moment, then gave me a big grin showing teeth so white they looked like my friends' who'd had theirs bleached. The landscape architect no doubt. He seemed awfully young.

Eulalee called the meeting to order and announced that we were going to open with the pledge of allegiance to our lovely flag we'd been given by General Davis, who was the head of the Davis Landing VFW. We all stood and faced the flag and put our hands over our hearts. I hadn't said the pledge of allegiance since I was in first grade. Stumbling through it, I was touched to the point of tears at the sight of my fellow members leaning on their walkers and their canes, earnestly proclaiming the words that politicians were using to get themselves elected. The Garden Club *meant* it. We sat down. I wiped away a tear, uncomfortably aware that the landscape architect was watching me. Of course, I stood out in that group. Nobody else was crying over the pledge of allegiance for one thing. And I could stand and even walk without assistance. I was the youngest woman in the room and the slimmest, although that wasn't terribly visible in my navy sweatsuit. I sneaked a look at the boy. He winked. My head snapped around.

After the minutes of the last meeting had been read and approved there was a limited discussion of where we were going for our day trip and Eulalee urged everyone to think hard and come up with some great ideas. The beautification committee was called on to report. Effie told us two dogwoods had been planted in front of the courthouse to replace the one that had been blown down in the last storm, one pink and one white and everyone said that was a good choice instead of a magnolia, which had been considered for a while but everyone decided they just got too messy shedding their leaves all year long. Then Eulalee got around to introducing the guest, Mr. J. P. Jones. And, she said, he'd told her to just call him JP but we could call him Mr. Jones or JP, whichever we wanted.

Of course he said that he wanted us all to be real friendly and to call him JP when we came to the shop for plants, seeds, or advice and he hoped we'd all find our way there so often we'd trample a path to the door, whole crowds of us. There was a slight murmur among the ladies, but it was hard to tell if they were murmuring that'll be the day or what a dear boy. He said Eulalee had asked him to talk about herbs that day— that Eulalee never gives up, she is *determined* to get this town converted to healthy eating habits—and he was happy to do that as he felt it was a really interesting topic, but he hoped we'd all let him come back another day and talk about southern plants and shrubs and flowers as he felt he was well qualified and that would give him a wider range of subject. Then he got on to herbs in cooking.

Well there wasn't much he could tell *me* about herbs in cooking. After all, I'd taken cooking classes in north and south Italian, French, Spanish, Chinese, Mexican, Indian—I probably knew more than he did. At least as much. So I concentrated on JP himself. He looked almost as much of a misfit in this place as Warren and I. In fact, he looked more like a beautiful Italian jet setter than a Georgia cracker. His mouth was definitely out of a Michelangelo painting, add that to olive skin, huge hazel eyes, the style and grace of an aristocrat, and the body of an athlete and you come up with a hot twenty-year-old with more than a touch of sexy machismo. He'd be blond if he'd just let his hair grow out of that military cut. He'd look as if he should be stepping out of a Porsche or a Gulfstream or a long white sailing vessel with a large crew. He did anyway. He looked like money. It took the assurance of money to appear before the Garden Club in chinos and a raggedy navy crew sweater. He seemed to be speaking directly to me, but that was probably his public speaking technique, making eye contact with this one and that one and the front row and the back of the room and so forth. Except he was mostly making eye contact with me. Shifting uneasily on the hard, little chair, I wondered if anyone else had noticed.

I was also wondering why my two daughters hadn't married something that looked like that so I'd have grandchildren who looked like Renaissance putti, when I suddenly realized that he was warning us about poisonous herbs and plants. Things like mistletoe berries and poinsettias and what else? . . . I really hadn't been listening. But then he said he'd wandered off his subject and would get back to herbs.

Like a flash it hit me that whoever had killed Miss Emily and Sammy Jo could have used something as untraceable as a leaf or a berry. . . . Something that was right under our noses. In just about every house. Indians would know all about those things. . . . We were close to the answer. Luther could have slipped Miss Emily a little something with Sammy Jo's help. Simple. And then he could have done Sammy Jo in. What better cover up than the solicitous lover? The self-sacrificing nurse? And all the time he was killing her. To get the house and the car and the money in the bank! It was common knowledge in town that none of the Tryons had any cash. When they wanted to buy groceries at Piggly Wiggly, they'd go around town with their lawnmowers looking for grass that was longer than a crew cut. And they'd work just long enough to get the grocery money and that was that. But now Elvira Lewis? What connection did Luther Tryon have with Elvira Lewis? None that I knew of. I'd have to ask Sarah Taylor, who never came to Garden Club, saying she was too old to have to do anything she didn't want to do.

The landscape architect had finished without my noticing and Eulalee led the applause and thanked him for his very interesting talk. Flushed with success, he glanced at me and grinned before he sat down. She said the coffee urn was over there in the corner—decaffeinated and she hoped no one objected—and to please help ourselves to a cup of coffee and some of Emily Bell's delicious miniature cheesecakes. She thanked us all for coming and Emily Bell for her little cheesecakes and the meeting was over. She asked us to excuse her to get back and see how Elvira was getting on and of course they all made their way to the cakes while Eulalee ran out to her big black van.

While we were still living in the penthouse, we entertained an upper upper type English *jeune fille* whose parents were friends of our agency and had seen fit to give this creature her airfare and just enough money to travel around the country by Greyhound bus but not to eat. She managed, being a resourceful little Brit, because they'd also given her a list of friends and acquaintances in various cities where she was fed and given a bed. By the time she'd returned to New York and was about to fly back to the UK, she'd seen a lot of things like the Grand Canyon, Las Vegas, Mount Rushmore, the Mississippi, Harlem and Broadway, but what had made the deepest impression on her was the look of Americans. She kept telling us of the obesity she'd seen all over the South and the middle west. She said in California they seem to care about their looks, and in New York, but everywhere else your people are grotesque! And this is why. Even into senior citizenship they were scarfing up those cheesecakes at eleven o'clock and they'd be having "dinner" at eleven-thirty just the same. Probably topped by Moon Pies and Twinkies.

I went to the urn for a cup of decaf and waited for the crowd to clear around JP. When it thinned he turned to me and asked if it was possible, anywhere in Davis Landing, to get a cup of espresso. Or even to buy espresso coffee and make one's own.

I told him it wasn't.

He said, "You're probably surprised that I like espresso. Or even know about it." He was so young and eager and ingenuous.

"Not a bit."

He was disappointed. "Well, if you ever should wonder— the answer is—my mother is Italian."

"Really."

"You know what my name is?"

"Jones."

"What did you think the JP was for?"

"I didn't." He was closer, his eyes smiling into mine. I backed away.

"Were you thinking the JP was for John Paul?"

"I hadn't given it a thought."

"Well, it's not. It's really GP. For Giancarlo Paolo."

"Oh?" What I was feeling was definitely not maternal. Keeping a distance between us I said, "Mr. Jones, do you know of many poisonous plants around here?"

"Planning to get rid of someone?"

"No."

"A husband, maybe?"

"I am researching an article."

"Sorry. I didn't mean to offend you."

I managed a "Nothing you could ever say could get to me enough to offend me, sonny" look. "Would you have that information available? Like in a book?"

"I can whip together some pages for you. And you'd better have the antidotes too. In case you change your mind. You could come to my office and we could go over the material together. . . ."

"My husband is working on the project with me."

"Hm—uh—bring him with you—"

"Look. Don't bother. I can go to the library." I moved away from him quickly.

He followed me to my car. "Please—"

I turned on him. "You please. I don't need some kid young enough to be my son—"

"Twenty-five last Friday—"

But I was in the car and away, conscious of my heartbeat. It was really knocking in my chest. I felt out of breath. Good God. Sex. Turned on by that child! Warren and I hadn't given it a thought since we'd gone broke and depressed.

The next morning I drove an hour and a quarter to meet Dolores at the airport, risking a speeding ticket because I'd forgotten about the roach traps and it had taken me some time to collect all of them and put them away out of sight. I chose Warren's "workroom" in a shed behind the house where he'd collected some tools and baling wire and a lot of stuff that should have been junked or put in somebody's yard sale. Dolores would never spot them there. Nobody could find anything in that place including Warren. Driving along I was so relieved that I'd remembered. We'd never had roaches in New York thanks to Bliss Exterminators' monthly visit. Dolores wouldn't have understood. And when we went back to New York, as I hoped we'd do very soon, I'd never be able to control her. Because I'd been in such a rush, I threw some cold water on my face, pulled a comb through my hair, grabbed the dogs who always enjoyed a ride to break up the boredom of life down here, and went tearing off without a thought to how I looked.

Chapter 11

♦

• We made it just in time to see the passengers descending from the plane. A lot of blacks, a lot of military (this is a military state), and Dolores, a vision of urban chic Madrid style. She'd cut her hair just like *Vogue*'s editor, and it was hennaed, gleaming in the sun. She was wearing a suit of black Spanish leather, high-heeled black leather shoes, very simple gold jewelry, a wonderful leather shoulder bag, and carrying a small leather suitcase. She could have just come off the Concorde. I was waving and calling and generally making a fool of myself before she was in the airport building. When she saw me she stopped dead.

"Dolores," I shouted. "Here I am."

She walked toward me slowly. "What happened?" she said.

"Oh Dolores, I'm so glad to see you—I'm so happy to have you here—oh Dolores—"

She held me close, then pushed me away for another look. "What happened to you?"

"Nothing!"

"Look at you! Look at your hair! You need color. You need a cut! Look at your hands." She picked one up, turned it over. "You need a manicure. When you last have a manicure? You don't have rubber gloves? You should always wear rubber gloves. And what you're wearing? What is that?"

"Dolores, everyone looks like this down here—"

"Why?"

"Because it's very casual. Very casual life-style." I tried to take her luggage but she tore it out of my hand. I tried to get her to walk with me to the car, but she stood rooted, shaking her head. "No makeup—You need blusher—I never see you look like this—never!"

"Dolores, there's nothing and no one to dress up for. You know my husband, he never sees how I look—"

"You do it for *yourself!*"

She was happier to see Jackie and Mathilda, said they'd grown and gotten fatter and looked very good. They were ecstatic to see her again, jumping and jumping and going out of their minds in silent joy. Once we were all in the car and starting on the long ride to the coast, Dolores resumed the attack, insisting she couldn't believe that everyone looked like me. I looked at her, her flawless creamy skin (all that olive oil), her pretty shiny hair, her beautiful suit. . . . My only defense was to inquire about her husband's health (he was older) and how things were in New York. She was off. The subway fare had been raised again, the streets were dirtier, people from El Salvador, Nicaragua, all over Central America, all coming to New York. Why? she wanted to know. Selling dope, living on the streets—her indignation carried us to the coast.

After an enthusiastic hug and kiss for Warren she went to her room, unpacked our presents: Spanish soap for me, Café Bustelo for Warren, rawhide chewing sticks for the dogs, then reappeared in a cotton housedress and rubber gloves. "Where is a broom?" she demanded. "Give me a hard brush for the floors, the pail, rags for dusting, Lysol . . ." We couldn't dissuade her.

She fell to her knees and stayed there until she'd gotten the house up to her own standards. Two days of scrubbing, airing, polishing, scouring toilet bowls, criticizing, and rearranging furniture. . . . When everything had been turned upside down and put back together again to her taste, she announced that we would give a little dinner. She would cook paella. Dolores is an irresistible force. I called a few neighbors. We would be eight. She made flower and leaf arrangements all over the house, put out the best towels, polished the silver, and announced that now we would go to the store.

Her pronouncement on Piggly Wiggly was that what we spent forty-five dollars for in New York would have cost over a hundred, but the meats! . . . She frowned at the meat counter with the pig snouts, cheeks, feet, and tails. "For poor people," she said.

We cooked all the next day, having a rousing battle over the shrimp for the paella. Dolores peeled them and used the peels to make her stock for moistening the rice. That was all right. But then she insisted on putting the shrimp into the dish and cooking the hell out of them. For the flavor, she said. I argued to have them put in at the last minute, but I should have remembered it's impossible to win with her. Especially when she'd brought me four ounces of saffron. Our guests all enjoyed the food enormously. As much as they enjoyed meeting Dolores. And after they left I got another calling down. "You say everyone look like you? These ladies don't look like you! They have manicures. They take care of their hair. They wear pretty silk dresses. Don't have to cost a lot—"

Gunfire sounded from Miss Emily's house across the street. The Tryons shooting at the moon. Dolores crossed herself and said it was just like New York. But cheaper to live here. When I took her to the airport I promised her, amidst tearful good-byes, that I would get my hair colored and cut *somewhere*—manicure and pedicure seemed to be going too far. But that morning I'd used a blusher and she was mollified. Driving back I felt that I understood, for the first time, the Brits who always dressed for dinner in the jungle. Once you let the side down it was difficult to pull it up again.

During her visit JP Jones came to call. It was in the middle of our discussion (Dolores's and mine) over the shrimp for the paella and I was flushed and disheveled from the heat of battle, trying to ignore the knocking at the door. If you waited long enough they went away, leaving a note or a plate of cookies or maybe nothing. But Jackie and Mathilda barked so frantically that it was clear this caller was not about to retreat. Flinging open the door I was confronted with JP. Dolores was right behind me. The sight of him silenced her, the first time in my experience anything had had this effect. His chinos were clean though worn at the bottoms, the same ragged sweater over a faded blue shirt with a frayed collar, and the same unquenchable look in the eyes. He was carrying a brown manila envelope. And then Warren, who had come up behind us, invited him in. Warren said he'd thought I was going to the door and he was sorry we'd kept him standing there so long. I backed off but Dolores stood her ground.

JP looked directly at me. "I brought the pages you wanted," he said.

Warren held out his hand. "I'm Merrie's husband, Warren Spencer."

"JP Jones." They shook hands.

"And I am Dolores!" she announced.

"Nice to meet you, ma'am. Miss Merrie, you asked—"

"Thank you," I said, snatching the envelope from him. "Thank you very much. 'Preciate. And now, if you'll excuse me, we're in the middle of a cooking project—"

But Warren wasn't about to let him go. "You live here?"

"Now I do. I've opened a landscape service. Up at the crossroads." He felt around his pockets. "I was sure I had a card on me—"

"Do you know anything about tennis courts?" Warren demanded.

I was backing toward the kitchen.

"Do you play? I've been trying to get a game since I moved here—"

"We have to talk," ushering that boy into his study where no one was allowed.

"Warren," I said softly, shaking my head, wagging a warning finger.

My husband gave me one of those blank blue-eyed stares

and shut the door behind JP. I hurried back to the kitchen with Dolores at my heels.

Dolores said for her thoughts she should go to confession. She asked if he was American, saying he looked like Julio Iglesias but blond. Spanish. Maybe Italian. She said, "He likes you. I see in his eyes." I finally got her back on track with the shrimp. But then she suggested asking JP to dinner that night. I told her the people who were coming were all older. I didn't have a chance to look at the contents of the envelope until I'd delivered Dolores to the airport, still scolding, lecturing, and advising. Like my mother, she needed constant attention. But I cried when we hugged good-bye. She cried too, telling me over and over we should come back to New York, we didn't belong here with all those old people. Mr. Warren maybe but not you. I miss you, she said. You are my mother, my sister, my daughter, my friend, I love you. In her lisping Spanish it was beautiful. Even as she was climbing the stairs to the plane, she was insisting, offering the sofa bed in her living room. Bless her heart. Jackie and Mathilda and I watched the plane take off and disappear into the sky. And then I felt even lonelier.

Chapter 12

◆

◆ That night we had leftovers for dinner. Dolores had done so much cooking and in such massive amounts that the refrigerator was overflowing. There was enough paella for three nights and there was her wonderful tortilla and her stuffed squid (which they use for bait down here) with the inky rice and her Basque chicken.

That was one good thing about Warren. He'd eat leftovers and never quibble. Warren would eat garbage without noticing. His mind was on other things. His novel and his small remaining investment in the stock market. And of course his new interest in rebuilding the town tennis court. You didn't even have to serve him the leftovers—just tell him what was in the fridge, which bowls and containers it was in, and he was now able to locate the food, put it in an appropriate dish, and pop it in the microwave.

The microwave has changed our lives. Faced with an antique kitchen we hadn't yet brought it into the twentieth century. It would cost a fortune which we didn't have. But there was a gas stove on bottled gas with two working burners. After Dolores cleaned it all four worked. We had been considering a new stove—everyone down here uses electric—but knowing how frequently Davis Landing loses power during a storm or even when some DWI runs into a power pole or a squirrel electrocutes itself trying to chew on one of the terminals—we'd operated on the two units and bought ourselves a microwave. I'd always lobbied against them, but once Barbara Kafka came out in favor of them with her recipe book we took the plunge. It works. On some very hot nights I even cooked spaghetti in it. Twelve minutes. Start with hot tap water, zap for six, stir, zap for six more. Came out fine. And Warren— Warren fancied himself as an independent chef. We'd come a long way from his eggs over easy. He could now heat up whole meals. And corn on the cob? That was a dish he could prepare himself from scratch with no help from beginning to end. He'd put six unshucked ears into the microwave, push the button, and when the bell went off, take them out, shuck them, and all the silk came off with the shucks. Nothing to do but butter and enjoy. When we could get corn down here. There were two farmers who raised eating corn and their crop lasted no more than two weeks. The corn crop down here is and always has been field corn for animals.

Warren had zapped his food and was eating his dinner. I had lost my appetite over all the cooking and all the food that had been consumed in the week that Dolores was with us. He was telling me what they—he and JP, his new playmate—were going to do. First they were researching, consulting the experts, and then—

I was leafing through the pages JP had given me. "Warren," I said, "you're not going to believe this! Mistletoe berries can be fatal—poinsettia—*philodendron*—oleander—*oleander?* There isn't a house in Davis Landing without oleander— *holly.*"

"Merrie—"

"Warren, do you realize that when Miss Emily died and when Sammy Jo died every single house in Davis Landing was draped in holly?!"

"Merrie, you're shouting—"

"They may not have had mistletoe or poinsettia but *holly*—"

"Merrie, do you want to hear about the tennis court or don't you?"

"Yes! But not right now! This is important!"

"We're going to go to town meeting and see how much support we can get for the basics—"

"Philodendron—"

"JP and I are willing to do the physical work, if they'll pay for the new surface and the net and the backstops—"

"Spider plant—"

"That's a fair proposition, don't you think?"

"Azalea—"

"The cheapest would be clay because it's here all around us but that's not the best. The best—"

"My God, daffodils—"

"Merrie, you haven't heard a word I said!"

"I was listening I was listening—"

"What did I say?"

"Clay isn't the best."

"And?"

"It's all around us but it's not the best—"

That was once when *he* walked out of the room. But I was absolutely stunned at the lethal qualities in all these common plants surrounding us. I took JP's pages and went out into the garden to study the perennial border. Iris. Hyacinth. Larkspur. Lily of the Valley. Christmas rose. Christmas rose? The church was full of them at Miss Emily's funeral. Bleeding heart. Four o'clock. So ingenuous. Morning glory. Innocently cheerful morning glory—English ivy?! Obviously, you didn't have to be a master of Indian lore to knock somebody off in this town. *Anybody* could do it. Granted they'd need access but that was easy in a place like this where all doors were unlocked and everyone invited you in for tea or coffee or whatever. It would have been easy to get rid of Miss Emily and there were plenty of locals who would have liked to do just that. The lethal dose or doses could have been delivered right to the door in any one of those numerous casseroles. Same with Sammy Jo, although that would have been a little trickier with Luther on guard unless of course he did it himself. My God, that parade of casseroles! It was dizzying to think about.

Warren was now busier than ever since the tennis court project had been added to the novel project and the stock market project and there was always something that had to be fixed in the house. He didn't want to hear *anything* about the so-called murders or my half-assed theories about who might have committed them. He was constantly having meetings with JP either in JP's shop (I had yet to set foot in that place) or in his own library with the door firmly closed. He did everything but put up a KEEP OUT sign on it. They, or he, I had no idea who was the guiding light in this venture but I could make a guess, had drawn up a plan to submit to the town commissioners. I knew there were three possibilities, cheap but not good, medium-priced but slow to drain, and expensive but ideal. He didn't discuss this with me, saying I could come to town hall and hear them present their case. Thanks a lot. Naturally, under the circumstances, I was seeing rather more of JP than I'd have wanted, but it was always in fleeting glimpses as he entered or exited and I was almost always busy somewhere else in the house, usually the attic.

That place was enormous and full of treasures, like Grandmother Lavinia's eighteenth-century silk dress and matching mob cap. I tried the dress on. A little short but the waist was okay when I pulled the corsets tight. The blue was nice with my eyes, but the general effect was a tall, thin Martha Washington with her own teeth. Or was that George with the wooden teeth? And there was so much furniture! Country antiques. And spinning wheels and chamber pots and old ledgers and quilts and hope chests and diaries and love letters and uniforms and hats and bonnets and dolls and baby clothes and trousseau underwear and hand-woven sheets with beautifully worked monograms . . . I could and did spend hours up there just looking through boxes and chests, hoping to stumble on an original copy of the Declaration of the War Between the States, or something worth masses of money that would immediately free us from this place with enough loot to live in New York, hire limos, pay Dolores, travel on the Concorde, whole days at Kenneth's, a personal trainer, a week at the Golden Door—luxury! I was starved for luxury. Meanwhile I considered opening an antique shop somewhere but pushed that off for the time when our cash flow got down to dribbles and drops and I'd be baking my brownies and English muffin loaves to sell out of the front parlor. Didn't seem right somehow to sell off the family history even though no one else cared. But it was sort of reassuring to know that I could if I needed money.

Sarah Taylor dropped in for a visit right about then. She was calling and *halloooing* all over the house until I came down out of the attic at about the same time Warren opened his door. I arrived at the bottom of the stairs just in time to see Sarah Taylor at her most coy. Head tipped to one side, high, sweet, soft voice, smooth and slow and syrupy, all for the benefit of JP, whom she'd not met before. He gave me one look and I felt it in my groin. All these weeks Warren had never noticed, but Sarah Taylor did. Warren excused himself and JP—they were working, he said—and closed the door firmly on us.

"Well, Miss Merrie Lee!" Sarah Taylor said in her normal rasp. "Just how long has *this* been going on?"

"Oh, they've been working on the tennis court project for a long time," I said. "Would you like some tea? Coffee? Pepsi? Come in and sit down! I've got something to tell you—"

"Have you been keeping that beautiful boy locked up here?"

"Warren has. That 'beautiful boy' was on the Italian Olympic tennis team and he and Warren are just dying to get the old town court reactivated." She'd followed me into the kitchen. "And I have *nothing* to do with it! As you can see!"

She looked at me. "I can see a lot. I saw the way he looked at you—"

"Oh, come on! We've hardly said two words to each other. He's the horticulturist who spoke to the Garden Club a couple of meetings ago and if you weren't trying to match Miss

Pearl's record you'd come to meetings and *learn* something. Sure you don't want anything? The coffee's all made. . . ."

"Well I don't mind if I do. Now Merrie Lee don't you go keeping things from me. He looked at you and you looked as if someone had just cut off your air—"

"Look, I spoke to him after the last meeting and asked him if he knew of any poisonous plants around here. That's all. You know, following our line of thinking? And did he ever!" I retrieved the pages from the drawer in the kitchen table. "Here's the list he gave me."

Sarah Taylor glanced through the pages muttering, "I declare!"

"So you see, anyone of those casseroles could have been poisoned. A single cup of herbal tea—it wouldn't take much—and you don't have to be Indian to pull it off—"

"I declare! And now Elvira Lewis is getting weaker and weaker, I'm told." She said this without any feeling, a pleasant expression, the suggestion of a smile. I remembered that I'd heard her husband had been suspected of fooling around with Elvira too. And then I looked at Sarah Taylor, a sweet, neat, unsubstantial little old lady, stirring her coffee daintily and helping herself to an oatmeal crisp from the cookie jar. Was it more than coincidence that Sammy Jo and Elvira Lewis had both been rumored to have been fancied by the late Itney Lee, Sarah Taylor's husband? But then what about Miss Emily? I tried to picture Miss Emily in flagrante delicto. Impossible. Although according to her portrait and the faded photographs she had been a good-looking young woman . . . forceful even then. . . . No, not Sarah Taylor. But she didn't like Miss Emily at all and couldn't stand Sammy Jo, said she simpered. I looked at my friend taking tiny bites out of her cookie and sipping coffee and I could no more think of her taking another life than my Aunt May. Less. Aunt May was a wild little woman capable of anything. Sarah Taylor was reclusive, quiet, thoughtful, and careful. No. Not Sarah Taylor. I asked what was wrong with Elvira Lewis.

"Merrie dear, we're all of that age."

"What age?"

"The age when we're supposed to go. It doesn't matter much how we go. The important thing is that we go when we're called."

"Some people live to a great age down here. Like Miss Pearl."

"Would you want to live to a hundred and five like Miss Pearl?"

"Miss Pearl could dance all night!"

"Most of them have stayed too long. When my time comes I want to go. My darling Itney Lee is waiting for me."

Itney Lee, the late philanderer. And she still loved him.

"With my darling Shenandoah." She'd had to put Shenandoah to sleep. A very painful thing. She'd closed herself in the house and not answered her phone for days.

"Sarah Taylor, how about we go see Miss Pearl?"

"Whatever for?"

"To shed some light. To get some answers."

Sarah Taylor put down her cup and saucer and stood, brushing cookie crumbs from her lap. "I'm afraid I've lost faith in that particular oracle," she said. "Merrie Lee, thank you so much. It was delicious. Did you make those cookies yourself?"

"Yes, but—"

"I declare. You are so clever." And she was out the door. I hurried after, but I wasn't quick enough. The image of Sarah Taylor's long, aristocratic fingers with the gold and diamond rings mincing herbs and brewing potions stayed with me. Every time I closed my eyes I could see it.

My international friends always want to know what I do "down there." But when I tell them their eyes glaze. Actually, there isn't time enough for everything and the days are very short. Partly, I suppose, because I'm up at five-thirty or six and can't stay awake long enough to watch prime-time television. I make a vast effort for the PBS programs, but have been known to nod off and then stumble up the stairs and fall into bed without cleaning my face, only the air is so clean down here it never gets dirty. I don't know what it is. Maybe all that fresh air. Maybe depression. At the agency I was accustomed to eight- and ten- and sometimes twelve-hour days and was *stimulated*, had to take an occasional sleeping pill.

But down here Jackie and Mathilda need their exercise and I am the dog walker and it's just the three of us. Not as much fun for them probably as that great girl who could walk ten dogs in New York and never get their leashes tangled. The walk is best had in the cool of the day, and dawn, during the hot months, is the cool of the day. We walk for a couple of miles every morning. Which gets us back to the house at six-thirty or seven. Ravenous. They eat and I fix the coffee and make my own toast and juice and read the local paper and check supplies and make a shopping list. They sleep while I have a shower and change from the walking sweatsuit and Reeboks to a slightly less ancient sweatsuit and Reeboks or, according to the season, jeans or shorts and sandals. And tidy the house a little. By then the Stockbroker is up and about and gets the mail from the post office. He chats up people there. I chat up fellow walkers. (That's the extent of our social life.) Then there's the reading of the mail and the *New York Times*. We get the mailed edition, which arrives pretty reliably two days late. Phone calls. I get off to do the shopping around ten or ten-thirty. It's leisurely, what with all the visiting in the aisles. Everything is leisurely here. Bringing me back with a trunkful of supplies around eleven at which time everyone is ravenous again. Jackie and Mathilda have a snack. I prepare lunch for the Stockbroker and myself. Then it's time for the afternoon walk. Followed by their afternoon nap and my session at the desk, paying bills, working with the checkbook, which never comes out right, notes to friends around the world, and then it's time to start dinner, which has to be timed so that we can watch "MacNeil/Lehrer" and according to my stomach, which has been gnawing since around four-thirty. After Jim and Robin and Charlayne and Judy sign off my husband trots off to the kitchen to do the cleanup for which I bless him every day of my life and I go through the bed preparation of toothbrushing, face-washing, etc., and fall into bed to "read," but a couple of pages of anything will put me right to sleep. Short day, as the parrot said.

We brought our VCR down but we don't have the same tastes. I loved *A Room with a View*. He walked out in the first five minutes. *My Dinner with André* he called talking heads. What he does like to watch is anything with James Stewart, John Wayne, or Gary Cooper. Or World War II. Anything about World War II. I usually watch with him as I have a certain morbid fascination in watching his lips move with the actors'. He knows all the lines just as I know *Casablanca*. So we don't rent videos. You know, I'm beginning to think it's not fatigue at all. Probably if I got out of this place I'd have as much energy as Aunt May.

My plan was to bring my poison theory to the attention of Chief Samuel Pollock. But I had learned when I first came down here that any idea to a man or a committee has to be presented through a man. Although the mayor of Davis Landing, when we first arrived, was a woman. That was all right apparently. They came to order when she called them to order. Of course she was a Davis. Married a Colby. But when my husband and I made the rounds for the telephone, correcting the address on the utilities, a question about the boundaries, even to the town hall to inquire about garbage collection, it was always the same. He would do the friendly western bit, introducing himself and his wife. Or as I'm known down here, *et ux* (and wife). In this state they have this strange law that if I buy a farm with my own money and want to sell it I have to get his permission! Not fair!

The courtly gentleman would then offer a chair for me which was always carefully and quite deliberately placed somewhere behind Warren's. Or in a corner. Warren was directly across the desk so that they could do one-to-one easily. I was out of the sight line. The gentleman spoke only to Warren. If I ventured an opinion, a quip, a question, it went unheard. And I knew damn well Warren heard me. My role was to sit quietly where I'd been placed, legs crossed at the ankle, until the conversation was finished. At that point we all stood, the gentleman said how nice it had been to meet me, ma'am, and I followed Warren dutifully three paces behind. My rotten husband *loved* it! I went along with it because I tend to be an observer. I was still in the sociological research phase, which didn't last much longer. Sociological curiosity gradually evolved into acute paranoia.

When I suggested to him that we go to the police together, his eyes closed down and I knew it was a lost cause long before he told me. "You think I'm going to make a fool of myself over some cockamamie idea of yours? Forget it! They're old ladies! They're dying! They're supposed to!"

Sarah Taylor told me the police would listen because "our men have manners. But they'll never do anything about it. They'll just say that damyankee is crazy!"

If I asked JP to go along with me . . . of course he'd do it. I knew he'd do anything to be with me. But a., he's a foreigner in this county, and b., he's young, and c., my instinct told me to stop before I started. My instinct was spelling *t-r-o-u-b-l-e*. JP had already requested, through Warren, that I head up a fund-raising committee for the town tennis court and I had already denied the request. If I asked his help now I'd be bound and beholden to give him mine on his project and endless days together were spinning out in my mind. I was toying with the idea of enlisting Luther's help. . . . Luther!?

Chapter 13

◆ Much to everyone's surprise Elvira Lewis got herself out of bed and practically crawled to Garden Club. Well, actually Eulalee brought her along in her van. I have never understood why a sweet-faced, little, white-haired lady would choose to drive that kind of vehicle and I asked a few people but they looked at me strangely without answering. One woman said something about Eulalee likes to carry things around. It was so big and black with those blacked out windows it could have been carrying the Grateful Dead. But Elvira really looked dreadful. We were all hovering and offering tea and coffee and Josie Ann's miniature pecan tarts when Elvira gave a long sigh and fell off her chair. Dulcy Lee Jones, who had been a nurse, administered mouth-to-mouth but Elvira was gone. We got the Emergency Rescue but they said she was gone. They took her to the Emergency Room but the doctors there said she was gone. They said DOA. Heart failure. Well that meeting was over before we had even pledged allegiance to the flag.

I went home and told Warren. "Heart failure," I told him. "That's what Dr. Wilson said about Sammy Jo. Heart failure. But isn't that what everyone dies of? Heart failure? What kind of a cop-out is *that*?"

For the first time Warren looked almost interested. I seized the opportunity. "Would you come with me after lunch—we'll just talk it over with Sam Pollock—"

"JP's coming over. We're planning the campaign. Going after the churches and the Rotary and the Chamber of Commerce and the banks—"

But he didn't say no. I was encouraged. But thinking how little it took, I got depressed and into one of those Where am I going? moods. That carried me right over to Miss Ophelia's hair salon. She said Joy (pronounced *Joey*) was their color expert. Joy could do *anything*. When Joy was finished with the color, I told her to take off a quarter of an inch all around. Mary Farr in New York always said a quarter of an inch makes an enormous difference. Well something did. According to Joy's mirrors. Recklessly, I asked for a pedicure. I knew they could do a manicure, as I'd seen them doing them, but I could push the cuticle back too, and I used a clear polish, which I could also do myself if I wanted to. But the pedicure—bright red toenails!

Miss Ophelia rose to the challenge. She phoned someone who had been known to do an occasional pedicure and in half an hour there I was back in the storeroom with some poor soul kneeling over my feet, which were soaking in a plastic bucket. Miss Ophelia went all out. She installed me in a sort of a deck chair so that I was reclining at the kind of angle that made my back and stomach hurt like too many sit-ups after months of no exercise. "Now you just relax," she said, hooking up a record player placed on the top shelf. "You're going to have music with your pedicure." And she started a long-playing Glenn Miller album.

It was almost bearable. By gripping the arms of the chair I could pull myself up and off my lower spine. My mind drifted to Miss Ophelia and Joy and all of the Garden Club shagging in their ponytails way back then. But then the needle got stuck and played the same phrase over and over and over.

I looked at the head bent over my feet. "Sounds like the needle's stuck," I said.

"For sure," she said cheerfully.

After a pause I asked if she didn't mind.

She was intent on cuticle snipping, but after a while she said that you couldn't really expect it to sound like a CD—old album like that—and went on snipping.

I asked her if she'd mind turning it off.

"Yes, ma'am." She—I'd never heard her name—dropped my feet back in the bucket with a splash and climbed on a chair. Couldn't reach. Piled one chair precariously on another—at last the sound stopped.

"There," she said, climbing down to take her pedicure position again. She took my foot in her lap and said with an anxious smile, "I haven't done one of these in a long, long time." Her upper lip beaded with sweat, poor thing.

But eventually it made me feel good to know that hidden under my Reeboks and white sweat socks were shiny red toenails. The kind I used to wear under my sheer black panty hose with high-heeled strippy black sandals. I felt so good I went home and poured some bubble bath in the old claw-footed tub and soaked, holding my feet up to admire. They inspired me to apply a body lotion when I got out. That's when I caught a glimpse of myself in the steamed up old pier glass in the corner of the room and moved closer for a better look.

You have to understand that most of my life I have been thin. A tall, gawky, skinny child, growing into a tall, thin girl with protruding hip bones, no stomach, no hips, and no breasts. Great for showing clothes but then so was a hanger. Twice in my life I had breasts, each time I was pregnant. But then back to the flat stomach and the flat top. I always felt a need to apologize to my sex partners who generally were kind and said it didn't matter. After an infusion of feminism, although I was still sensitive, I no longer apologized. Women envied the fact that I could dress in seconds. Panty hose, shoes, and a dress. Or slacks and a tee shirt. But what I was seeing in the long mirror was something else. I don't know how it happened—lack of stress, three regular meals a day, no more lifting weights, maybe all those poor little hormones sitting around waiting for sex to happen again—whatever, there seemed to be a roundness. I had hips. I had breasts. Quite an improvement over the last time I looked. I tried to remember when that was. Must have been during the warm weather. I didn't spend any unnecessary time without clothes in this house. No insulation. Minimal central heating. Lots of drafts. I looked again. Hot dog! Warren would say, Great piece of ass. If I could get his attention.

I descended the stairs at five o'clock promptly wearing my sheerest black pantyhose and highest heeled black sandals. The dogs came running at the clatter. A cotton sarong, a white silk tank top, red lipstick, a dab of Obsession on the inner thighs, and I was there not to cook, but to seduce. Gliding to his door, I knocked. Repeatedly.

The door was thrown open. I could see JP. He saw me and his mouth curled into an appreciative smile. My husband saw only someone who had interrupted his train of thought. "Merrie, I hope this is important!"

I gave him a slow smile along with a model turn while murmuring seductively, "So do I . . ."

He noticed. He said, "What are you doing in that outfit! Put on a sweater before you catch cold!"

I came to a dead stop.

"Did you want something?" he demanded.

"Not really. Just wanted to tell you you'll have to cook your own dinner tonight. I'm going out." I had *never* "gone out" since we moved to Davis Landing. He didn't ask where, why, who—nothing!

Pure cold rage carried me out the door, into the car, and fourteen miles to the nearest movie I could sit through. It was chilly but the car has a heater. Once there, I sat for two hours without grasping what was on the screen, jamming popcorn between my red lips to keep my teeth from chattering. There I was in my sarong and bare arms covered with goose bumps while around me people were cozy in anoraks and down jackets and that made me even angrier.

By the time I got home I was ready to cry with rage and

misery. My entire body was numb and shaking with cold. Locking the car door (force of habit after all those years in New York and having three cars stolen from under the eyes of the doorman—at least that's what he said—it was probably collusion), I turned to go into the house and found myself in his arms. I pushed against his sweater. "You! I'll probably die of pneumonia and it's all your fault!" But it wasn't Warren.

"Merrie," JP said.

"What are you doing here?" I said through chattering teeth. "You'll catch your death!"

"And will anyone give a damn? Will anyone *notice*?"

"I will—I care—I love you, Merrie—"

"Go home, will you—"

"I love you—I said it—I love you I want you—"

I ran into the house and slammed the door, but Warren never even looked up from his novel or his stock project or whatever he was creating on his computer. Damn his soul. It wasn't until later, when I'd been under my down comforter long enough to stop shivering, that I started to think about JP and what he'd said.

It wasn't exactly a surprise. I'd guessed a long time ago. Silly boy. But drifting off to sleep it was amazing how much sensual pleasure I got just remembering how his hard, young body had been shaking almost as much as mine when he held me.

The next morning I was too sick to get out of bed. Jackie and Mathilda gazed at me in silent accusation. They knew I knew it was long past walk time. Warren slept peacefully beside me. I hoped he caught it too, whatever it was. I kicked him and told him he'd have to walk the dogs.

He wanted to know why.

"Because I'm sick!"

Semiconscious, he got to his feet and pulled on his jeans, looking at me with one eye closed. "You look awful."

"I feel awful."

I woke and slept and woke and slept and no one came near me. Filled with self-pity and wearing two pairs of sweats and Warren's heavy ski socks I thumped downstairs. The dogs barked. Warren looked up from the computer. "People asked me where you were. I told them you were sick. So there's a bunch of stuff in the kitchen."

We looked in the kitchen. "Lot of sweet potatoes," he said.

"I can't eat anything. I'm sick."

"You look awful," he said, and left me for his computer.

I swallowed two aspirin. I made some hot tea, mixed it with honey and lemon juice and added a large amount of dark rum, poured the whole brew into a thermos carafe and carried it upstairs where I fell on the bed with the latest *New York Times.*

All day I woke and sipped and slept to wake and drink some more. The *Times* fell all over the floor, unread. Two thermos carafes later I woke to see Warren peering at me.

"Eulalee is here. She brought some herb tea."

I sat up, trying to say I don't want to see anyone, but nothing came out. It was like a person who'd had a stroke and wanted desperately to communicate but couldn't. Maybe I was drunk. I had been at various times in my early life too drunk to speak or function in any way. Or maybe it was the aspirin. Or maybe it was the aspirin and the rum. My eyes refused to focus but Eulalee seemed to be standing in the doorway. Holding out a steaming mug of something.

"Merrie Lee," she said in her sweet, soft, little drawl, "I've brought you some herb tea, honey," approaching the bed. "You just drink this down and you'll be better in no time." She held it to my lips. It smelled godawful and when she tipped the mug so that some of the stuff slid between my lips it tasted even worse. A brew to gag over. Which I did. And just managed to make the bathroom. When I staggered back to bed, groaning, she was still there. "Now let's try a little more," she said with infinite patience, and brought the cup to my lips again.

I pushed her hand away. The mug fell, the herb tea was all over the floor, and I passed out.

After that came a period I think of as the Dream Sequence. Warren was in and out of it, hovering. Eulalee was there too, scattering herbs, trying to shovel evil-smelling stuff down my throat. JP, proclaiming his love. Eulalee was a constant. Luther. Luther?! And then one morning I woke up to find Eulalee beside me on the floor, scrubbing in wide circular strokes. I watched her for a while. She was a good worker. There were a lot of flowers and plants. It looked like a hospital room. But it wasn't. I was in Lavinia's four-poster, propped up with a lot of pillows. Wearing a flannel long-sleeved gown from the attic. It was soft from centuries of washing and very comfortable. Eulalee got to her feet and proceeded to scatter sweet-smelling herbs on her clean floor. I wondered if I might be dying. She was smoothing the sheets over me.

"Am I dying?"

"I declare!"

"Am I? You can be straight with me—Am I dying?"

"I declare! Are you feeling better?" She didn't exactly look joyful.

I started to get out of bed, very weak in the knees.

She rushed to my side, protesting, but I shook her off. Jackie suddenly appeared, jumping with silent joy. And then Mathilda. Warren came up the stairs. "Sorry, Eulalee, they just bolted out of the room—Merrie! Are you all right?"

"Am I dying?"

"Of course not! You're looking . . . well . . ."

I got back into bed and demanded a mirror. "God," I said. "What was it? Plague? Or cholera?"

After she left Warren told me that Eulalee had been feeding me her herb gruels and teas, which I regularly threw up until he'd asked her to just leave them as I was sleeping and Dr. Wilson had said I needed all the rest I could get. And then he'd thrown them down the garbage disposal. Dr. Wilson had prescribed antibiotics and that's what I got. He and JP had seen to that.

"JP?"

"He was my assistant nurse."

"He saw me like this?!"

"JP is not about to tell everyone in town that Merrie Spencer looks like hell—"

"Lost my looks. . . ."

"Listen, we've made a lot of progress with the tennis court—"

I closed my eyes. He was going on and on and on something about the less desirable court would be around twenty thousand, the one we should have is somewhere around thirty thousand and that doesn't include the net, the fence, the landscaping—Something about pipes underground to sprinkle it. Nothing about drainage. We have to wet it because it's a clay composition and if we don't wet it the surface will blow away in millions of tiny particles. And I'm thinking behind my closed eyes that the really important thing is my hair is all stringy and sweated up and badly in need of a shampoo. That sexy little JP taking care of me . . . with my yucky hair. . . .

In a couple of days I was out of bed and Jackie, Mathilda, and I ventured out for a walk. As we walked along people waved and tapped their horns and waved and Eulalee's black van stopped so we could talk. She said I was sure looking better, sugar, and I said it was all those good herbs and I really did 'preciate. (I've gotten so southern, lying comes naturally.) She frowned and wanted to be sure I was really well enough to be walking all over town again. She seemed worried. And she was telling me that she was going to brew up something that would strengthen my blood and I was thinking that she'd called me "sugar" and remembering her opinion of sugar, when all of a sudden there was a racket and a pounding from the back of the van. Like two dogs trying to get out. Big dogs. And Jackie and Mathilda started a racket and jumping up and down. I said she must have a really big dog back there but she just said she'd talk to me later and took off.

Well two days later Sarah Taylor and I were at our usual table at the Harbor View slurping down the she-crab soup that Penny had recommended—it wasn't quite as bad as the clam chowder—and I asked her what kind of a dog Eulalee had. She said Eulalee didn't have a dog.

So I said, "Well what's she carrying around in the back of that van? A pony?"

Sarah Taylor concentrated on the hush puppies. She said they were really good that day. She said that there was a rumor going around that Judge Davis was looking for a legal reason to evict Luther Tryon and his family from the Davis house and was ready to carry it to the Supreme Court of the United States. And I got distracted from Eulalee's dog. Or pony. Or mountain lion. Whatever.

And then we got on to Elvira Lewis's funeral, which I had missed due to my pneumonia or whatever lethal virus I had had. Sarah Taylor said it was very quiet. Elvira's son had come up from Texas and as he'd never married and there weren't many left in the Lewis family to mourn Elvira. It was a subdued funeral. "Sad to see all your peers dying off," she said.

I was thinking about all the AIDS funerals that had been going on in New York since I'd left. My friends said it was always the same people at those funerals. Rows and rows of death heads, all of them dying. But it was getting pretty lethal down here. For a small town. Since Christmas Miss Emily, Sammy Jo, and Elvira Lewis, and the crocuses were just beginning to show. Sarah Taylor said the altar guild had been hard put to come up with flower arrangements they hadn't already done for Miss Emily or Sammy Jo.

Elvira Lewis had instructed her executor to cremate her and scatter her ashes from a small plane over the ocean. Unexpected coming from that little lady who had never been up in a plane in her life. Sarah Taylor said Elvira had often expressed a desire to fly but she'd never had any place to fly to. And the ocean—Well, that wasn't too surprising as Elvira had confided that she believed that we all came from the sea and it was only fitten that we go back to it. I thought the small plane idea was very Hollywood. But into the sea . . . Yes, Elvira was a devout Episcopalian but she had also taught science at a high school level for years.

At dinner that night I reported everything I'd learned at lunch. His only comment was, "What kind of dog does Eulalee have?"

I asked him if I'd been dreaming or if Luther had actually

been upstairs in the bedroom when I was ill. He said he was. Just came to see if there was anything he could do.

The next day when Jackie and Mathilda and I passed the Davis house Luther was on the porch with his regular group, all of them sitting quietly leaning on their rifles and staring into space in their morning calm. I thanked him for his offer of help and he came down from the porch and told me to be sure and put some Epsom salts around the roses April first. We got into gardening hints and I began to feel that he was almost a friend. In that mood I asked him about Eulalee and what kind of animal she carried around in the back of her van.

"Ain't no animal, ma'am. That be Bubba. Havin' a bad day. Bad days she carry him with her."

I couldn't wait to tell Warren.

Chapter 14

◆

◆ Warren thought about Bubba but not for long. Seems that JP had an assistant—a graduate student name of Lisa from Atlanta—and they'd invited us to go out with them Saturday night. If I was up to it.

"Out where?"

"Some place on the beach. I think it's called The Club? Seafood place. Or maybe it was pizza."

"If you want."

"Do you?"

"I don't know. I haven't met Lisa."

"Who's Lisa?"

"Didn't you just tell me JP has an assistant named—"

"Oh! Lisa!"

"I swear you're mind's going soft."

"Do you want to go out with JP and Lisa or not?"

"I don't know. . . . I'm still weak in the knees but it doesn't sound too strenuous. . . . Maybe it would be good for both of us to get out of here. . . ."

"Is that a yes?"

"God, I can't seem to make a decision anymore!"

"Is that a no?"

"You decide."

"Okay. Let's go. What have we got to lose? . . . Couple of hours. . . . anyway, you should meet Lisa. She's a cute girl—"

"Where did you meet her?"

"At JP's shop."

"What does she look like?"

"Great legs! She wears these little miniskirts!"

". . . Saturday night. That's such an awful night to go out."

"Down here it's the night we do it."

"Do what?"

"Carry on. Go straight to hell."

"We do?"

"It's the American way."

The arrangement was that they were to pick us up in Lisa's four-wheel drive at five-thirty. "So we can get a table right on the dance floor," Warren said.

"We're *dancing?*"

Warren did the two-step and that was about it. Dancing with him I felt like an extra in a scene from *Urban Cowboy* and I didn't like being held by the back of my neck. Anyway, in New York, the places we hung out, they didn't dance. Just sat around and talked themselves to death and did deals and coke and drank. Saturday night would be in the nature of more sociological research. I let Warren take care of all the arrangements while I tended to pushing back my cuticles.

Warren wore his usual jeans with a blazer. I thought I looked fairly normal that night. I dressed as I would to go to dinner in New York and then took a lot of extra things off. I'd learned long ago that it was possible to look well dressed in any old thing (and I do mean old) if you carried a really good purse and wore really good shoes and of course Warren's pearls. I threw on strand after strand after strand and felt ready to face whatever the evening might present. But when I heard a car screech to a stop in front of our house, car doors slam, and guns go off across the street I suspected it would be a little more than I was prepared for. Then Warren opened the door.

Lisa was tall, tanned and toned, exuding health and energy

in tight, faded jeans stuck into cowboy boots worn with a man's undershirt over nothing (clear display of dark nipples) and a wide leather belt with a huge brass buckle reading "Montana." A man's flannel shirt hung open and masses of dark shiny hair blew and bounced around her shoulders. Her smile was a toothpaste ad, skin flawless. She was the epitome of health and youth. And very pretty. What they call down here "a mess." Like if you peer into a carriage and say, What a beautiful baby, the mother smiles and says, "I'nt she a mess?" While we were standing at the door doing the introductions the guns went off again. All the Tryons were on their feet staring over at our house. Lisa turned, did a little entrechat and bowed. There was a lot of slapping of thighs, whistling, and another five-gun salute. She laughed good-naturedly. "Nice to be appreciated," she said.

She drove out to the beach. Fast. We let the men do most of the talking. I said, "So you're a graduate student?"

She said she had two and a half years to go and was interning with JP for a semester. That she cared about the planet and hadn't yet decided where she could do the most good. As an environmentalist? Horticulturist? Botanist? Maybe even a marine biologist! Anyway, this opportunity had opened up and she thought six months of practical experience—like in the world of commerce—would be helpful in coming to a decision. JP reached over and tousled her hair.

"And besides," she laughed, "he cooks Italian!"

JP laughed with her. Same old JP in the same torn sweater and frayed shirt. With a difference. I'd always seen him in a deeply yearning mood and tonight he was happy.

As soon as we got there and got our table and Warren ordered his bottle of Coors he went up to the band leader— they were tuning up their instruments: two guitars, a harmonica, and a bass fiddle—and asked them if they could play a two-step and before I knew it there we were circling the floor with my neck in his grasp. Warren doesn't say anything when he dances. And rarely at other times. When it was over he hugged me and reminded me that our first dance had been a two-step. First and every one since.

We went to the band and told them "Appreciate" and went on back to the table. Lisa was exploding with enthusiasm over our dance. She begged Warren to do a two-step with her. And off they went. While I rubbed and stretched my neck and drank a little beer. "You can get a real thirst from a two-step," I said.

"Wait till you try shagging," JP said, taking my hand and looking at my rings.

"Shagging?" I pulled my hand away.

"That's the specialty here. After six-thirty."

"I thought the specialty was pizza. Or is it seafood?"

"People come here to shag, not to eat. . . . They have contests—it's fun. But for now"—he pulled me to my feet—"I don't two-step, but let's slow dance. . . ."

Over his shoulder I saw Lisa dart back to the table for Warren's hat, jam it on, and rush back into his neck hold. With that face she could wear anything. JP was breathing into my ear saying how much he wanted me and how he'd been longing to hold me and make love to me—I pulled away from his obvious sincerity. "JP, get a new writer! Your dialogue's terrible! And I'm probably as old as your mother," I said.

He pulled me back. "I can't stop thinking of you. It's been like that since the beginning—"

I was watching Lisa stroking the back of Warren's neck.

"There is no beginning—"

"The first time I saw you—"

"You're just missing your mama—"

He looked directly at me. "I see you in the face of every flower. I hear your voice in the song of every bird. I long to worship your beautiful body—"

The kid was definitely more Italian than American. I broke away and headed for our table. Lisa and Warren followed as the music stopped. She was still wearing his hat. It looked great. I whipped it off her head saying the hat smelled.

"I don't care," she laughed, "I love it," and whipped the damn thing back on her head.

We all ordered hamburgers. As usual Warren had got it wrong. There was neither seafood nor pizza. Nothing but hamburgers. And shag. They assured us that we'd love shagging. Warren said he didn't know if I was strong enough, being just out of bed after a really heavy illness. I immediately felt like someone on medicare.

Then the music started, the floor filled, and the place shook. Warren watched for a moment then said with delight, "I can do that! That's like the lindy!" and grabbed Lisa and there they were doing it along with everyone else. JP was saying something but it was too noisy to hear human speech. "Let's try it!" I shrieked. "Come on! I want to try!"

He was a wonderful dancer and once we got into it I realized that once upon a time a long, long time ago, I'd moved to this beat, danced these steps—not for long as I didn't have that much time to be a teen before I became a mother, but it all came back to me. Basically, it was totally aerobic and when we got back to the table after the first set I realized pearls were too hot for shagging, and threw my pearls into my purse and the Chanel earrings on top of them. After the second set I peeled off my shoes and my panty hose. Shagging was for flats and bare feet, not high-heeled Chanel pumps. As the evening wore on I borrowed a rubber band from the management and scooped the hair off my neck into a ponytail and hiked my skirt all the way up with a safety pin from the same source. It was wild. JP was very good. Warren was better. Warren did things like sliding me along the floor between his legs and throwing me around his shoulders and over his head and spinning me along his arms. Things I'd never done. I was better at it than Lisa because I was about four inches shorter and ten or fifteen pounds lighter.

And maybe I was a better, more responsive dancer. Anyway, Warren preferred shagging with me and after every dance he hugged me even though we were both dripping with sweat and I knew my makeup had long since melted but it wasn't even worth looking for a mirror. We were having fun! Oblivious to everyone around us. After nothing but debts and lack of cash flow and boredom and melancholy we were having fun!

We went outside for a minute to cool off and look at the ocean from the parking lot. "Look at you," he said. "You look like a kid." The wind felt good on my bare legs and the sand was cool between my toes. I felt alive. Like after a couple of sets of tennis. "Look at you," he said, and kissed me. Like he used to all those years ago. Like he had when I'd completed the circuit of the island by leaping from rock to rock. It was like being in love again. But he went zooming off to get his jacket for me against the wind. Not that I'd asked for it. Right then I would have liked being held against the wind. But that was Warren's way. Very considerate.

So I was standing there with my skirt all the way up and my hair in the rubber band, and along came JP with Warren's jacket.

He said Warren would be right out, he'd just stepped into the men's room, and put my arms into the sleeves and pulled me to him by the lapels and kissed me smack on the mouth. It was a nice kiss. I didn't move away and I didn't feel at all guilty. I was enjoying being alive and feeling all sorts of emotions and sensations, but mostly just being fully alive. Then somebody's brights shone right on us. JP and I stared into the lights like deer on a country road. The driver switched to his parking lights. It was Eulalee's big black van staring at us. Nobody got out. I shivered and ran back into the restaurant.

"Well!" Warren said, "There you are!" He looked a little uncomfortable. Maybe because he was leaning against the wall with Lisa leaning on his front with her arms around his neck. She had the grace to step away. I snatched his hat off her head. Warren said he was just coming out to look for us. Then we all laughed. JP said it was about time to get Merrie home. Of course smart-ass Lisa had to say something about my turning into a pumpkin, but JP explained that I'd just had a very severe pneumonia. Then she became so solicitous you'd have thought I was her terminally ill grandmother. Asking me if I was all right, warm enough, trying to help me walk to the car—I wanted to smack her.

Warren got my belongings and we walked with his arm around me to the car. We sat in back and he kissed me again. Guilt? Whatever, I liked it. I looked at beautiful JP and felt nothing but pleasure. Like looking at a sunset. When we got home I took a long hot shower and washed my hair and put on a black lace nightgown and moisturizer and lots of blusher and waited in bed and finally fell asleep waiting. The only warm body anywhere near me was Jackie's on the floor on my side of the bed.

Chapter 15

◆

◆ The next morning Warren said he'd worked on the novel until after three. Had a real breakthrough. I said I was happy for him. Then I mentioned seeing Eulalee's black van out there. "Maybe she and Bubba were out for a night of shagging." We laughed together, friends again, our fleeting romantic mood quite shattered. It was back to Grim. With one difference.

JP kept trying to get me alone and I was beginning not to mind as much. I really liked kissing that boy. Nobody mentioned Lisa. I assumed she was out at the crossroads minding the store. At the town hall meeting where Warren and JP presented their tennis court plan—very professionally too, complete with drawings, projections, descriptions, specifications and budget—I didn't see her. And if she'd been there I would have. There were never more than four or five people in the audience and they were only there to present their own projects.

Not much public spirit in Davis Landing. I'd spoken to a few people about helping the watermen and their families. People I knew could afford to make a gesture. When the red tide killed the fishing or when the winter was really bad and killed the fishing and they couldn't make the payments on their boats. They had no other resource but the water. And they were very proud people, refusing to accept charity. One man took his four children and went to the town dump to salvage tin cans and bottles for whatever they would bring. Young Mark knew who were the neediest families. The church would make up baskets of food and clothes and blankets and sheets and Mark would carry them out to their shacks. He'd always say, "If you know of anyone who might be able to use these things I'd like to leave them with you." And the man would say he didn't know of anyone while the barefoot children of the house would gaze longingly and silently at toys and sweaters and shoes and turkeys and hams. Then Mark would ask permission to leave the things should the man hear of any needy person. I helped him collect the contributions and sometimes I went with him to help deliver them and my heart broke for those good people, especially the children.

I told Sarah Taylor I'd been shagging out at The Club. She said it sounded like fun. Mixing with the riffraff. But when I mentioned Eulalee's van being out there too, she said it couldn't have been. Said she'd been with Eulalee that night. They were having the Davis Landing Book Club reports at her house and she knew who was there and what cars they'd come in. Eulalee had picked up Anna May Duncan and they'd been at Sarah Taylor's from six-thirty for refreshments to nine listening to the book reports. They'd had some very interesting discussions about Barbara Taylor Bradford's new book and Danielle Steele's new book. Very interesting evening. I said then there must be another black van just like Eulalee's and she said not in this county. Very definitely. I even asked Eulalee. Not if she'd been out at The Club parking lot, but if there was another van like hers. She said if there was she didn't know about it and then went in to a long, convoluted story of how she bought the van. It was previously owned by these people in Columbia who had a catering service and had several of these vans with white lettering on them but then with the recession they'd gone out of business as people weren't using caterers except for big things like weddings and they were few and far between. And how she was so happy with it, never any problems and at a good price too. And then she shoved a cup of blood strengthener at me and I threw up. Warren came away from his desk to explain to the poor woman that I had certain allergies and he told her about ant bites and going into anaphylactic shock and always having to carry this kit with me that had Adrenalin and a needle in it and how I could die from an allergic reaction. But Eulalee just went out to the van and brought in about a pint of the stuff and told Warren to get it down me. I needed it to build up after my illness. Before he could dump it, which is what he regularly did with Eulalee's brews, Luther appeared with some New Zealand spinach he'd been growing behind the Davis house in the perennial border and asked what that stuff was.

"Eulalee's blood strengthener," I told him.

He smelled it and said "Whew! For Japanese beetle!" and made a gagging sound.

I said, "It does smell bad, doesn't it?" and we laughed.

After he left, Warren said I'd better be careful, but then we both agreed that I wasn't about to consume any of the stuff Eulalee brought over as he threw it all down the garbage disposal. "It's just one stinking cup of muddy bouillon to me! And I don't ever want to hurt her feelings letting her know I never swallowed any of her prescriptions."

To no one's surprise the commissioners vetoed any town money for the tennis court. They raised the taxes this year and cut services so what could we expect. I mean, if they feel they can no longer support a dog catcher, how could they explain a tennis court. But to everyone's surprise Warren and JP raised the money. All the churches contributed and so did Rotary and so did the PTA. Not vast sums. But lots of little monies together added up to one high-grade tennis court. Almost all of it came with the expressed hope that the youth of Davis Landing would spend time on the court rather than drinking, drugging, and driving too fast while under the influence. It was decided by all the donors that the original name be kept, The Davis Landing Tennis Courts. At one time there had been three and we all hoped that at some time in the future there would be three again. If not more.

Now Warren and JP were seeing contractors about a bulldozer. They were both busier than ever and Warren had forgotten all about romance if the idea had ever flitted through his thick head. JP of course was still grabbing at me whenever he got the chance and we were kissing a little behind doors. But it all amounted to nothing more than a friendly indoor sport.

My new fan was Luther Tryon, strangely enough. He'd convinced himself that someone was trying to do away with me and he'd taken to coming over every day, all cleaned up, to see if I was all right, bringing a bouquet of herbs, or a basket of spinach or seeds or seedlings. Once it was a topiary rosemary that was a work of art. Really touching. I brought the rosemary to the next Garden Club, in the spirit of show-and-tell, because it was exquisite. Unfortunately, the ladies misinterpreted my motives. Yes, Luther was absolutely gorgeous but. . . . There was a lot of sniffing and muttering and whispering and sidelong glances at me and my poor little tree and no one paid much attention to the lecture on dried flower arrangements by Ardis Davis, the former president of the Davis Landing Arts Guild. I didn't pay much attention myself as every flower I'd ever dried turned brown.

And the Arts Guild hadn't charged enough for the magnificent wood carvings the watermen had been doing to turn an honest penny. They were mostly decoys and mostly wild ducks of various kinds although there were some shore birds carved of silvery driftwood that would have sold for hundreds or even thousands in New York galleries. I considered them sculptures by gifted though as yet unknown artists, but when I said thirty-five dollars wasn't enough for a work of art that had taken hours and hours I was told by this same lady that "we can only charge what the traffic will bear." I didn't have the money to prove that some people will pay more so they are still charging thirty-five dollars for a month's work.

It wasn't that I didn't want to kiss Warren or wouldn't have liked very much to get back to the superb sex we'd always enjoyed until we lost our money and came down here and got depressed, but he'd developed a blind spot on the subject. Even when I went and sat on his lap he scratched behind my ears. Like Mathilda. Not that we could discuss it. He never could. He could just *do* it and he was great. But now if he felt in a talkative mood all he ever wanted to talk about was the tennis court, the hourly price of a bulldozer, the stock market, or his novel. Oh, yes, and JP. What a great kid he was. Why didn't we have one like that was his favorite rhetorical question.

The days were getting a little longer and all my friends were either in Gstaad or St. Moritz or Aspen or Palm Beach or Barbados or Tunisia. Luther brought me some branches of quince to force in the house. A couple of days later the dog doorbell went off and wouldn't stop. I ran to see what it was about and found another one of those notes stuck in the screen—nobody ever takes their screens off down here due to the fortitude and good health of the bugs and the vagaries of the weather—and a white paper stuck in the windshield wiper of my car. This time they'd written YOU HAVE BEEN WARNED. Same on both notes. Of course, there was no one to be seen, not even any of the Tryons across the street. It had a chilling effect. On me. Not so Warren, who just glanced at it and said, "Another one of those things?" and tossed it aside.

The next morning I showed it to Luther. After he'd finally figured it out sounding each syllable silently including "warned" he became mildly agitated. Said I'd have to be very careful. Never to be alone. The end result was that we had at least one armed Tryon on the front porch at all times. Sometimes two. When I walked the dogs we were trailed by a gun-toting Tryon. Sometimes on foot, sometimes in one of their scabrous cars. I appreciated their solicitude but, prompted by them, Warren had reactivated his hovering and now he was joined by JP and I was being smothered by their collective caring.

Right about then Aunt May phoned and insisted I come up. Right away. She was in the hospital after being mugged waiting for a cab at the Carlyle. Nothing serious but she needed me to get her out of there. She was vague about X rays and damages and doctor's names but not about hospital food and regulations. "They won't even give me a drink in this goddam place" was the way she put it. Her closest kin except for me was a great-grandson who in an idealistic moment had volunteered as a teacher in a black school in Mississippi and couldn't leave his post.

Aunt May alternated between ordering and wheedling. I said I'd speak to Warren. She said "Oh, I'd much rather have him!" But he had to oversee the tennis court and the house needed more work and and . . . His excuses were endless and sounded reasonable but I knew he just didn't want to go. So it was up to me. After all, she was *my* aunt. None of my friends would be there and New York in the winter with slush melting in the streets knee deep at the corners and cabs splashing by and always taken by luckier persons than I—well, this is not the time I would have chosen. But I dearly loved Aunt May and she was the last of her generation of my immediate kin and even at Lenox Hill Hospital she'd be more alive than 90 percent of the people in Davis Landing.

Preparations for leaving Warren in charge of Jackie and Mathilda and the house for any length of time require a great deal of organization, a calendar of events in a conspicuous place and quite a bit of cooking. It's the sort of thing one does for a baby-sitter from whom one can't expect too much. Jackie and Mathilda had a checkup due and they seemed to need another worming. The fleas down here carry a particularly stubborn kind of worm egg along with countless other unattractive and uncomfortable afflictions. I marked the date of the checkup on the calendar in marine blue acrylic along with quick dry-brush sketches of two little terriers. Their food would have to be replenished in another week or ten days—Science Diet kibble. And the heartworm preventive pills were to be given on the fifteenth of each month. So much for Jackie and Mathilda, my chief concern.

They were my children, like two angelic three-year-olds who never had temper tantrums, had superior intelligence, wit, understanding, and a large vocabulary. When my young unmarried women friends asked me, as they were wont to do, what to do about the dilemma of the biological clock since they wanted children but didn't have the prospective father, I always told them "Have dogs!" With Jackie and Mathilda at my feet watching the news on TV I never felt alone. They were a constant comfort and joy. Along with the calendar/chart a nightly phone call was necessary to remind Warren to *look* at the chart and be sure the dogs were in the house before he went to bed.

After Jackie and Mathilda came the feeding of Warren. If I didn't leave prepared food he'd never complain, just spend a week or two living on beer and cheese. So I usually cook up a large vat of chili. It's his favorite food and one he doesn't mind eating steadily until I return to cook again. I make it from scratch including the beans (down here I sometimes use black-eyed peas cooked with ham bones and garlic) and have been known to throw in a square of unsweetened baking chocolate for a deeper flavor. And four dried red peppers because he likes it hot enough to bring out the sweat on the top of his head. I make individual portions in plastic boxes, carefully labeled, and freeze them. Of course, before I leave I show him where they are in the freezer. I also write notes fastened to the refrigerator with magnets: CHILI IN BOXES ON TOP SHELF. That sort of thing. Then I bake up three or four loaves of Myrtle Allen's Irish brown bread and freeze them.

It's so quick and simple and you don't have to knead it. You just take a big bowl and put seven and a half cups of whole wheat flour in it. Then add two tablespoons of salt or less if you're on a salt-free diet. Turn the oven on until it's just barely on and stick the bowl in there. Then take three packages of yeast and put them in a bowl along with one cup of very warm water and four tablespoons of molasses. Then grease up two loaf pans. The flour should be warm at about the same time as the yeast is bubbling. Take out the warm bowl, pour the yeast in, add three more cups of very warm water, stir the whole thing up and spoon it out into the pans. It'll be wet and sticky but not to worry. Cover the pans and let the stuff rise which it does fast enough to surprise you. I mean, sit down for a cup of coffee or a telephone call, don't go away. It'll come about up to the tops of the pans. Turn on the oven to 450 and when it's hot stick the pans in and bake for forty minutes. They should be done. Warren loves that bread and it's nourishing enough to keep him going all by itself.

Then I make many batches of oatmeal cookies and bars, fill the cookie jar and freeze the overflow, notes on the freezer door, etc. etc. etc. This way I know he'll have nourishing, cholesterol-free food while I'm gone, because I do love him and I'm used to him and I certainly wouldn't want to be left alone in this swamp hole.

Luther and JP approved vociferously of my leaving town. We drove to the airport in a convoy. Luther's horrible car and JP's pickup and Warren and me in ours. They all kissed me good-bye. Luther's was especially interesting. I think I'm in a chronic state of horniness. Luther!?

Chapter 16

♦

♦ After an uneventful flight that took the usual eternity—I could have walked to New York in the same time—I settled in to my room at Aunt May's and phoned a man Warren and I had gotten to know rather well during our series of car thefts, a very nice New York City detective from the nineteenth precinct, Lieutenant Meneguzzi, who'd asked us to call him Johnny. My plan was to buy Aunt May a gag gift to make her laugh. What I had in mind was a bulletproof vest and what I wanted from Johnny was the price of these things, and if possible, maybe the police department would have a somewhat cheaper previously owned garment. Johnny said he'd get back to me. I told him I was now on my way to Lenox Hill and I'd be either there in Aunt May's room or here in her apartment. Then I went out to buy flowers and her favorite candies.

All the papers are full of the terrible things that have happened in New York but it looks pretty much the same to me. Oh, lots of empty shops and closed restaurants, but there are small compensations. Like the proliferation of rose shops under the names of ROSES ONLY! or ROSES ROSES! or ONLY ROSES! And roses are Aunt May's favorite flowers. I've been told they're flown up from Colombia every day (probably with tons of cocaine), picked fresh that morning.

They're very good quality, all colors, but the best thing about them is the price. As little as six dollars a dozen when regular florists are selling roses for six dollars a *bloom*. Longer stems are as much as ten or twelve dollars a dozen, but it's possible to make a real splash with three or four dozen short-stemmed roses. I invested in a dozen each—red, yellow, white, and pink. Then I stopped at William Poll on Lexington Avenue. Aunt May doesn't like to chew on nuts and hard centers as she has a problem with her bridge but Poll's thoughtfully stocks delicious chocolates and bonbons that melt on the tongue and not too fast.

Of course when I got to her room at the hospital it was filled with flowers. The television was blasting away, Aunt May was sitting up in bed frowning into a magnifying mirror, and the first thing she said to me was, "Did you bring me a drink? Why not?" I told her I would have to speak to her doctor. After all, that's why I was there. She said, "What does *he* know?! Dr. Whitney says a drink every day is good for my heart, but he's off skiing somewhere and these people are good for nothing!"

"Aunt May," I said, "if you have a skull fracture nobody would let you drink, even Dr. Whitney—"

"It's only a hairline!" she said with a great deal of irritation. "I was standing under the canopy at the Madison Avenue entrance to the Carlyle Hotel waiting for a taxi. Rosabelle and I had just had lunch there—"

"Rosabelle?"

"You know. Rosabelle. Whatshername. I've known her all my life. She lives in Santa Barbara. You know who I mean. Anyway, she came into town on her son's jet to have an eye lift. It's amusing, isn't it? The New Yorkers go out there for their lifts and the west coast people are coming here. Anyway, she was here for an eye lift and we decided to have lunch at the Carlyle because we like that room. You know it's quiet and the service is good and they have that wonderful buffet— things you can eat without too much chewing or cutting, not like lamb chops. So anyway, we've finished lunch and it's raining and we're standing outside next to the doorman to whom we'd just given five dollars to get us a cab when this—this person came walking by real fast and he took my shoulder purse right off my shoulder without stopping. Well, of course I shouted at him but he just kept on walking and then I took after him—"

"You didn't—"

"Oh yes I did—I'd just cashed a check for two hundred dollars and it was all there except for the five I gave the doorman because Rosabelle signed her son's name for the lunch so it was on him. That's another reason we like to go there. It doesn't cost us anything. We even put the tip on his account. Another reason we like to go there is sometimes we get to see Robert Redford. He eats there a lot just like a plain person. We've never seen him with anyone but other men. Like business lunches." She took up the magnifying mirror again. "Rosabelle is going to mention me to her doctor. I'd like my chin line cleaned up and a really good lift to get rid of all these lines around my nose and my mouth and of course an eye lift too—"

"Aunt May, how did you get hurt?"

"Maybe a tummy tuck—"

"Aunt May—"

"Yes. Well, I was running up Madison Avenue after him—I mean he had all my cash and my credit cards and my phone card and the key to my apartment and my drivers license—"

"You're not supposed to drive—"

"That's beside the point. Anyway, I'm running up Madison Avenue in the rain shouting, "Stop thief! Stop that man!" And some people stopped him and I ran up and hit him with my umbrella and pulled my purse out of his hand but he pushed me and I fell and hit my head on the sidewalk. If I hadn't been wearing my mink hat my head would have cracked wide open and spilled whatever brains I've got left all over the sidewalk! But I was wearing the hat because I needed my hair done so I got this tiny tiny nothing fracture—"

"Is that all?"

"Is that *all?* Enough to deprive me of any semblance of civilized living! Have you ever eaten hospital food? They send around the dietician to ask what you'd like—oysters and champagne, I said, like Isak Dinesen—and what do you get? Garbage. Macaroni and cheese. Noodles. Soft garbage. And no Scotch. I told her Dewar's. It's just unbearable! Merrie, I want you to get me out of this place. Immediately! I insist on going home—Haven't had a decent night's sleep—Lights out at nine—Temperatures at five o'clock in the morning—I won't have it—"

"I'll see who's in charge. And meanwhile, I brought you these roses."

"Oh, how lovely—Don't take them out of the wrapping, we'll just get right into a cab and arrange them at home—"

"And some of these little goodies I know you like."

"Thank you, dear—You can give me a couple of those right now—"

"Do you have a nurse, Aunt May?"

"No! And that's another thing! I asked for a private nurse and they said they were in short supply and only for really sick people! Well if I'm not really sick then what the hell am I doing lying here in this hospital bed, forgotten by everyone—"

"I'll go and talk to someone—Be right back."

No one seemed at all anxious to keep Aunt May in the hospital. They used words like uncooperative and difficult. But they said her doctor would have to discharge her and they didn't expect to see him until tomorrow morning when he did rounds. His telephone was answered by a service, which told me essentially the same thing. When I went back to Aunt May's room she was threatening an aide with her magnifying mirror. The poor woman had just brought the supper tray with baked macaroni and tapioca pudding and Aunt May was highly indignant. And justifiably so, from what I could see. I told her we'd have to wait until the doctor saw her in the morning and I would be there definitely at eight-thirty and talk to him myself. Then we phoned Le Cirque and ordered oysters on the half shell and poached bass to be delivered at eight o'clock along with a bottle of Dom Pérignon. That taken care of we settled down to a nice gossipy chat about lifts and surgeons and prices and recovery times and Aunt May dozed off in the middle of it. I stayed to have a taste of her fish and several glasses of champagne and then left. She was going to be ninety-four in August and I only hoped that if I had the misfortune to live to that age I would be half as sharp and fierce.

Before I left I managed to find some vases and arranged the roses. If you use really warm water they do better. And several colors in one bowl are nice. Pink and white in one bowl, red and yellow in another. Then I went home, a little squiffy from the champagne, as I'm not accustomed to drinking anything and have lost my tolerance, and very tired. I couldn't wait to get into bed.

After cleaning my face and marveling yet again at how much dirt it had picked up in a very short time, I climbed into one of Warren's tee shirts and phoned him. The phone rang until the answering machine answered with his message. After the beep I said, "Warren where are you? Where are the dogs? Are they in the house? How was the chili? Love you," and turned off the light.

The next morning I asked the staff, the butler, the cook, and Harriet if anyone had phoned me and was told no one had. I had juice and coffee and called home. Once again I got the machine. Frustrating. And off to the hospital to do battle.

It was a little like Desert Storm. I was ready to wage war but they were only too happy to surrender before a shot was fired. Aunt May was discharged. They needed the room, Aunt May was raising hell and seemed to be perfectly all right as well as very troublesome. She wasn't even having headaches. I had a number to call should she develop any unexpected aches. Meanwhile two aspirin would take care of anything. She was so determined not to stay in the hospital that she'd already ordered a limousine for ten o'clock. "They're lucky they decided to let me go," she said, "because I was leaving anyway." She told the nurses to take all her flowers to the children's ward (including my roses) and, carrying her candies, walked regally to the elevators, nodding and waving as she went, occasionally darting into some man's room to say good-bye.

The car had a bar, which pleased her, but she gave the poor driver hell because there were no bottles, no ice, nothing but empty glasses. Then she picked up the phone and called her house to announce her imminent arrival. The butler told her there'd been a message for me. A Lieutenant John Meneguzzi.

"Well," she said. "Lieutenant John Meneguzzi. Army, Navy, or Air Force?"

"New York City police," I said. "A friend of Warren's and mine."

As soon as she got settled in at home, we had the obligatory Bloody Marys. Then she changed into her jogging suit and while she was running a large circle between the hall, living room, and dining room, I phoned Lieutenant Meneguzzi. He'd found what I was looking for—previously owned if I didn't mind some soil and the price was right, but I'd better have a look at it before he made the deal.

Aunt May was having a bath before her lunch date.

"I run for twenty minutes every morning after my breakfast. Get the heart beat way up there. Blood circulating. Then I have my bath. Rosabelle and I are going back to the Carlyle. I want to give that doorman a piece of my mind. Standing there like a lump of lard—not lifting a finger to help me. We're going to have the lobster salad with champagne. On her son. And maybe see Robert Redford." She slid down into the bubbles. "You know, Merrie, life can be damn good even at ninety-three. Not that I feel ninety-three. If it weren't for my damn eyes (deteriorated retina) and my goddam bridge I don't feel older than I did when I married my second husband, thirty-five . . . Whatshisname? . . . Whatshisname? That's the only thing. I don't remember names."

She didn't mind at all that I'd be out to lunch too, but she wanted to meet the gentleman. "Have him come up here so I can look him over and see if I approve. After all, I adore Warren."

She approved. She sparkled. Johnny Meneguzzi was a big good-looking man in a turtleneck sweater under a sport jacket. He told her we were going to have lunch in Little Italy because we had to do an errand downtown. She invited us to join her at the Carlyle. Johnny said he couldn't. Had to be downtown. She offered us Rosabelle's son's limo. He thanked her, but we had a department car. She insisted on seeing his guns. She started wheedling for something small and neat that she could carry in her purse. He said he didn't think she could get a license. Aunt May said she was sure he could manage one for her. For her safety and security.

She told him in great detail about the mugging and offered to come down to a lineup any time to identify the man, said he got away because after he knocked her down everyone was more interested in her. So all she got was a hairline skull fracture but if she hadn't been wearing her mink hat her head would have cracked wide open. And if she hadn't had her mink coat on to cushion her fall she would have broken her back or her hip or one of those things old people break. She invited us to join her in a glass of champagne. A Scotch? A Bloody Mary?

We rode downtown in an inconspicuous dark sedan of an indeterminate age. Not young for the doors wouldn't open unless you hit them hard in the right place. Hard. Then they opened grudgingly. I asked Johnny what he did if he was chasing someone and got there and the doors wouldn't open. He said they opened from the outside and there was always someone standing around who'd open them. But since the mayor and the governor had made all the budget cuts he couldn't complain about it. "They're closing the *libraries*," he said.

We had lunch in the place where Joey Gallo was shot. I think it was Joey Gallo. Anyway, it was really authentic Italian food and it was great. Mussels with red sauce (they don't eat mussels in Davis Landing or even pick them though, now that

I think of it, I've only seen silver mussels, not the blue ones that are so good for eating), escarole sautéed with garlic and oil, even the bread was great—and the espresso made me think of JP and thinking of JP made me wonder where Warren was and how my dogs were. I wanted to get to a telephone. But Johnny wanted to know all about living in Davis Landing.

"You wouldn't like it," I said. "No opera."

"No *opera?*"

"I listen to the radio on Saturday afternoons when Texaco does opera. And I have some wonderful tapes: *Tosca* . . . *Aïda* . . . Oh, you wouldn't believe the library. There's nothing to read."

"No culture?"

"Johnny, in a place where you can't buy pancetta or arugula or DeCecco pasta or *espresso coffee* how can you expect culture?"

"I could never live there. The hell with the clean air and no crime. I could never hack it."

"They don't even have *garlic!*"

He slammed the table. "That does it! You gotta get outa there!"

From lunch we proceeded to one of the reputed Mafia social clubs, familiar to me from *The Godfather* movies, a place with blacked out windows and no signs of life except for the number of men in black caps (I don't mean baseball) who were standing around outside. They looked at us impassively, nodded at Johnny. One of them even opened the door for us. Inside there was a bar and a number of tables with middle-aged men playing pinochle with their caps on. The bartender produced the vest. He said, "We cleaned up the sweat. There wasn't much anyway."

Johnny examined it carefully. "Try it on, honey."

I did and understood why cops didn't want to wear them. It felt stiff. Moving around in it one was very confined.

"How much?" he said.

"For you, Meneguzzi—*niente.*"

"Come on."

"I want to pay for it," I said.

"Come on, Giuseppe, how much?"

"You done plenty for me. Forget it."

I wore it back to Aunt May's under my raincoat.

All the way up the East Side Drive Johnny and I talked about Davis Landing. He said we were wasting our lives down there. "No theater? No opera? No libraries?"

"The living is cheap."

"Call that living?"

He assured me that if I wanted to reach him I had only to call—day or night—"They can always find me. I got the beeper. Anything. I'll send it down to you. Pancetta. Parmigiano. Espresso. DeCecco. Garlic! I'll send you a whole damn necklace of garlic!"

While he was becoming more and more upset about our horrible fate I was looking out the car window at people living in the street—drug deals on the corners—and I'd say, "Look at that, Johnny! We don't have anything like that!"

"So you don't have crime! Booorrring! You've got such low energy down there, they can't even get themselves geared up to do a little break-in—a little murder! Merrie, you need intellectual stimulation. Don't tell me how clean it is! You're only half alive!" And more and more. Nagging. The minute I got back to the apartment I phoned Warren. And spoke to the machine. Damn. Aunt May had left a note for me. "I have theater tickets for us tonight and I've booked you for a day of beauty at Kenneth's tomorrow. My treat. XXXOOO."

A day at Kenneth's included massage. Of course I'd stay. The hell with Warren wherever he was. If he didn't care enough about me to—to even *try* to talk to me—after all the times I'd called him—I'd taken to saying, "This is your wife, Warren!"

I was gift wrapping the vest when JP called. He was in New York and could I have dinner with him. I said I couldn't. And I couldn't join him for lunch the next day. But I could probably do lunch the day after. I asked him how Warren was and he said fine. And the dogs? Fine. The tennis court? Fine. He was staying at a newly redone former fleabag hotel near Times Square, checking out the town with Zio Roberto, his uncle from Milano, and shopping for tennis nets. Lights too, so they could use the courts at night. We arranged lunch for one-thirty the day after next at a place to be decided upon. The way I was feeling about Warren I didn't care if I never went back to Davis Landing. He could send the dogs up here.

Aunt May said, "People don't dress for theater the way they used to but I refuse to wear Reeboks and a tee shirt. I'm wearing my black Valentino dinner suit with a white sequin tee shirt."

"I didn't bring anything that dressy—"

"You can have whatever you need out of my closet. But make it gala, not the sort of thing you wear down there in that dreary place. I've ordered the longest stretch limo they've got with blacked out windows and a sunroof so the waiter can stand up."

"What waiter?"

"From '21.' They're sending him along with the champagne and caviar and it would be ridiculous to have the poor man serve us bent double."

When we arrived at the theater she told Felipe, the waiter, to be sure and keep the champagne on ice and the caviar too. "Come along, dear"—pulling at my arm—"we'll just whip out here and refresh ourselves during the intermission. It'll be such fun guzzling with no one knowing what we're up to."

After the show (costing eight million, lavish, deafening and forgettable, like all the new musicals) I asked if we could drive past JP's hotel so I could see where it was. The whole Times Square area had changed so drastically, in fact all of New York, things disappeared overnight and new things replaced them and it was all very confusing. We went past the hotel, which had been duded up on the exterior but had the same drug deals going on at the entrance. Aunt May said I was not to meet anyone in that dreadful place.

"That dreadful place is probably charging two hundred a night—"

"Who in God's name would stay *there?*"

"A young man from Davis Landing. He's been helping Warren with the tennis court—"

"Name?"

"JP."

"That's not a name."

"Giancarlo Paolo Jones."

"Age?"

"Twenty-five. We're only having lunch, Aunt May—"

"That's the way they all start. We'll have a drink and canapés at my place."

The day at Kenneth's was heaven. They all made much of my southern accent, which I didn't know I had and the massage was ineffably soothing. Every muscle in my body relaxed. I hadn't realized how tense I'd been and how tacky-looking until I got into that place with all the power ladies. Mary Farr snipped away, criticizing all the time and the ladies gossiped. The newest separations, the reasons, injecting silicone in the upper lip instead of collagen, the best man for a clean chin line, some said Donald Trump was tacky, others said Ivana was a heroine to have stayed with him so long. Mary Farr and I said we were sorry for their children.

After Kenneth's, I met some friends for tea at the Regency. Crumpets and scones and Devonshire cream and the hell with the cholesterol and lots of gossip about the Southampton/ Park Avenue group. They were all being photographed nude by an artsy *Vogue* photographer who'd done Madonna. They were doing it with their husbands, their children, and their lovers. And planning for London in June in time for Ascot and the Hamptons in July and Scotland in August for the shooting—They wanted me to stay and join them in Jamaica but I told them I had to go back.

I walked up Park Avenue to Aunt May's, enjoying looking at the people and what they were wearing and listening to snatches of conversation in every language in the world. I love New York. Our old doorman said hello. He said all the people in the building missed us and wanted to know when we were coming back. When I got home the butler said Warren had phoned. No message. Damn! I phoned back and spoke to the machine again. Damn damn damn! Where was he? That night Aunt May wore her vest to a Japanese restaurant. She and I sat cross-legged and shoeless on a tatami mat eating sashimi and sushi with chopsticks and drinking hot sake. I did more drinking in those two days than I'd done in the previous two years. We finished our meal with mung bean ice cream, which seemed to be a healthy thing to do and then went to a movie Aunt May had especially been wanting to see. It's all about life in Beverly Hills, she told me.

It was. According to some writer's coke-induced dream? In it everyone was doing it to everyone including the dogs. I whispered that it was a porno. Aunt May laughed. She whispered back that those Southern Baptists had got me. She thought the movie was very funny and laughed all through it. When the lights went up I realized she was the only white-haired person, at the same time I was receiving almost unanimously disapproving looks from the audience for corrupting this sweet little old lady. The butler said Warren had phoned. The message was everything was fine. Bloody hell, I said.

I phoned JP. He was actually in his room. He said he'd been enjoying New York. Zio Roberto (Uncle Roberto) had worn him to a nub. Wanted him to come back to Milano. Wanted to meet me.

"Why?"

"I told him about you."

"What did you say?"

"That I was in love with you. That you kissed me as if I were a child."

I hadn't thought he was that sensitive.

"He wants to meet you. To take us to lunch."

"Fine. Bring him along. Aunt May has invited you here for a drink before lunch. One o'clock. Park and Sixty-first. Twelfth floor. I'll tell the concierge downstairs we're expecting you."

"*Va bene.*"

"By the way, what's Warren been up to? I haven't been able to get up with him yet (a southern way of saying I haven't been able to reach him—talk to him—whatever)."

"He's fine."

"You keep saying that. Why doesn't he ever answer the phone?"

"Maybe he's out."

"Obviously he's out. Out where?"

He hesitated. "Probably at the court. See you tomorrow. One o'clock."

Everyone knows Italians are never on time. Or should. I kept telling Aunt May one o'clock probably meant two o'-clock. All right, one forty-five. One of my closest Italian friends told me years ago in Rome that if one is invited to dinner at eight-thirty, it is extremely rude to arrive at eight-thirty. "The host and hostess are not yet dressed! The food is not prepared! The table is not set! Eight-thirty means nine-fifteen. At the earliest."

"JP is on American time," I said, "but his uncle is here from Milan."

"One-thirty," she said, nibbling at the canapés. "And if I eat all of these it's their tough luck. But if I like your friends I can have Whatshername—Cook—do up some more."

By one-thirty Aunt May had had two Scotches. When the doorbell rang fifteen minutes later she would have welcomed Godzilla with open arms. She took one look at beautiful JP and elegant Zio Roberto and told the butler to have Cook make some more canapés.

JP was dazzling in his city blazer and gray flannels with a muffler around his neck. I'd never seen him out of his raggedy clothes. But Zio Roberto . . . ! Zio Roberto was JP thirty years from now, thirty years of the good life and good food and wine and many loves and never any lack of money . . . dressed by an English tailor, wearing a discreet French cologne. When this very tall, very distinguished, very elegant gentleman bent over my hand and carried it to his lips while gazing into my eyes with a meaningful twinkle, I realized that I must get myself back to New York somehow. When he bowed over Aunt May's hand she reached up to stroke his cheek. He laughed.

We laughed a lot, managing to consume two bottles of champagne as well as numerous canapés, until the butler announced that madam's masseuse had arrived and was waiting. Aunt May made her excuses and reluctantly toddled off, but not before she got Zio Roberto and JP to promise that they'd come back to see her. In fact, that they'd come and see her whenever they were in New York. She tried to get JP to move out of his "dreadful" hotel and into one of her extra bedrooms but he said he was only staying one more day. Next time, she said, don't you forget! Now remember! You promised!

The three of us decided unanimously to go to an Italian place as who else would understand lunch at three-thirty except perhaps the Brazilians but they might be having breakfast and anyway we didn't feel like eating Brazilian food. We went directly to Harry Cipriani's latest branch of his place in Venice and ordered Bellinis (puree perfectly ripe and perfect fresh peaches and add good champagne) and risotto. Nothing mattered. Money . . . Warren . . . The dogs . . . Nothing. We ordered a lovely, clean Pinot Grigio with the risotto and a green salad. To be followed by espresso. I don't remember what we talked about. Nothing of any importance. Zio Roberto spoke a perfect British English—he said the family always had English nannies for the children—and JP and I were trying to demonstrate southern speech to him. . . . Anyway, whatever it was it was very funny or at least we all thought it was hilarious. And then the six o'clock cocktail crowd was pushing through the doors and, although JP and I didn't have any immediate plans, Roberto did. He said he had to check his fax machine and make some extremely urgent calls that he should have made hours ago. JP wanted to show me his crazy art deco closet of a room but I thought I'd better check Aunt May.

Before we left the table Roberto brought my hand to his lips and told me, with that devastating twinkle, how much he regretted leaving. He offered me a lift, saying his hotel was very near Aunt May's apartment. We said good-bye to JP and got in a cab but the address he gave the cab driver was not Aunt May's apartment.

"The food," he said, as the cab drove off, "is very good there. As good as his place in Venice."

"Yes," I said.

"It was a good choice," he said, looking out the window.

"Yes," I said, looking out my window.

He took my hand, turned the glove back and kissed the palm. There was no need for speech.

When we reached his address, one of the city's best residential hotels, he paid the driver and helped me out. He took my arm. The doorman tipped his hat. We went through the revolving door into the lobby and directly to the bank of elevators. Riding up to the fifteenth floor in silence we both stared straight ahead. When we stepped out, the maid, her arms full of clean towels, nodded to him. "Your rooms are made up, sir."

"Good," he said. He put the key in the door, held it open for me, put his coat on a chair, took off my coat and put it beside his. He took off his suit jacket. I stepped out of my shoes. He loosened his tie. I peeled off my panty hose. He picked up the phone and said that he would not be taking any calls that evening, he was not to be disturbed.

Around eleven o'clock I phoned Aunt May. She wasn't home. I told the butler I would be returning in the morning, hung up and was suddenly very hungry. Roberto said he was too.

"What do you feel like eating? Omelette? Steak frite? Pasta?"

"Pasta's always good. But what would you like?"

"The one thing it is impossible to get in Italy. Do you know what that is?"

"I can't imagine."

"Jewish delicatessen."

We laughed.

"It would be amusing to have a pastrami sandwich on rye bread."

"Make it two."

"Champagne?"

"Would it be too gross if I asked for water?"

"Fiuggi?"

"New York tap water is good enough for me."

"Fiuggi is better for the digestion."

The next morning when we were leaving he said, "It would be very nice if we could meet again."

"But not very likely."

"What will you do?"

"I'm going back to Davis Landing. This afternoon if I can catch a flight."

"I shall think of you." He kissed my hand. "Thank you."

And we stepped into the corridor, walked down the hall and rode down in the elevator in silence. It was a cold, gray day with a slight mist in the air. Already the traffic was heavy. He bowed over my hand and turned south. I walked swiftly in the opposite direction.

Chapter 17

♦

• Aunt May was still asleep. I phoned the airline and booked a flight for five o'clock that afternoon. Then I called Warren and by some miracle he answered.

I said, "Warren! This is your wife!"

"Merrie! How are you?"

I told him I was coming home that afernoon. My plane would be getting in about ten-thirty that night. "No," he said, "you mustn't."

"Mustn't what?"

"Mustn't come home yet. Stay up there awhile. Enjoy yourself."

"Warren, where have you been since I left? This is the first time I've been able to talk to you in *days*—"

"I've been working hard—Merrie—I'm coming around to your way of thinking."

"My way of thinking about what?"

"The poisonings."

"What changed your mind?"

"Things."

"What things?"

"I'll tell you when I see you."

"But you just told me not to come back—"

"For your own safety—"

"Where are the dogs?"

"Around."

"Where around? In the house?"

"How do I know?"

"Warren, I'll be on that ten-thirty flight tonight."

"Merrie—"

"If you don't want to meet me I can always thumb a ride.
With some truck driver."

"Merrie!"

"See ya!"

After I was all packed I went to ROSES ROSES! and
bought Aunt May a dozen red, a dozen white, a dozen flesh,
and a dozen pink. Massed together they'd be nice. And some
more candy. That about used up the money I'd brought with
me, leaving just enough for a taxi to the airport. I hadn't
bought anything for myself. Clothes were priced beyond me.
I couldn't believe little nothing day dresses for nine hundred
dollars. Anyway, where would I wear them? The weather was
getting nastier, and by the time I reached the house it was
snowing and Aunt May was up.

"Where were you last night?"

"At a friend's apartment."

"Which friend? The old one or the young one?"

"Neither."

"I don't believe you. I peeked into your bathroom. You
took the red ones *and* the blue ones."

"Aunt May, you're a naughty old lady. Zio Roberto
took us to lunch at Cipriani's and I ran into an old school
friend. She dragged me home with her and we sat up all night
reminiscing."

"It must have been a hard choice," she said as if I hadn't
spoken. "Do I have to guess?"

I ignored that and went off to arrange the flowers. While I
was busy massing roses, a package was delivered for me. From
one of New York's most prestigious jewelers. I opened it with
Aunt May at my elbow. It was a very large, white, and perfect

pearl to hook on to my triple choker. No card. My aunt whistled. "You know," she said, "I would have chosen him too. Time enough for the young one."

I felt no guilt. Just very relaxed and lighthearted. As Aretha's song goes, "He made me feel like a natural woman." And as Shirley MacLaine said when she accepted her Academy Award, "I deserved that."

When I finished packing the few clothes I'd brought, Aunt May had a limo waiting to take us to the Metropolitan Museum for the new show of Impressionists, but it was too mobbed to really see the paintings. She said she'd had no idea or she would have arranged for a private showing, which she could do since she'd been on the Board for so many years. So we went on to Bergdorf's to buy Warren some of the cologne Zio Roberto had been wearing which I'd checked out in his bathroom. They did a beautiful gift wrap for me and then we whipped out to the limo and over to Le Cirque for lunch. Aunt May had oysters and champagne à la Karen Blixen. I had linguine with butter and lots of grated white truffles. Unforgettable. She sent me out to the airport in the car, which was nice since it left a small balance in my wallet, and begged me to come back and stay with her again.

At the airport I checked my one piece of luggage and bought all the New York papers for Warren, who didn't mind yesterday's news. Then I hurried to the boarding gate. Davis Landing was so far away—I'd become a New Yorker again—that I was startled when a young man strode up to me and took my newspapers. It was JP. Then he kissed me. I drew back.

"Warren told me you'd be on this flight."

"You talked to him?"

"Sure. You look different."

"Just city clothes."

"What's different about you?"

"I can't imagine. Three, four days of intellectual stimulation, breathing energy in the air, seeing old friends, lots of good food and wine, and laughs—I guess it shows. When I'm in New York I'm fully alive."

He wanted to switch seats so that we could be together. I told him I planned to sleep all the way but he managed to sit beside me.

I closed my eyes.

"Your aunt is great."

"So's your uncle," I said sleepily.

"People say I'm going to be just like him."

"JP. If you want to read the papers, please do. Or watch the movie or—"

"There isn't any movie—"

"I'm going to sleep."

He woke me when it was time to debark and change planes. In the airport he bought us Pepsis. I looked around. There we were back in the Southland surrounded by obesity and no one I knew.

JP said we had two hours to kill. "We could go to a motel," he winked.

"If you'll watch over my belongings, I intend to sleep right here under the fluorescents." And I lay down on the floor on my coat and went right back to sleep.

JP woke me. "Time for our flight." He leaned down and pulled me to my feet. "I got some great shots of the very elegant Mrs. Warren Hancock Spencer resting between flights."

"You have no camera."

"Oh but I do." He waved a Polaroid shot at me. It seemed to be either a corpse or a woman derelict who happened to look exactly like me. "I thought I'd send this to Zio Roberto."

"You fiend. Give me that thing." We were both laughing when it tore in the struggle. He said, "I've got lots more."

We boarded the little commuter plane. The pilot was a woman. I couldn't help noticing, even in my wiped out condition, how many passengers inquired as to the age of "the vehicle" when they boarded. And each time the programmed stewardess chirped something about it being "a new vehicle. Two years old." Anyone who flies today has to be a fatalist. I was rested and relaxed. What will be will be. My fingers played with Roberto's pearl at my neck. I wasn't happy about going back to Davis Landing but I longed to see my dogs.

Lisa was right out in front, looking great. She threw herself on JP, hugging and kissing and whimpering just like a hound dog. Warren was out at the truck with Jackie and Mathilda. They jumped and jumped and jumped straight up in the air. Warren said, "You look different," and kissed me.

"So do you," I said. "Are you thinner?"

"Shit, no," he said.

"Have you been eating?"

"Of course I've been eating, you silly woman." He looked pale and tired. The truck started with a roar.

"This thing is beginning to sound illegal."

"Prob'ly needs a new muffler."

"Why didn't you want me to come back?"

"I did. Of course I wanted you back. I missed you all the time you were gone."

"You said—"

"Forget it. You're here, aren't you?" He turned the radio to a country station. It was hard to talk over it.

I switched it off. "Anyone die since I left?"

"Not that I know of." He switched it back on again.

I switched it off. "Has Lisa been here all the time?"

"Sure." He switched it on again and started to sing "Lucille" along with it. He has a nice tenor. I gave up.

It was a moonless night and very, very dark. Everything on our street looked exactly as it had when I'd left. It didn't seem possible that it was less than a week ago.

He welcomed the newspapers and the cologne with equal enthusiasm. His favorite was Hermes but I told him this was something new.

"Everyone in New York is using it?" he chuckled.

"Not everyone."

I went right to the kitchen to check the food. Almost everything I'd left for him was still there. He was already deep into the New York papers but I managed to get his attention. "You didn't eat anything!"

"Sure I did."

"All the boxes are still in the freezer."

"Well now you won't have to cook for a while."

"You haven't been eating!"

"I ate some. And Lisa's been fixing things."

"Lisa?"

"She's been helping me."

"How?"

"I got a glitch in the word processor and she fixed it. I would have had to stop working on the novel if she hadn't. Prob'ly would have had to drive a hundred miles somewhere to find some guy to fix it for me."

My fingers went to Roberto's pearl. "I thought Lisa was a botanist or a horticulturist or something."

"She is. But she's had a lot of computer training. And she's very handy mechanically. She's got JP's business all programmed. Client list, billings, accounts—"

"And she cooks, too?"

"She microwaves. Like me."

He went back to the newspapers and I went up to bed. Just before I fell asleep I wondered at my hypocrisy being jealous of Lisa after my own experience with Roberto. I didn't feel the least bit guilty about that and was quite sure Warren was being truthful about his glitch . . . or was he . . . ?

Chapter 18

•

• When I woke the next morning Jackie and Mathilda were sitting beside the bed waiting silently for their walk. I was rested enough to feel up to it. Warren was still sleeping. The three of us were especially quiet. The sun was just rising when we stepped outside. Everything was in place on the porch. I checked my Mediterranean fern, which after blooming profusely now had been blessed with a crop of red berries. Probably poisonous. Down here during the winter you can leave them outside and untended. Then in the spring, water and there they are. Mine is two years old and enormous. When I stepped off the porch and turned toward the water I glanced at the house. It had peeled! It was hideous! The white paint had become scabrous, bare in patches, flaking in others, and spotted with red and yellow and green and deep blue. Well, I'd just have to wake up Warren and find out what had been going on.

As we walked we met the usual people and got the usual greetings. "Bin away?" "Where ya bin?" And to all I said how glad I was to be back in lovely Davis Landing. One of the postal workers was running the flag up on the pole in front of the thirties brick building, with a Morgenthau plaque on the front, which had replaced an orchard. The wind caught it as it reached the top and it blew straight out against the blue of the sky. We said "Moanin' " and as he finished tying the line around the cleat he said, "Look at her! I'nt she the most beautiful thing you ever did see?" I agreed.

The Stockbroker was up when we got back and had already made a pot of his awful coffee. "Did you notice the house?"

"What *happened* to it?"

"I wanted to surprise you. But we didn't have enough time."

"Who's *we?*"

"Lisa and me. She was helping to scrape. There's hundreds of years of old paint on those boards. They're heart pine when you get down to them. We could leave them bare if you like. It was interesting to see what was underneath. This house wasn't always white with green shutters. One time it was red and another time yellow and once it was blue and then there was cream. We thought you might want a color this time around. Instead of white."

I fixed the dogs' breakfast and we went out to look at the colors. I couldn't believe the first settlers had used blue. Red, yes. It was easy to see it had been a barn red in spite of the fading. The yellow was more of an orange, like a pumpkin yellow. I liked white with green shutters myself. The way it had been. But as Warren pointed out, unless the white was kept really white and clean it looked like hell. He said it would have to be power cleaned every spring because of the mold it gets from always being damp from the humidity.

You could put something in the paint against the fungus, but it didn't work all that well. He was thinking about an off-white, like a cream. Which after all, it had been once. With darker green shutters. With a touch of black in the green, to bring out the contrast. Sounded good to me.

We went back inside to have our breakfast. He said he'd go buy the paint as soon as the hardware store opened. I told him I appreciated his working so hard to make the house look better. He said why live in a shit house long as we own it.

Might want to sell it. I'd never thought of that. Gave me a twinge. . . . This house was family.

He went off to the post office for the mail while I went through the stack of bills and junk that had come in while I was away. When he came back he said, "That van just went by again. Eulalee must be mighty busy with sick people if that's who it is. At the post office they were saying everyone's got an intestinal virus and some people are down with a bronchial virus too. If she's so damn busy what's she doing cruising the streets?"

I was frowning over the bills and he was busy with his calculator figuring out how much paint we'd need. Undercoat was going to be white. One undercoat. Two top coats in cream. At nine o'clock sharp he left for the paint. But he came right back in. Another note had been stuck in the screen. Now it hasn't seemed worth mentioning, but they've been coming fairly regularly, always with the same message, telling me to mind my own business. To stop meddling. And since I wasn't *doing* anything, that is, other than researching local horticulture in the library, and native American folk lore, and talking to all the pharmacists in the county, and anyone else who would talk to me on the subject, I really felt . . . forget it, this must be some nut. So here was another one telling me to mind my own business. Well, thank God, we still have the First Amendment and I intend to use it.

We opened the note together. This one consisted of letters cut out of newspapers and glued to a large piece of paper. It said: MRS. SPENCER MAY GOD HELP YOU NOW. I felt a definite chill. This one was different. This one seemed serious.

Warren looked disturbed. He put his arms around me and said, "Merrie, you've got to go right back to your aunt's."

"You're really worried about me, aren't you. That must mean you care."

"Of course I care you stupid woman."

"That's sweet. But I'm not going to let them run me out of town. This is *my* town . . ."

"We'd always keep this place—We could come back whenever we want—"

"Takes money to run two houses, Warren. But instead of us leaving town why don't we both go see Sam Pollock and show him this?"

He said right after he got the paint. And meanwhile I was to stay in the house. Which I would have done anyway. The place was a record of Warren's days. The junk mail he received, opened, and balled up to toss into a waiting trash can. He usually missed, sometimes quite widely as could be seen by all the balled up papers on the floor. It wasn't that he was too lazy to pick them up, it was just that once they left his hand he no longer felt connected to them. So they lay there until I came along. Bending from the waist could be done in all sorts of therapeutic ways; straight down, swinging to the side and then down, sideways—all very good for the waistline. I could have swept them up but why sweep when there was all that good exercise available?

And there was a pile of filthy jeans and work shirts and socks and towels . . . and two practically unused jockey shorts. He only wore underwear when he went out on what he considered formal occasions like weddings and funerals. So he must have gotten dressed twice. For some important occasion or occasions. Which he'd never mentioned. I would ask him when the time was right.

When he came back with the paint I reminded him that he'd said that he was coming around to my way of thinking.

"Never!"

"When I was in New York. On the phone. You said Merrie, I'm coming around to your way of thinking about the poisonings."

"Oh, that."

"Did something happen while I was away?"

"Nothing. Well . . . the cat over at JP's shop died. The one he used to take with him in the truck like a dog."

"Ohh! That was a great cat."

"Yeah. Lisa said she'd been trucking out all the leftover

Christmas trees and she'd planned to take out the leftover Christmas decorations—the mistletoe and poinsettia and holly and Christmas roses and a couple of oleanders that hadn't sold—had them all in a pile on the floor, and she'd noticed the cat was playing and nibbling around the pile, chewing on the oleander branches, but she didn't pay much attention. That cat was always into something. And then it went into convulsions and foamed at the mouth and died."

"I'm so sorry . . . that was a nice cat. . . . It was more like a dog than a cat. . . ."

"Anyway, that got me thinking. Merrie, all those plants—they're all on your list. The Latin for Christmas roses is *hellebore* and Lisa said they've got an insecticide at the shop made of *hellebore* dust that's got all kinds of warnings. Merrie, there's someone in this town using plants to kill *people!*"

"Oh? So it's not kid stuff? It's not me writing my own scenario! It's not—"

"All right all right all right." He never likes to be reminded of when he's wrong.

"And all those warnings? Game playing?"

"All *right*, Merrie! We'll go see the chief."

That was one time when I sat right up beside Warren instead of being relegated to a dark space behind him. Sam Pollock listened. I'll say that for him. He didn't interrupt once, looking into Warren's face and shifting the wad of tobacco from his right cheek to his left cheek. He spat and asked to see those notes we said we got. We looked at each other.

I said, "They were so—so yucky—"

"Distasteful," Warren said.

"So distasteful that we threw them out."

"You never thought to keep one of these threats you allegedly received?" he asked Warren. "Mr. Spencer, without proof it's just your word." He spat again. "You askin' us to start investigatin' these alleged threats without no proof—"

"I saw them—My wife saw them—"

"That ain't good enough. Next one you get, you keep it. That's evidence." He pushed back his chair.

"But Chief, the last one said, May God Help You—It said, 'Mrs. Spencer May God Help You.' "

"Hearsay. You tellin' me. Look, I'd like to help you, I really would. I believe Miz Spencer is kin to my wife. She was a Davis. I'm from Alamance County myself, originally, but I bin here twenty-five years, don't feel like a foreigner no more—"

"Chief, Merrie's already been hurt once. You know about that—When the truck hit her—"

"No proof of malicious intent there. That one's on the books as a hit-and-run accident. We need proof of these things you're alleging."

My stomach was feeling very queasy. "Warren! The one we got this morning—Mrs. Spencer May God Help You. I threw it in the trash!

"The truck hasn't been around to collect yet, maybe we could still find it."

We were out of there in a flash. But when we got back to the house our two trash cans were standing neatly side by side on the curb. Empty.

"Maybe we can catch them," Warren said, and we took off up and down the neighboring streets. And there it was. Just ahead of us on Queen Charlotte. Big Sam who always waved to me and the dogs on our morning walks was more than happy to let us look through the collection. We looked.

The note, which we knew was in there with all the stinking garbage (it was only collected twice a week), was hard to distinguish from papers and newspapers covered with slime and muck and rotted food. Warren thanked Sam and the truck moved off.

I was so angry I couldn't speak until we got home. Warren picked up our trash cans to carry back into the yard and I exploded. "You know there's a recycling post! I've told you over and over. I've separated the papers from the cans and the plastic and the glass—"

"Dammit Merrie, shut up!"

"No I won't! I'm tired of separating every little thing and then having you throw them all together."

The Tryons had come out on their porch.

"Get off my back," he shouted.

"Don't you shout at me."

He carried the trash cans into the backyard.

I pulled some weeds because I had to do something physical.

Luther appeared at my side, beautiful as ever. "Howyadoin'?" he said in greeting.

"I've been better."

Two of his brothers loomed behind him. "If you got a problem—"

"I don't have a problem, Luther. Whyever would you think I have a problem?"

He looked down at his boots. I saw that his brothers had brought their rifles with them.

I was suddenly aware that I loved Warren. "Luther, just because we raised our voices a little—Well . . . married couples don't always agree on everything, do they? . . . You should know that. . . . But there's no problem. No problem at all."

Warren burst out of the house, still shouting. "I work my ass off for you—I do everything I can to protect you, and all you do, all you do is nag and criticize and ignore and—"

"Warren," I said sweetly, "the Tryons have come over to protect me"—moving swiftly to his side—"I told them it was just nervous tension," managing a quick kiss.

He pulled away.

The brothers went back to their lookout on the porch. Luther asked if we were planning to paint the house. Warren said we were.

Luther said if that girl—the same girl?—was going to help? He might just lend a hand too.

Warren said he thought Lisa was busy but . . . " 'Preciate."

I spent the rest of the day in the attic. My time in New York had made me want millions even more than I had before. Aunt May was so generous I knew I could ask her for a loan, but she was actually pretty much hogtied by trusts and trustees and foundations. There wasn't that much cash around and all of her estate had been assigned. Scratch Aunt May. It was up to me. And to Warren. He had the novel, the pile of manuscript was getting thicker, and his stocks. I had nothing.

Warren worked hard to finish the scraping. Then we both stared at the bare wood for a long time and discussed applying a sealer and letting it weather.

"It won't turn silver," he said, "like cedar."

"I know. It'll just darken like the floors."

"Reddish brown."

"With a red trim? Green trim?"

"You want an Adirondack cabin?"

We decided to paint it. He worked until dark applying the white undercoat on the front of the house.

While we were watching "MacNeil/Lehrer" over dinner he asked me what I'd ever done for or to Luther Tryon and Bubba to elicit their apparent devotion.

"I didn't have to do anything," I said. "I happen to be a very attractive woman." After New York I was able to say that with confidence. "Remember when you thought so?"

He looked away from the television set. "I'm glad to see you're wearing some of your pearls. What's that thing hanging on the front?"

"Costume jewelry. Everyone's wearing them."

"What is it?"

"A pearl drop."

"When I sell my novel I'll buy you a real one."

"Don't worry about it. Everyone thinks this one is real."

"I'm not going to buy gallons of paint until we're sure cream is the color we want. I'll get just enough to do the front of the house."

"Fine."

Under the Tryons' supervision he worked all the next day.

The house was cream and so were the porch rails. We stood across the street admiring it.

"Looks pretty good," he said.

"I like it. You did a great job."

Chapter 19

♦

♦ The next morning when I opened the front door to go out with the dogs there was a notice nailed to it forbidding any further work on the house and ordering the owners to appear before the town commissioners. I ran upstairs to wake Warren with Jackie and Mathilda at my heels. "I don't know what it's about," I said, "but I've got to get these dogs out for their walk."

By the time we returned Warren's rage had attracted a goodly portion of the neighborhood in spite of the fact that it wasn't even seven o'clock yet. I pushed my way through the crowd. The dogs had to be fed, coffee made, juice squeezed, bread sliced. Life goes on.

Warren stormed into the kitchen. "There isn't one single goddam person who doesn't think our paint job is a fucking improvement. Not one."

"Warren," I said, "as soon as the Town Hall opens you can call and find out what that notice means and who put it up and sort the whole thing out. Until then, your breakfast is ready."

We got the answers. The commissioners put the notice on the house. We had neglected to ask their permission to change the color—"What change! The white was practically worn off!"—and we would have to attend the next meeting on Friday at seven o'clock and tell them what we planned to do and bring samples of the colors we planned to use. If they approved we could go ahead with the painting after we had paid a fifty-dollar fine for ignoring their rules.

Warren screamed at that piece of news. "Fifty fucking dollars!"

I was furious. I mingled more with the town than Warren did and I knew all the commissioners. I knew who had had a hysterectomy and why. Whose daughter had a fertility problem and then it was found not to be hers but his. Who never came to meetings because he was home drinking. Who came to meetings and should have stayed home drinking. Who was angling to build a development in the wetlands. And more. I knew them all. And I was very angry. Cars were constantly slowing down outside our house to view the new cream paint. Early morning walkers stopped me to tell me how great the house looked. A lot of people I didn't even know, who weren't even kin to my knowledge, were on our side.

Warren was cleaning his guns, which made me very nervous. I asked JP if he'd accompany me to the trial. That's how I thought of it. Would he accompany me? He'd carry me on his shoulders, he'd pull my chariot, he'd cover my path from our house to the town hall with rose petals! . . . I phoned Lisa to my own surprise and asked her to come and baby-sit Warren while the trial was going on. Told her he was cleaning his guns. She said she'd be happy to accommodate. I told Warren to stay *home*, him and his .357. If I needed him I'd call. I was surprised that he agreed.

The town hall was filled that night. The Tryon brothers stood against the back wall with their guns stacked in the corner.

The commissioners sat on one side of a long table. I sat on the other. They appeared to be looking at someone they'd never seen before, arms crossed on their chests, stern and unyielding as New Englanders. The meeting was called to order. The charges were read. I was asked if I had anything to say in my defense.

"How were we supposed to know about this rule of yours?"

"The notice was sent out with the summer water bill."

"The summer water bill?! I always throw those notices away without reading them."

"Didn't your painter tell you about the proper procedure?"

"My painter is Warren Spencer, my husband. He wasn't aware of your requirements any more than I was."

"Did you bring your color samples?"

"Yes."

"May we see them?"

I laid two sticks on the table. One cream, one blackish green.

"This is the color of the house?"

"That is the color we intend to paint the house. Cream."

"This is the color of the trim?"

"The trim will be cream like the house. The shutters and doors will be green."

They passed the sticks around and all of them examined them intently, as if they'd never seen cream and green paint before. Then they voted a muted "Aye."

The chairman or whatever said the colors seemed to be in order and had been approved.

I asked permission to speak. It was given.

I looked from face to face as I spoke. "I have thought of you as my friends. Mary and Ruby and Gloria and Earl and Gerry and Johnny," and I went right along the table. "I just want you to know that if any of you had been on my side of the table and I had been on yours I would have found you to ask if you knew about this ruling and to tell you what the penalty was. I would not have allowed anyone of you to step out on your porch and find a cease and desist order on the front door without warning."

I looked from face to face. They stared back at me.

"Have you finished with me?"

"Soon's you pay the fifty dollars."

"I have a check here." I drew it from my pocket and placed it on the table. Then I walked to the door and out of the building followed by JP and Sarah Taylor and all the spectators with the Tryons bringing up the rear.

It was over. The Tryons took up their watchful posts on their porch. Sarah Taylor came home with us. She and JP told Warren and Lisa they should have been there. "Merrie Lee was great. I was real proud of her," Sarah Taylor said.

JP said, "Merrie did good. Real good."

"If I'd gone I would have shot those sumbitches. All of them," said my husband.

Chapter 20

◆

◆ Beginning the next morning I picked up all the g's I'd been dropping for so long and deliberately erased any trace of a drawl from my speech. I walked briskly and I didn't say "Moanin'." My greeting was a clear-cut, hard-edged damyankee "Good morning!" letting everyone know what I was and proud of it. I may have been born to Davis Landing but I no longer wanted to be one of them.

Warren finished painting the house. It looked lovely. Worth all the money for the paint and all the labor he'd put into it. And wouldn't you know, he'd no sooner put the ladders and paint cans into his "workroom" than the historic preservation committee came to call and asked us to open our house for their annual tour to raise money for the town's historic preservation. Some of them were the same commissioners who'd glared at me across that damn table and not a word was said about the last time we'd met (across that table). You never saw a more affable group of people in your life. Including Eulalee, who was president of the Historic Preservation. They even carried on about how lovely the house looked inside and out and what wonderful things we'd done with "this old house, one of the first houses built in Davis Landing, built by the founding Davis, constantly lived in by Davises and still owned and occupahd by a Davis," and unchanged all this time except for the indoor plumbing. They declared about this and they declared about that and how we'd bothered to preserve the old wooden fixtures with the pull chain facilities and the pump in the kitchen. And, of course, they wanted me to be right there in one of Grandmother Lavinia's dresses of the period. Warren had raced out the back door the minute they were seen coming down the street with the excuse that he had to go to the post office. Anyway, he disappeared. No help as usual.

I managed to be as southern as they were. Not in speech, in hypocrisy, or as it's known down here, manners. I smiled and smiled, covering the hostility I felt. Speaking through smiles. I invited them all to sit down but I quite pointedly did not offer any food or drink, which I hoped would give them a clue as to my true feelings and the fact that I had not forgiven anything. Then I said it was a great honor but I would have to speak to my husband before accepting it and I was sure they all would understand. The privacy of our home was a sacred thing. They declared of course they understood.

The tour would be the last weekend before Lent, same as always, and they were hopin' we'd say yes as soon as possible so they could announce and do a little publicity. Each year, as I must know, there was a star house and our house was to be the star house this year if we consented. And they'd like Warren in costume too. Revolutionary costume, that is. There weren't any cowboys in Davis Landing. I told them I didn't know about getting Warren into costume but I'd let them know about the house as soon as we'd had a chance to discuss it and eased them out on to the porch while they were still explaining how simple it would be for me—that they'd all make the punch and cookies and cakes and set the table, and the Garden Club always did the flowers and the stair garlands and around the doorways, and there would be a hostess selected by them in every room so that we needn't worry about anything goin' missin' and some of the men in costume would be on the porch checkin' off the tickets and keepin' out any undesirables, they went on, interrupting each other, although there never *were* any undesirables because we got the nicest people every year and that our fame had spread across the state so we were sellin' more tickets and raising more money than evah and, all speaking over one another, they told me how easy and absolutely painless it would be and that the churches would be offerin' fish frys and barbecues and all I'd have to do was put on one of my grandmother's dresses and a mob cap and look pretty and that certainly wouldn't be hard for me—

"Who cleans," I said, "after all these people go thundering through the house?"

There were a lot of shifty looks between them and a gradual seeping into the street in twos and threes leaving Eulalee to tell me that although the question had never arisen, people cleanin' their own houses, she was sure somethin' could be arranged. "Although," she added confidentially, "havin' seen the housekeepin' in Davis Landin' I'd rather clean my own."

When Warren came home I told him about their visit. He looked grim and said he wasn't giving up a day's work on the novel and checking the market so hundreds of people could snoop through our house!

"It won't be the only house—just the star house—"

"I don't give a damn if it's the whorehouse, the answer is emphatically No! No no no and no!"

I told him they wanted both of us to wear Revolutionary costume and laughed.

"The answer is fucking no!"

"Okay. That's what I'll tell them—fucking *no!*"

"Don't say fuck. What's another word that says the same thing? Clean it up a little."

"I wasn't about to quote you exactly, Warren. I'll just say my husband and I talked it over and we decided we'd rather not have a public showing of the house. This year."

"*This* year? That leaves an opening for them for next year or the year after or—"

"I hope to God we won't still be in Davis Landing!"

"You really hate it?"

"Warren! Why do you think I've been in this depression?!"

"What depression?"

I toyed with the idea of getting into that, but no. "Warren, I said not this year so it wouldn't sound like a cold turn-down. Think *I* want strangers wandering through this place and seeing the way we live? That we can't afford decent plumbing? Can't afford to redo the kitchen? And I'm certainly not going to climb into old Lavinia's clothes and make an ass of myself for hundreds of people from God knows where—"

"Why would you be in your grandmother's clothes?"

I screamed. But only for a second. "Because, as the owners we're supposed to look like we're still back in the seventeenth century along with the house. Perfectly preserved, all of us."

"All of us?"

"You, me, and the house. We're all supposed to be dressed up."

His face went red. "Did they think I was going to wear Lavinia's clothes too?"

"Warren, they don't think that's funny. Up in the attic there's a complete selection of uniforms from all the wars—"

"The Revolution too?"

"Yes."

He considered this. Then ventured, "You know that old musket I've got over the mantel in my workroom? That's a Revolutionary musket."

"Really." I try to humor him.

Chapter 21

◆

◆ He *had* gone to the post office when he said he was going to go to the post office. And he'd brought a package for me from Aunt May. The bulletproof vest. With a note:

> Merrie dear,
> I have enjoyed wearing this so much and have amused my friends and acquaintances but I now return it to you as I no longer have need of it. Your friend the lieutenant has managed to get me a gun permit and a darling pearl-handled Smith & Wesson .25 caliber formerly owned by a gangster's girlfriend who no longer needs it as she is the former girlfriend of the former gangster. I carry it in my purse at all times even to the opera for you never know. John also introduced me to a shooting club downtown and I'm pretty good although I have to use two hands but then so do the players at Wimbledon. So I want to thank you for your thoughtfulness and am sending it on should you need it down there in that godforsaken place. Hahaha!
> Your loving
> Aunt May

I went upstairs to try it on. It smelled wonderfully of Joy and made me homesick. Twirling around in front of the old bathroom mirror I decided to show it to Sarah Taylor. We hadn't had a chance to really talk since I'd been to New York and I needed to catch up on the local news. I felt with the perspective of my absence I'd be able to detect from our conversation whether she was up to anything. Like killing off her friends. No one else had died during the interval. At least she hadn't mentioned anything about funerals. I told her I had a big laugh for her.

She said she could use a big laugh or even a little one and that she was just about to phone me when I phoned her. She had some very important things to tell me. Surprising things: Evidence Sam Pollock wouldn't be able to dismiss so lightly. And then added that they had crab cakes on the menu at the Harbor View that I wouldn't be able to turn my nose up at. I asked if they were frozen and she got huffy and said no one went crabbing in this weather. "You and your fresh foods! It's an obsession!" We arranged for her to pick me up at eleven-thirty as usual.

I turned away from the phone to be confronted by my husband as Revolutionary soldier, arms and legs sticking out of a uniform that was once worn by a much, much smaller man. He was carrying his old musket.

"How do I look?" he wanted to know.

"Terrific. But I don't think you should try to wear that, Warren."

"Why not?"

"Men were smaller then."

"I like it."

"You can carry the gun with something else."

"What?"

"Something more . . . homespun." I don't know why I ever expected him to notice my vest. "Maybe you could be a pirate and still carry that musket."

He considered this. "I could wear an earring."

Now Warren is the one man in the *world* who should not

wear an earring. I could not in a million years imagine Warren in an earring. He's too tall. He's too bald. But then so is Mister Clean. He can carry it. Sean Connery is bald. He can wear an earring. Warren is a pale Norwegian blond. Not really bald. Thinning. He cannot wear an earring. It's not his look. Oh well. "Sarah Taylor's picking me up. See you later."

"When is Lent? Would I have time to grow a ponytail?" I just kept going.

When the big black car stopped outside the door I was ready, wearing a skirt and sweater, my choker with Roberto's pearl, a touch of eyeliner, and Aunt May's vest. I strolled leisurely down the porch stairs to the car, giving her plenty of time to get the full impact.

"I declare!" she said. "Aren't we smart!"

I waited but she had started the car and we were moving down the street. "What did you want to tell me?" I asked.

"Not here!"

"You think the car might be bugged?" An amusing thought. "We could play the radio real loud and talk over it or under it or whatever—"

"Merrie Lee, I'm driving. And I have these new progressive focal glasses so I have to concentrate. I'll tell you when we're settled at the Harbor View."

We drove on. "You've had a perm," I said.

"Ophelia's revenge I call it. But while I was over there a lot of the girls were talking and Merrie Lee, I don't know whether you're aware of it, but all of old Davis Landing is on your side. Who the hell do those commissioners think they are? Some of them haven't even been here ten years! And they only came to Davis Landing to buy up old houses and restore them to sell and make a pile of money. And get themselves elected to town offices. And raise taxes. It's a disgrace!"

"It's nice to know some people are on our side. But I'm still angry. And would you believe that as soon as poor Warren had finished, the historic preservation committee came around and asked us to open the house this year. And get ourselves into costume!"

"There's no shortage of old clothes in that house. The Davises never threw out a thing! All those uniforms from all the wars—But"—she laughed—"you'll never be able to get Warren into costume!"

"You think so? He's even decided to let his hair grow into a ponytail. Maybe wear an earring."

"I don't believe it!"

"I didn't either. I think it's because he wants to carry that old musket that his family took out west. And not wear a tie."

"I don't believe—I wonder where Eulalee's bound for." The black van was almost abreast of us. Sarah Taylor waved. Did Eulalee wave back? We'd never know. "Busy woman," Sarah Taylor said. "There's been so much flu around this winter. Everyone's had something."

She parked the car. The van pulled in behind us.

"Sarah Taylor, you haven't said anything about my vest!"

"I was being polite. What *is* that thing?"

"My bulletproof vest. I just wanted you to see how people dress in New York."

"Well, I don't think it goes with pearls. Since you asked me."

"I thought you'd laugh! It's supposed to be funny! I hope Penny will appreciate it."

"You forget people down here have manners. They might think your clothes are funny but they'd never laugh. Not in your face. And we've all seen a lot more outlandish getups than that thing, haven't we?"

We were out of the car, starting into the restaurant. Eulalee's van left the curb and hurried down the street. We looked after it.

"I do believe I've left the key in the ignition." She turned back to the car.

I followed with the idea of being helpful. I was just standing there thinking what a pretty day it was and looking at the Davis Landing flags in front of the bank and the American flags on the sterns of the boats and the rows of seagulls facing into the wind, inhaling the sea air and thinking how lucky we were to be living in one of the few unspoiled places in the United States even without culture. It had rained during the night and everything smelled fresh and clean.

I turned. Sarah Taylor was leaning across the front seat, grappling with her ignition key. I said, "There's a mud puddle right behind you when you step back."

She retrieved the key and said, "There! I swear I get more absentminded by the day!"

And I said, "No one's going to steal your car, love. Warren says they're all afraid of hell—"

Then she said, "Oof!" and dropped to the ground with an arrow in her back, her face in the puddle.

I didn't hear anything. There should have been a whizz or something—the street was empty. "Sarah Taylor! Sarah Taylor! Sarah Taylor!" I was kneeling beside her, screaming.

I woke up the dogs who left their places in the sun in the middle of the street to come over and sniff at her face and neck. "Sarah Taylor!" I screamed. "Help! Nine-one-one! Help!"

Verla Mae Corby, who hadn't been a police person for too long, came along right then on her motor scooter, doing her regular patrol. She dismounted.

"Verla Mae—She just fell down with that arrow in her back—Do something! Get EMERGENCY RESCUE!"

Verla Mae remained calm. "This is my first real case! We're trained to keep our heads—"

"Will you *do* something—PLEASE!"

"Your name?"

We were kneeling beside Sarah. "Merrie Lee Spencer I was a Davis—Can't you get Emergency Rescue on your radio?"

"Merrie Lee Spencer—"

She was a slow printer.

"And the victim?"

"Don't you *know* her? It's Sarah Taylor Millet—She could be *dying* right there—PLEASE HELP HER!"

"Sarah Taylor Millet. And the perpetrator?"

"VERLA MAE FOR GODSAKE—"

"Ma'am, I have to make my report."

Doctor Wilson was parking his car for lunch at the Harbor View. I shouted at him. "DR. WILSON—DR. WILSON—OVER HERE—IT'S SARAH TAYLOR!"

He ran and was on his knees feeling for the pulse. At the neck. The wrist. "Verla Mae," he said, "get Emergency Rescue over here right away!"

"I will do that, Dr. Wilson, but I have to make my report before the witnesses leave the scene—"

"THERE WEREN'T ANY WITNESSES—NO ONE BUT ME AND THOSE DOGS—"

I was screaming and crying. My nose was running.

Sarah Taylor looked so pitiful lying there, all crumpled. Her face was turning gray-blue with a small trickle of blood running from the mouth to the chin.

Dr. Wilson tried to wiggle the arrow slightly. It wouldn't budge. He turned her on her side. Her face was muddy. And her new glasses. And her new perm.

"Must be a hunting arrow," he said. "Sharp as a razor. That bow must have taken sixty pounds of pressure to fire."

Verla Mae took off.

"But she'll— It won't be—"

"Pray for her."

My first and only true friend down here. Even if she had had something to do with the recent rash of deaths. She was my friend and my confidant and she always said it like it was. No southern mealymouthed pussyfooting. Always a comfort. Even if she was a murderess.

The regular eleven-thirty lunch crowd was gathering. Instead of going in to the Harbor View they stood around Sarah Taylor cutting off her air. Emergency Rescue arrived. Dr. Wilson directed the men as they slid my friend and the arrow into the ambulance. He ran for his car, tossing back answers to the shouted questions: Can't tell anything yet . . . no way of knowing at this time if any vital organs have been penetrated . . . perhaps none if we're lucky . . . and he was away. Nobody believed his optimistic projection.

I followed him in Sarah Taylor's car. By the time I parked that monster and got to the emergency room, Dr. Wilson had whipped her into surgery.

Suddenly, as I was pacing, I thought of the dogs. I phoned Warren. He said he'd be right down.

I have never been able to cry like Meryl Streep. I didn't have to check a mirror to know; red swollen eyes, blotchy face, dry lips.

My husband put his arms around me. "Is she still alive?"

"I don't know. Who would want to kill that poor lady? She never hurt anyone."

"For sure."

"How could she have killed anyone? She didn't know that much about plants—didn't even go to Garden Club—"

At which point Chief Pollock arrived. He looked into the emergency room, said, "Hey! How'ya doin'," and disappeared.

"Did you see anything? Anyone?"

"There was no one there, *nobody*—seagulls and dogs,—that's all—then suddenly she fell down—with her face in that puddle and mud all over her new glasses—"

"Is there anyone we should call?"

"The whole town was about to go to lunch. Anyone who doesn't know by now isn't worth telling."

"There there there." Lots of patting and holding close.

"She—she should have been—wearing Aunt May's vest—not me—"

"It's real good against bullets, Merrie, but arrows, they'll cut right through that plastic fiber—slice right through."

"Dr. Wilson said it was a hunting arrow."

"Vest wouldn't have helped her."

A nurse with a serious expression arrived. "Dr. Wilson wanted you to know your friend won't be suffering any more."

That's one of their genteel ways of saying someone's d-e-a-d. Although it was not unexpected it threw me into fresh paroxysms of grief. Warren drove us home in the truck and phoned

JP and Lisa to collect Sarah Taylor's car and put it in her shed. Then he put ice on my forehead. Then, sitting on the bed, he phoned the police and demanded—*demanded*—protection for me. Warren can get really motivated when it's absolutely necessary.

Chapter 22

◆

◆ The porch was full of armed Tryons when Chief Pollock
arrived. I was told that Luther actually challenged him. Of
course there was no love lost between them since the whole
Sammy Jo affair.

Right then Lisa, having taken care of Sarah Taylor's car and
given the keys to Lula, was applying cucumber slices to my
eyes while Warren and JP hovered, and I lay there knowing
that I'd miss Sarah Taylor terribly and that I looked like hell.

Chief Pollock stood in the doorway. Said he'd like to ask
me some questions. Warren said I was in no condition to be
put through that kind of an ordeal. Sam Pollock said that he
had the law on his side. Warren said he didn't give a shit who
was on Sam Pollock's side but I sat up before there was any
blood shed and said I would submit to any ordeal, but I'd like
to wash my face first and if they'd all get out we could carry
on downstairs if they didn't mind.

Actually the cucumber slices did more good than makeup.
And dark glasses helped even more. My dog Jackie came
closer. We walked down the stairs together.

Warren was accusing Sam Pollock of negligence, indiffer-
ence, and not doing the job he was paid to do. Sam Pollock
was looking for a place to spit and finally opened the door and

spat out in the midst of the Tryons who misunderstood and raised their rifles, so I got there just in time. The chief had brought a patrolman, Joe Donovan, along as a witness to whatever I was about to say. Warren was still shouting and Joe was standing there with his arms crossed on his chest like he was getting ready to stop him with a fist in the mouth. Mathilda decided to bark at Joe and the chief. Jackie intelligently lay down at my feet.

"Warren . . ." I said, tugging at the sleeve of his denim work shirt, which I noticed needed mending. "Warren? My head is really hurting from all that crying . . . please . . . I can't take this noise . . . it's going to split wide open. . . ."

Then we all sat down. Chief Pollock said he didn't care for any iced tea and opened his notebook. He already knew the time and the place from Verla Mae. What he wanted to know from me was what I had seen.

"Nothing," I said.

Joe's eyes rolled, which he tried to change into a blinking frown when he noticed our noticing.

"What were you and Miz Sarah Taylor doin' in front of the Harbor View?"

"What do you *think* they were doing?"

"Warren! . . . We were going to lunch."

"All right. The vehicle belonged to—"

"Sarah Taylor Millet."

"Take me through the whole thing. . . ."

He sounded as patient as Andy Griffith did when he was the sheriff of Mayberry.

"Come on now. Did you walk to her house? Did you walk to the Harbor View? How'd you two get out on the boardwalk there?"

"Sarah Taylor picked me up in her car at my house at eleven-thirty."

"That's real good. Let's have some more of that."

"She drove down to the Harbor View and parked the car where you saw it."

"What time was the parkin'?"

"I didn't notice. However long it takes to drive from my house to the restaurant at ten or fifteen miles—"

"Ten? Or fifteen?"

"*I* don't know. She drives very slowly—She drove very slowly—" Pause for sobs.

"Do you *HAVE* to do this *NOW?*"

"Yes, sir. Whall the facts are still fresh in the witness's mahnd."

"It's all right, Warren. Sarah Taylor always drove very slowly so as not to disturb the dogs—The dogs that sleep—in the sun—in the middle of the street—"

"You're doin' good, Miss Merrie Lee."

"Okay. Then we got down there—I already told you that—and parked the car—Sarah Taylor parked the car, and we started inside, but then she said she'd left her key in the ignition, and she went back—to get it—and that's when—when it happened."

"Where were you?"

"Right there. Behind her."

"Did you see anyone?"

"No. There was no one else."

"How would you know that, ma'am?"

"Because I was looking around. Waiting for her I was looking at the boats and the gulls and—and there was no one else there!"

"Nobody else parkin' their car? Nobody gettin' in or out of their boat?"

"The street was deserted. You know how it is this time of year—"

"Yes, ma'am. Any traffic?"

"Nothing!"

"You sure?"

"Yes, I am. Nothing moved that I can remember."

"And then?"

"And then—the arrow—and she fell—and Verla Mae came along and she can tell you what happened after she got there."

"Yes, ma'am."

"There can't be too many people in a town this size with hunting bows—it should be easy—"

"Yessir, that's true, i'nt it. Now we bin seein' you and Miss Sarah Taylor aroun' together for a good whall, Miss Merrie Lee. Would y'all know of anyone would want her daid?"

Pause for sobs.

"Any enemies? Any person or persons who would wish her ill? Want to do her bodily harm?"

"No."

"You sure now?"

"Yes."

"Someone's been harassing my *wife* since Christmas—we told you about those notes—"

"Yessir but you said you didn't keep any of them—"

"We didn't, but she's been receiving them—all sorts of warnings—we both read them, and that black van is always around—"

"Black van?" Making a note of black van.

"Oh—"

"Eulalee Merrill's black van—"

"Warren—"

"My wife has been receiving threats, and if *she* can have an enemy then why not—"

"Sarah Taylor knew about my threats and she never said she got any—if she had, she would have told me."

"You have to have proof—"

"Wait a minute—I just remembered—when we were arranging to have lunch today she said she'd found out something important—about the threats? And what we suspected about the murders? But she wanted to wait and then she didn't want to tell me in the car because she was concentrating on her driving and she had new glasses—Warren! The van! The black van!"

"Yes, ma'am? The black van?"

"I saw it again this morning—It was right there behind us when we got to the Harbor View and then when we parked and got out of the car it drove down the street very fast."

Chief Pollock was writing.

Warren erupted. "Goddamit, that fucking arrow was meant for my *wife*. Now what are you going to do about that? Do I have to send her out of state?"

The dogs barked frantically.

"We're doin' the best we can, Mr. Spencer. Ouah budget's bin cut so bad cain't hardly tell it's theah! We need another man even on the off-season when theah ain't nobuddy heah. Theah's allus the boat people and they kin suah stir up a mess of trouble without even tryin'."

They finally left without Warren hitting them.

Chapter 23

♦

♦ And life limped on. Warren was furious. And nervous. And overprotective. I was nervous but more than that I was sad and lonely and very, very depressed. Barely able to talk. Just sitting around moping. One of those Where am I going with my life if I have a chance to live it? times. Warren and I were barely speaking. That Warren wasn't speaking was not unusual. But there was usually sound bouncing off him—my cheerful chatter. Attempts to be funny. Unable to rise to it I sat and stared into space. Warren thought I should get out of town. Go to Aunt May's. I hadn't the energy to agree or disagree. It was grim.

All of Davis Landing was at Sarah Taylor's funeral, black and white, Episcopal, Baptist, Methodist, and even a sprinkling of Catholics from out of county. People were standing in the rear of the church and along the sides and the pews were really crowded. Most everyone sat in silence waiting for young Mark's entrance, but some woman in the pew behind me was giving her companion a rundown of the best funerals in the last ten years, ending with a sigh. "I just don't enjoy them the way I used to." Big John Bell, the lawyer everyone used, said she had made her funeral arrangements years before. She'd conferred with Beau Johnson, the undertaker, and they'd gone over the various options, including cremation, which was by far the cheapest, and she'd told him she'd "like to try that." And she'd stuck with it, being famously frugal. But she'd changed her pallbearers almost monthly depending on her mood. They were all honorary, as there was nothing to carry, but Warren had survived the last draw. He was one of twelve very distinguished southern gentlemen. I mean the others were. Warren was Warren and growing his ponytail at that. I saw Chief Pollock leaning against the wall in the back. And Big Sam, who drove the sanitation truck, and Darleen from the Town Hall. They were all there to pay their respects to one of the last of the southern ladies and to observe the passing of one of the last remaining shreds of the Old South. They didn't know that but I did. Sarah Taylor was the last of her kind. I'm sure I wasn't the only one looking around surreptitiously to see if the murderer—whoever he might be—had dared to show his face.

After, Lula and her kin had fixed a feast. Platters and platters of her famous fried chicken and mashed potatoes and gravy, casseroles of macaroni and cheese, fried bread (those delicious little cornbreads), field peas, country ham, her own pickled peaches, and bread pudding with bourbon sauce (one of Lula's numerous nieces married into a New Orleans family). Soul food. Lula could open in New York City—Soho or Tribeca or anywhere trendy there was a reasonable rent—and make a fortune.

The house was filled with flowers and plants and some people we'd never seen before. Distant relatives. If Sarah Taylor had had time for second thoughts she might have changed her will and left it all to a dog home. We'd discussed that once. She was seriously considering it. And if she could have seen these people, kin of her second husband's from Alabama, examining the furniture for scratches and looking at the backs of plates and balancing the silver forks and trying to see the signatures on paintings—she would have tossed them all out. Most of Davis Landing left sad and early with the almost certain knowledge that the carpetbaggers would sell everything for the best price they could get. All the family history Sarah Taylor had cherished and guarded for so many years. Including the house. It was very depressing.

When we went home we found one of Bubba's garlands on the front door, like the first of May. Luther and his group, fully armed and surrounded by beer cans, were dozing on the Davis porch across the street. Warren and I went into the house and immediately lapsed into our familiar silence. Suddenly I couldn't stand it. I had to talk to someone and, without thinking, I dialed Sarah Taylor's number. When Lula answered I realized what I'd done and burst into ferocious sobs.

Warren came out of his office dressed for tennis. I stopped. He went back in. The tennis court was finished so he had tennis to stretch his muscles, and balls to hit to vent his hostility, and people to play with. I could have but I was out of practice and not good enough at the moment for their game. When he wasn't playing tennis or fixing the house he was watching his investments and/or writing his novel. Warren was *busy*. And apparently happy although it was very hard to tell with Warren. I watched him leave in his whites and his sweater I had meant to wash, with his rackets and a can of new balls and I hated him. I had to be busy too at *something*, some form of legal, gainful employment. There was no chance of a vice presidency of anything down here but there had to be something. It was the only way out of anger, depression, bitterness, self-pity, all the bad things I'd been doing to myself. . . . I sat down to make a list of possibilities. . . .

I could: open a bakery. But people who opt for Twinkies and Moon Pies would never appreciate French baguettes, lemon curd bars, whole wheat bread, or any of my specialties, except the brownies and you can't run a bakery on brownies alone.

I could: open a travel agency and advise people where to go. I'd been all over. But my taste was very sophisticated. I cared about food. And I'd heard the more affluent people down here who'd gone on a tour to China telling how they'd cleverly carried lots of peanut butter along so they never had to eat the food. Scratch the travel agency.

I could: represent the local wood-carvers in New York galleries. But I'd have to truck all the carvings up there. I'd have insurance. Probably lots of breakage. Expensive insurance. Scratch the artists' representative.

I could: sell real estate. Lots of housewives sold real estate down here. I could do that in New York but down here what and to whom? And the real estate market was very bad. Almost every house had a FOR SALE sign. Bad as New England. The interest rate was down but the banks weren't giving loans. Real estate wasn't selling. Scratch real estate.

I could: sell antiques. Yes, I could put a sign up if the commissioners would permit and sell all the stuff out of the attic. Dealers came from other places—like New Orleans and the Hamptons and Atlanta and Chicago, and carried off stuff that they sold for a thousand times what they'd paid. But it was those dealers who made the money, not us poor impoverished water people down here and why should I sell *my* family heirlooms to make those damyankees rich! Scratch the antique shop.

I could: sell clothes! Brainstorm! Not just any clothes. Previously owned New York clothes—clean, the latest fashions, the most expensive—my *friends'* clothes! But down here they're still wearing stiffly sprayed hair and skirts at that dowdy just-below-the-knee length. And they'd expect to pay no more than thrift shop prices. Scratch the clothes idea.

I could: open a club and serve illegal mixed drinks at high prices. (Davis Landing is still dry.) But they wouldn't pay high prices, they'd sooner bring a bottle in a brown paper bag. Scratch the mixed drinks.

I could: open a club and serve setups and hamburgers and have *entertainment!* But what besides a country singer? Maybe a blues band. A comic? Awful. A stand-up comic? That's a terrible idea. But I can make people laugh. I could maybe BE a stand-up comic. Merrie Lee's Comedy Club starring Merrie Lee Spencer—Herself—

"What's for dinner?"

That was jarring. I hadn't heard him come in and I hadn't given dinner a thought. What would he think about a Greek salad?

He patted his flat, flat stomach. I remembered from the last time I'd seen it some years back that it was muscular and ridged and it sure as hell was flat. "I just played a couple of hard sets and I'm feeling kind of empty. How about some chili?"

"Look in the freezer. Maybe there are some of those boxes I made when I went to New York."

"How about making some?"

"Takes too long. How about zapping some? It's the same thing."

"Merrie! I'm perfectly willing to do the cleanup but you're supposed to do the cooking!"

He followed me into the kitchen. I opened the door of the freezer, took out two boxes of chili and slammed them down on the table. "You can have two if you're hungry."

He followed me back to my lists. "That's not dinner—"

"It's *your* dinner. You know where the microwave is and you know how it works."

He stood there in his whites looking so attractive. My mind drifted to Zio Roberto.

"If you microwave some rice to have with it you've got a complex carbohydrate! That's very healthy. And there's a lettuce heart and the dressing's all mixed ready in a jar in the door."

"You're not eating?"

"Not chili. Not tonight."

"That's not very friendly."

"I don't feel very friendly."

"Why not?"

"I'm depressed."

"What have you got to be depressed about?"

Did he really say that? "Well, let me count the ways. . . . For one thing I just lost the only friend I had down here—"

"You've got me—"

"You're not my friend. You don't talk to me—We don't do anything together—All you do is sit at that fucking computer—"

"Which helped me to make fifty-four percent on my investment this last year! *Fifty-four percent.* Do you realize what that *means?* My stocks beat every pick—"

"Great."

"Merrie, it means we can keep up the mortgage payments on the New York place."

"But we can't live there."

"Is that what you want? To go back to *New York!* That hell hole."

"Warren, I'm in exile down here. And I don't see any way out of it."

"When I finish my novel and it's sold and we have millions then we'll talk about it. Right now, how about dinner?"

Oh God. "Warren, you do fantasize."

"And some of them have come true. Count your pearls."

"My pearls are beautiful. But I have nowhere to wear them. I'm dying down here. I'll die if I can't get out of this place. Warren, I cannot stay here year after year without a break— I'm suffocating."

"You just had a break. You can go back to New York any time you want. Stay with Aunt May—enjoy yourself."

"It's not the same. It's being a tourist. I want a life there. I want my own place and I need my work and money and clothes and—"

"If you'd stop sitting around feeling sorry for yourself you'd see that there's a lot more to do here than you think."

My mouth opened and closed again. "Warren go zap your chili."

"If you'd just *try*—"

"I *have* tried!"

"Not very hard. You sit around and mope. And what's this?" He jerked the pad off my lap. "Sitting around doodling—"

It was so unfair I ran upstairs and slammed the bedroom door and threw myself on the bed and burst into tears like an adolescent.

After a while the door opened. He walked around the bed and sat down beside me. Shoulder patting.

"That wasn't fair," I said, throwing off his hand.

"So you're thinking of being a stand-up comic?"

"I have to do *something*, and everything else I had to cross out for one reason or another."

"That's kinda cute. . . . Want some ice on your eyes?" Little kisses down the neck.

I lay still wondering what was next.

He pulled back the bed cover and lay down next to me, pulling my arms around his naked body. Holy shit! Back to the little kisses. "You'd probably be very good as a . . . stand-up . . . comic. . . . You used to be . . . funny as all . . . hell! . . ."

Holy shit!

After a long while of lying there holding hands and silently enjoying the afterglow I said, "My compliments."

"Likewise."

Propped on an elbow I looked down at his dear, adorable, familiar face. We smiled at each other. "You had some very interesting variations on the basic theme there," I said. Tracing his smile with a fingertip I said, "Who've you been fooling around with? . . ."

His eyes went opaque and I knew.

I climbed out of bed. "That bitch! That BITCH!" I was pulling my clothes back on.

"Wait a minute, Merrie, you're wrong—"

"Warren, don't try to lie to me. I can always tell." I walked out of the room with great dignity.

Messing around in the kitchen with coffee and scrambled eggs on toast for myself, I could remember every time I'd seen Lisa with him, every look exchanged between them, how she'd hung herself from his neck out at The Club when we went dancing, draped right down his front against the wall. . . . Knowing that he must have been as horny as I was I had gone to New York, leaving them together to do just as they pleased. In Lavinia's bed. Or—remembering all the times I'd tried to reach him by phone—it might not have been Lavinia's bed. Warren was basically a very decent man. . . . Or maybe he just wasn't answering. . . . When I was tried by the town commissioners I actually asked her to come over and baby-sit my husband! How could I have been that naive? I wondered if it had started before I went to New York. All those "conferences with JP. . . ." I was willing to acknowledge that the bitch was attractive, very attractive, and agressive, very aggressive, but that was no excuse. . . . She was not about to put any more cucumber slices on *my* eyes!

When he came into the kitchen showered and dressed in clean jeans and lightly scented with . . . Zio Roberto's cologne. (I had totally forgotten Zio Roberto!) But that was no excuse for my husband—And he didn't know about Zio Roberto . . . and never would! He tried to say something, but I gathered my supper on a tray and carried it to the library. And I didn't speak to him that day or the next day or the next.

We were right back where we'd been before that little incredible sexual episode, which I didn't regret one bit. It reminded me of why I'd married him. Besides he was a very sweet, decent, tender man—I HATED thinking of him being TENDER with that BITCH LISA!!

Chapter 24

♦

♦ I didn't go to the tennis court and Lisa and JP didn't come anywhere near our house. Bubba left daily wildflower garlands as offerings and the trashy Tryons continued their armed watch on our house from their post across the street. Chief Pollock came to call, with Joe, with the latest news on Sarah Taylor's murder of which there was none. He had a few questions, vague and general, for me. I answered them as best I could but the answers were as vague and general as the questions. Warren said it seemed very clear to him. The black van had been right there, Eulalee's brother was closely associated with her black van, and Eulalee's brother was a bow hunter. There it was. All tied up with a red ribbon.

"Yessir, it do look that way, don't it? But the thang of it is Bubba's innocent till proven guilty, same as anyone and no one has placed him anywhere near the Harbor View. He was seen out 17 East picking wildflowers at 'bout eleven o'clock. And Miss Eulalee's van? They be another black van in the next county just like hers they bought from the same people in Columbia. So we comin' up empty-handed all the way 'round.''

The monthly Garden Club meeting came along again and it was mighty sad. We pledged allegiance to our flag and said

The Collect and then had a little memorial service for those of us who had passed on, reciting a couple of their favorite psalms and singing "Amazing Grace." I cried, seeing Sarah Taylor with her face in the mud and the blood running from her mouth. We discussed a memorial garden for our loved ones: Miss Emily, Miss Sammy Jo, Elvira Lewis, and Sarah Taylor Millet. I could hear Sarah Taylor's derisive snort at being lumped with Sammy Jo and Elvira Lewis. And classifying Miss Emily as a "loved one." Eulalee allowed that JP, being a trained horticulturist, might be very happy to design one for us. That was all right with everyone but the question was where would we put it? Not in front of the court house where there was a sort of a park which they were thinking of paving over as they needed more space for cars. On the grounds of the Historic Preservation? We'd have to get permission from the dreaded and unanimously loathed commissioners who would probably deny it. Lucia Lee Dennison said that between the Davis Landing Tennis Courts and the other old cemetery, which nobody used and some people were thinking of cleaning up and replanting and generally making more presentable, there was a small piece of land that belonged to the town but nobody'd cared anything about it for as long as anyone could remember. She said if we offered to pretty up the old cemetery maybe they'd give us that little piece to pretty up too and it could be The Davis Landing Garden Club Memorial Garden. For all of us. They were very enthusiastic. Lucia Lee was appointed to check it out and report back at the next meeting.

When I drove home I found our street in an uproar. Patrol cars, the chief's car, a fire engine, and a lot of people. Warren was standing on our porch. There was some kind of a struggle going on across the street. Tryons and women and guns and police—it was a real melee. I couldn't even get into my own drive. Had to leave the car in the middle of the street and make my way through the struggle.

I wasn't speaking to Warren, only occasionally and minimally, but I asked him what was going on. He said he really didn't know. He'd been working (as usual) and he'd heard gunshots, come out here to look and there was some woman over there shooting at the other women over there far as he could tell and then the men got into it and then the police came along and there we were. "Seems to be quieting down."

I put the dogs on their leashes and went out to the water-front where I knew I'd meet someone who'd know what it was all about or a reasonable facsimile. Colonel Willis was real pleased to tell me the whole story.

"Seems Mary Tryon is back from Florida. Went right over to the Davis house to reclaim her children AND her husband. How about that? Hauled out her gun and started shooting at those women over there and at Luther's brothers, calling them trash! Then she told Luther to come on home and busy him-self making some money to support his family. See, the still hasn't been operating since they all camped out here. I know, causen I tried to buy some of that stuff and there weren't none for sale. Best moonshine south of Virginia. Mary say to come on home and get to work! Sam Pollock ask her what about givin' up her kids and goin' off to seek her pleasure and she say all men are rotten and Luther, he ain't no more rotten than the rest of them and she knows what to watch out for."

When we strolled on home the street was clear. Cleaned out of Tryon cars too. The Davis house seemed empty of all Tryons, large and small, male and female. I missed them. I felt a lot less secure without armed bodyguards. I missed Sarah Taylor. She would have enjoyed the trashy Tryon saga. And Warren wasn't talking to me. But then he never did. And I wasn't about to bounce any cheerful chatter off him. I couldn't get rid of the nasty image of Warren and Lisa. I kept seeing them together. Instant rage. I'd picture them together and it was like an automatic furnace turning on. Thunk. And burning and burning steadily hotter and hotter.

I phoned Aunt May to ask if I could come up to see her.

"There's no need for you to ask," she said. "Your visits are always such a joy! And you're such fun!"

"Well. I don't know. I'll try."

"What's wrong?"

"I just don't want to be anywhere near Warren. I want to put a large space between us. Maybe permanently."

"You're thinking of leaving *Warren?* Why?"

"He's been having an affair, that's why."

Silence.

"Practically under my nose."

Silence.

"With a woman?"

"Of course with a woman."

Silence.

"Merrie? Do you still have that marble-sized pearl? That little bijou you were given by a nameless donor the last time you were here? The morning after the night you didn't come home?"

Silence.

"Aren't you being a bit hypocritical?"

Silence.

"I'd adore to have you visit as long as you like. But aren't you leaving the field wide open for that person to move in on poor Warren?"

"Poor Warren!"

Silence.

"Is she dangerous?"

"She's young."

"Dangerous."

"And bouncy."

Silence.

"And tall and strong and healthy."

Silence.

"And she plays tennis."

"Merrie, would you rather be single again?"

"No."

"Remember what it's like out there?"

"Yeah, I do."

"I'm told it's worse than it used to be."

"It would be death down here."

"You could always move in with me. I'd love to have you for a roommate."

"I'd have cirrhosis of the liver in six months."

"No you wouldn't, dear. Our family genes have a natural immunity to cirrhosis. I'm the living proof!"

Silence.

"If you and Warren separated you'd have to split your assets. Sell the penthouse and the house down there in a bad market. I guess you could always get another job. Or marry money this time. Or just live with me and we could travel. You could be my companion and take care of the luggage. I'd like to go to Africa before all the animals are gone—I'd like to go to Tibet . . . and mainland China . . . and Kyoto . . . and . . . Merrie? Are you there?"

"I'm here."

"But you're not a woman to live without a man in her life for long. Who knows what the next one will be like? They all have their faults, don't they? You know Warren's faults and you've got him housebroken to your ways. It's a dreary prospect to have to go through that all over again. Isn't it?"

"An Indian woman just said that down here."

"What was that?"

"Nothing important."

"When shall I expect you? Rosabelle is taking her son's jet to Palm Beach and she's invited some of the girls along. His company has a huge house on the ocean. You could come with us if you'd like. There's all that wonderful shopping along Worth Avenue—"

"Aunt May, I'll let you know. I have some thinking to do."

"All right. We won't be Palm Beaching it for about ten days. We'll talk later?"

"We'll talk later."

I sat on the porch with Jackie and Mathilda watching the brown live oak leaves blow down the street. What a wise old woman she was. I loved her dearly but I could never live with her or off her. And she knew it. Warren was a lovely man. That afternoon in bed was spectacularly . . . intimate. No two people could have been closer or more loving. . . .

Chapter 25

•

◆ The next morning when I took Bubba's offering from the doormat along with the newspaper I was still thinking it over and still thinking when the dogs and I started on our morning walk. And still indecisive when we came back and I was fixing their breakfast and ours.

Jackie refused his food. He sniffed it and walked away a few steps and lay down on the floor. That little dog had an unfailing appetite and had never been known to refuse a scrap of food in all his ten years. He looked totally miserable.

Mathilda licked his face, the dog equivalent of "there there there." He whimpered. She sat down beside him, eyes fixed on me, opened her mouth wide and screamed. Not a bark, not a whine, a sound I'd never heard from an animal. An almost human scream of grief . . .

Warren catapulted into the kitchen. He thought it was me seeing a roach. He knelt to test Jackie's limbs. "Nothing broken," he said.

"We just walked for an hour and there was nothing wrong with him. He lagged a little, you know he's always the leader and I almost had to pull him along this morning . . . but he won't touch his food."

"Won't *eat?* . . . There's something wrong."

The vet said that he might have gotten into something, to mix up an emetic of warm water and salt or warm water and mustard and get some down him.

Warren said on a good day Jackie would lap up salt water chased with mustard water and enjoy it. "That's not going to work!"

Mathilda sat on the floor next to him. She didn't touch her food. She sat as close to him as she could get and screamed. Looking from Warren to me, her meaning was clear. Help him!

We mixed up some warm salt water and dribbled it into his mouth. It dribbled right out. He didn't or couldn't swallow.

I phoned the vet and told him we were on our way. Warren wrapped him in an old bath towel and I carried him with Mathilda at our heels. She screamed again. It's a terrible sound. Startling. Unearthly. I held Jackie on my lap, pulled the visor down to shade his eyes. We left Mathilda in the car, nose against the window.

Now you have to understand, which is easier for dog lovers or any pet owners to do than for those who have never experienced the joy of loving and being loved by an animal, including a horse. These little dogs are our children, the children of this marriage. We had our own children scattered around, but Davis Landing being remote from everything and difficult to get to, we had not received any visits from any of them, which was fine with us. They were grown, had their own lives, we heard from them at Christmas and on our birthdays. Whenever they phoned between times it meant trouble. But their lives seemed to be running smoothly in various parts of the world. None of the Davis Landing people see their children for the same reasons we don't see ours. Sometimes in the summer the children and grandchildren arrive, piled and heaped in vans and station wagons, and spend a lot of time on the water and in the boats and enjoy an orgy of seafood and then they pack up and go off leaving the parents exhausted and happy for the visit to end.

We'd raised Jackie and Mathilda since they were two

months old, all through mischievous puppyhood to half-sensible adolescence to thoroughly wonderful little adult dogs. Bright and obedient, considerate and quiet, they were like two charming little people. And Jackie, for me, was a warm body and an understanding heart. My very best friend and companion.

When we unwrapped him on the examining table his breathing was loud and uneven. He couldn't sit or stand. I walked out of the room the minute I saw the vet's face.

Warren found me leaning on an outside wall, crying. He said if I wanted to say good-bye I'd better come in now. There was nothing to be done.

When that little dog saw me crying he tried to crawl to me to comfort me as he'd done so many times during our life together. It broke my heart. I picked him up and kissed his head and held him close. The vet filled the syringe . . . and it was over. Warren wrapped the towel tighter and carried him out to the car without a word. I followed weeping uncontrollably. My husband was leaning against the car, holding Jackie to him, moaning. When I opened the car door Mathilda screamed. I held her on my lap in the front seat. She trembled and shivered all the way home. The mirror on the visor startled me with my reflection, a mask of tragedy, mouth stretched wide in an uncontrollable grimace.

Warren drove back to the house hugging Jackie to him in the crook of his right arm like an infant. When we got there he carried his package directly to the back of the house. I heard the saw. Mathilda wouldn't eat. The sound of a hammer tapping away. He was making the coffin. She sat near Jackie's dish and screamed once, then lay down beside it. I wandered through the house remembering how he'd liked to sleep under a skirted table or under the long fringe of the bed coverlet. Through slitted eyes I saw Warren digging the grave under the red tips and crepe myrtle in the back of the garden. Beside him was a little wooden box.

I walked out to tell him how much I appreciated his doing all this for Jackie (we both considered him my dog). Warren was dripping tears into the grave as he shoveled and measured. The coffin was beautifully crafted. On the lid he'd nailed Jackie's name tag. I tried to thank him.

He said, "Dammit Merrie, I *loved* that little dog! He was such an independent stubborn little cuss—" Just like Warren.

I said, "Warren, I love you," and we hugged and then he put the coffin in the hole. Warren said Jackie was lying on his side and he was careful to place the box so that he'd be facing the house and know we were there. After the hole was filled he picked a spray of holly and put it on the grave. This was a man to treasure.

I kept crying. My face ached from being stretched in that awful grimace. Mathilda's screams continued. Less often. More shattering out of the silence. Nobody ate much.

"Warren do you think someone could have . . . ?"

"Possible."

The only plus in all that misery was that Warren and I were close again.

Chapter 26

◆

◆ Walking Mathilda was an ordeal. People stopped me, people I didn't know and had never seen before, wanting to know "what happened to the other dog." Cars stopped. I hadn't realized that we were one of the sights, that people liked to see the three of us walking along the waterfront. One man said it had been a spirited and happy thing to see us. Drivers left their cars in the middle of the street to tell me how sorry they were about Jackie. People sent flowers. People sent notes. People came with cakes and cookies. Eulalee brought a rosemary topiary on behalf of the Garden Club. Rosemary for remembrance, trimmed to the shape of a little terrier. They paid condolence calls. And with them all, I cried. I couldn't stop crying. One morning on the waterfront, a woman from Garden Club who'd been away for a bit asked me about the other dog. When I burst into sobs she gathered me to her ample bosom and told me to remember death was part of creation. That was strangely comforting. I'd never looked at death that way. As part of life. Like most people I hadn't looked at death. I told Warren that the people in this town could be really nice. He said yes they could but not to forget they could be fairly rotten too.

Mathilda's screams had gotten down to one or two a day

but she was definitely a depressed dog, her tail at half-mast. She no longer jumped with joy. She moved slowly and sadly like an old dog. Most of the day she spent looking in all his favorite places, under the bed and under the tables, all over the house, and then sat backed into a corner, moping, gazing out at nothing in a state of acute melancholy.

In the beginning there seemed to be a presence. We'd try to coax her to eat with a dog biscuit. Both dogs had always considered them a special treat and fought over them ferociously. She'd take it in her mouth and then suddenly drop it and back off and scream. Warren and I were sure that Jackie was with us, growling and not wanting her to have the biscuit, the way they'd always done. . . . He stayed with us for a couple of weeks. And then he must have left, for gradually she accepted the fact that he was gone and not coming back and she started to eat and to carry her tail a little higher. But to this day she has never jumped for joy again.

Bubba's offerings were a daily event but I'd grown wary of them. They were exquisite little wreaths and woven lengths of all sorts of strange berries and dried flowers and leaves, which I'd been tossing on the backs of chairs and throwing out once they were no longer fresh. There was always another. But the berries had a way of falling to the floor and the leaves would crumble, and I was convinced that Jackie had eaten one or some and that may have been the cause of his death. I refused to lose two dogs that way, shouldn't have lost the one. But I'd been so preoccupied and self-centered and—and paranoid—I hadn't been careful enough about sweeping and vacuuming. Probably I shouldn't bring them into the house at all.

I measured time by Warren's ponytail. Those lank ends were now long enough to be held in a rubber band. He was thrilled.

Sam Pollock and Joe stopped by with a handcuffed prisoner whom they asked me to identify. A large, bulging-muscled tattooed man with an untrimmed beard and a massive head of hair wearing ragged jeans and a vest over a bare chest and bare feet in the middle of winter. He was a retired biker who'd been living out on the shoals in a tent. They'd happened on him because one of his arrows had hit a fishing boat and torn a hole in it. Subsequent investigation coordinated with the Coast Guard revealed a person swimming in the ocean with air temperatures hovering around thirty-five.

"I'm a polar bear," the man said. "I swim every day. In snow . . . I break the ice. The polar bear shot an arrow in the air—It fell to earth I know not where," he told us.

"Ever see him before?"

"Never."

"You sure?"

"Sam, I'd remember *him!*"

He said, "Miss Sarah Taylor, she had her back to the water?"

"Yes, she did."

"And this turkey's been shootin' those lethal weapons into the air for some time now. He had a lot of them out there which we have now confiscated. It's the same kinda arrow that hit Miss Sarah Taylor. Huntin' arrow. We're about to book him on suspicion of murder."

"You can't hurt me. I'm the strongest man in the world. I swim in the great Atlantic Ocean every day rain or shine snow sleet or hail. I could break these cuffs if I wanted to but I don't want to. I'm a good person. I'm a vegetarian—" And they led him back to the car. Just another crazy. So Sarah Taylor's death was a hideous accident in the midst of all those murders. I *know* they were murders. I'm totally convinced that they were.

Eulalee came to bring me some blood strengthener. A quart of it. She wanted me to drink it in her presence. I told her I'd just had breakfast. I'd have some for my afternoon snack instead of tea. She wasn't too happy about that. Grumbled something about, "When I go to all this trouble, finding the herbs and gathering the berries and steeping and grinding—"

"Eulalee," I interrupted, "I see someone's been cleaning the Davis house after the Tryons."

She was immediately distracted. "Yes . . . Mary Duncan Davis . . ."

"So the Davises have got the house back?"

"Mary Tryon, Luther's wife, she said she wouldn't live in another woman's house, especially Sammy Jo's. So Judge Davis made some kind of a settlement . . . and it's back in the family, thank heaven."

"Amen to that."

"Judge Davis wasn't about to sit still and watch his family home that his mama was born in and her mama and he and the whole family—you know they used to have a special room in the back near the kitchen for birthin' babies—and another room—a little parlor in the front for the layin' outs—he was not about to permit that house to be desecrated like that . . . not for long."

"It was fate that brought Mary Tryon back to Davis Landing, wasn't it?"

"No it wasn't. It was Judge Davis."

I stopped rocking.

"He has his ways. Her letter said she was goin' to Florida so it was pretty easy to have her traced down there. She was in Tampa livin' it up. Once he found her he sent her a photograph of the house. Just a snap he had someone take. What you get from a passing car. But it showed Luther very clearly and it showed those trashy women with him. And then he got another one of those young'uns and the car they'd bin drivin'. That one wasn't as clear, but you could see it was Luther's car and you could see it was Luther's young'uns. Judge Davis is one smart man, i'nt he?"

When she finally got up to leave she said, ever so sweetly, "Merrie Lee sugah, I hope you're not just throwin' out my blood strengthener once I'm outa heah . . ."

"Eulalee, how could you *think* such a thing—"

"Cause I'm lookin' at you, honey. All that good blood strengthener I bin givin' you, you should be a lot fu'ther along than you are . . . I may just have to hold you down and feed it to you myself."

Although it was said with a kittenish giggle and a coquette's backward glance over the shoulder, she left me with an uneasy feeling. I unscrewed the top off the jar, sniffed, and immediately hurried into the kitchen and dumped it. I told Warren how nervous I was.

"She's an old lady, for Chrissake! Look, if she tackles you, just give a shout."

"What if you're not here?"

"Merrie, you're not *serious?*"

"You're not always here."

"You could kill her with one forehand drive—"

"What if you're not here? Then what?"

"I'm always here."

Chapter 27

◆

◆ Warren had been talking to Sam Pollock and the two of them had come up with a list of the dead women. JP had been researching with Lisa's help, and according to Warren's computer, this is what it all added up to:

Miss Emily: Eulalee could have wanted her out of the way. Sam says the town expected Eulalee to take over from Miss Emily when the time came. Miss Emily's time didn't come. Eulalee became the perennial vice-president waiting in wings. Motivated by years of frustration Eulalee decided to kill rival. Administered lethal herb or flower potion? Death caused by heart failure. Could have been natural heart failure.

Sammy Jo: Too beautiful, too attractive to men, Eulalee was jealous, had access, was giving her home remedies. Death caused by heart failure. Could have been natural heart failure.

Elvira Lewis: Eulalee had access. Possible motive: Sam says Eulalee wanted to open herbal apothecary shop. Husband of Elvira willing to be principal backer. Elvira convinced him he'd lose investment, husband pulled out. Motive: revenge. Death caused by heart failure, could have been caused by Eulalee's remedies. Could have been just heart failure.

Sarah Taylor: Accidental death by arrow.

What it all added up to was a big fat zero. No conclusive evidence.

But Eulalee was always there, brewing up her medicines, scrubbing floors, Eulalee . . . it couldn't be possible. Saint Eulalee. The women were no longer young . . . their deaths could all have been due to natural causes, except Sarah Taylor's, of course. I wondered who the next one would be. Lots of people in town were wondering the same thing.

I'd taken to asking Warren what his plans were for the day and where he expected to be, and that made him very irritable as he didn't like to have to make plans for a whole day. He liked to "play it by ear." If I asked him his answer was always, "How do I know?" He said the best part of being down here was not being committed to a schedule. Free as air. If he wanted to do tennis in the morning, okay. If he wanted to write in the morning and do tennis in the afternoon that was okay. How did he know when he'd feel like writing? When you were writing a novel and working out plot points you never knew. It wasn't like sitting down with your calculator and working on numbers like the market. You never knew when inspiration would hit you. I wanted to keep things good between us so I tried not to ask him.

Eulalee came back with another quart of her foul brew and brought Bubba with her. Bubba brought an exquisite little colonial bouquet of dried flowers set in a lace paper doilie and a strand of woven leaves and berries almost a yard long. He seemed to be more agitated than usual. They were both immaculate and rather dressy. Bubba had his hair plastered down and his leather shoes were highly shined. Real leather down here is unexpected and signals a special occasion.

I was totally relaxed, as Warren was working away at his computer and would hear me if I screamed or even called, but just as Eulalee was asking how he was, he leaped out of the office in his tennis whites with all his rackets and a new can of balls, said a hasty "hi," and something about working out the kinks in his mind as well as in his neck and shoulders, and that would probably take all afternoon playing hard!

Eulalee said they were so sorry they wouldn't be havin' a chance to visit with him. I tried to send plaintive signals that

I didn't want to be alone with them but I never really expected him to get them.

As soon as he went slamming out the door she said she was so fond of Warren and people didn't see much of him anymore. I explained that this was because he was constantly busy at his computer when he wasn't checking the court or fussing over it or playing on it. She said all of Davis Landing appreciated what he'd done with the court and how hard he'd worked and the money he'd raised. They did appreciate. And now he and JP helpin' coach the young'uns. Everybody appreciated.

I offered them tea or Pepsi but they declined. We sat down to talk about the weather. Bubba had nothing to contribute but rapid breathing. Then Eulalee and I discussed what I planned to do to get the house ready for showing. Was that next month already? I told her I planned to clean it. She had thought I'd be doin' some paintin'. I said no, we didn't intend to paint. And the garden? Some plantin'? No, nothing out there. Maybe freshen up the pine straw mulch. That would be about all. Prune the shrubs here and there if they needed it. She told me most people, when they showed their houses, they dressed them up special. I said people would just have to accept us as we are.

Bubba kept up that fluttery breathing. I asked him if I couldn't bring him something? Iced tea? Water? An oatmeal cookie? He nodded to "cookie." I excused myself and went into the kitchen.

While I was fixing a tray with glasses and little plates and oatmeal cookies and iced tea, I was thinking how foolish I'd been to be afraid. Warren was right, I had gone over the edge into paranoia. Writing my own scenario about this little town. How silly to think that Eulalee, well-meaning, hard-working Eulalee, had ever harmed anyone. Or that there was anything to fear in poor Bubba.

We had a very pleasant little social hour, Eulalee and I, gossiping about the locals. How different it was across the street with the Tryons gone and Mary Duncan Davis there with the judge. She was a real good housekeeper and he was mighty lucky to have her there runnin' his life for him. She seemed content enough not to have a life of her own, but she wasn't young and Eulalee supposed it was more important at her age to have the security of a roof over her head. As for Judge Davis, he got the best housekeeper in town for free.

"Sometimes he gives her a poke," Bubba said, and laughed.

Eulalee said, "Bubba! Do you want me to lock you in the van for talkin' like that? Do you?!"

He was reduced to instant silence except for his breathing, which was even more agitated.

"Tell Miss Merrie Lee you're sorry!"

He stared at his shoes. "Sorry. . . ."

"Say it right, Bubba, or *you'll* be sorry! Say, Miss Merrie Lee, I'm sorry I said that vulgar, untrue thing. *Say it*, Bubba! If you want to keep your bunny rabbit—"

I protested that it wasn't necessary. I said, "I know Bubba's sorry he said that vulgar, untrue thing, aren't you, Bubba? I know you are!"

He nodded.

And I said, "Anyone like more iced tea?"

Eulalee said, "We'll talk about this when we get home, Bubba. You haven't heard the end of it yet."

He looked frightened.

"I think I'll get us some more cookies, okay, Bubba? Excuse me."

I could hear them arguing all the way back in the kitchen. They sounded very angry. I wondered what their home life was like and if it was true, what some people said, that for a long time she'd kept him chained in a small room at the top of the house. Poor Bubba . . . chained in the house . . . locked in the van. . . .

When I got back to my guests they were quiet and peaceful once more. Bubba reached for a cookie and Eulalee said she just couldn't say no, they were the best things she'd ever tasted. Besides my brownies, of course. She guessed *they* were

"Do you want it from the cup? By the spoon? Or you want to suck it up through the straw? It's up to you, darlin'."

"Eulalee"—I pushed the mug away—"I just don't want any now—I've been telling you—"

She was holding me down. "Bubba, you come on over heah and help me give Miss Merrie Lee her medicine. Come on over."

He walked behind me and put both hands on my shoulders.

"There we are." She spread the dish towel over my lap. "Don't want to spill, do we?"

"Eulalee, I don't want to play this game." I tried to laugh as I pushed the mug away.

"We don't want to do that, sugah, don't want to spill." She was laughing. "It would be so much easier if you'd be a good little girl and drink it down, now wouldn't it, darlin'?"

I tried to get up but Bubba's hands were very strong. He was quite determined to hold me down and his sister was equally determined to get the stuff into me. I didn't for a minute believe she would care that much about putting the roses back in my cheeks. But she was a sore loser, that's for sure.

"Eulalee." I pulled at the napkin, laughing. "I'll have it for a nightcap, how's that?"

She was laughing too. "This is so silly, darlin'. I'nt this just the silliest thing? Let's do it *now!*" She grabbed my head and held it with one hand while with the other she tipped the mug against my lips. I pushed at her hand and managed to knock the thing to the floor.

"Oh, I'm so sorry! I hope it's not broken!"

"It's not broken," she said. "But we have made a real mess on Miss Lavinia's oriental! Just look at that. I had better get somethin' to clean it up before it sinks in and makes a permanent stain."

"I'm really sorry—"

"That's all right, darlin'. I'll just he'p myself to some of your cleanin' things." She disappeared into the kitchen.

I took off my bib. Every drop of those calories had gone

211

into the rug. But when I tried to stand, Bubba's hands held me down. "Bubba, the game's over."

"No it ain't. She comin' back."

"It's over, Bubba. I'm not going to drink that stuff."

"Ma'am, this thing ain't over. I know."

"How do you know?"

"I see this game before."

"When is it over?"

"When sister say it is."

Now I was quite sure I was destined to go the way of all the others. Heart failure. So this is how they did it. The two of them. Although I was sure the other women hadn't offered this much resistance, if any. That stuff was *poison*. Probably fairly quick acting so I wouldn't have a chance to tell anyone. I tried to stand again. Not a chance. "Bubba, you like pretty things, don't you?"

"I like flowers and pretty leaves and grass and birds and little bunny rabbits—"

"And pretty kittens and puppies—"

"And bunny rabbits and baby squirrels—I like them a lot and if I'm good Sister lets me have a pet until I'm bad and then she makes me watch till it's dead."

"And you like pretty ladies, don't you?" I kept watching the kitchen door.

"I like you. You're pretty. Sister don't like it when I like a pretty lady. Then we have to hurt her. I don't want to hurt pretty ladies."

"Of course you don't. You're a lovely man!"

I was twisted to look into his face. That had struck a chord. What was the key word? Lovely? *Man?* "Bubba, you're a fine man!" That was it. He was beaming. "You'd never want to do anything bad, would you, fine man like you?"

"But I have to do bad things when Sister say to do them—"

Eulalee came bustling out of the kitchen. "Merrie Lee, honey, you changed everythin' around on me since I was heah takin' care of you. I swear I couldn't find a thing. You moved all youah cleanin' thangs to another cupboard." She was on her knees, scooping up the calories with a damp rag. "This is goin' pick up fine and it's not goin' stain. You'll see. I mixed up a little club soda heah, take it right out." She was on her knees, scrubbing away. "And you might just sprinkle some boric acid powder around in that kitchen, keeps down the roaches better than anything."

Was I imagining, or did she think I was stupid? I tried to stand.

Bubba didn't think so.

"I'll just take these rags inside and wrinch 'em out and then we'll be all ready for another try at the blood strengthener. Be right back." And she was off, busy as could be, back to the kitchen.

"Bubba, would you let me up, please?"

"Sister don't say."

"A fine man like you doesn't have to listen to his sister all his life. You're a grown *man*! You don't want to do bad things to pretty ladies, do you? You don't want to hurt me, do you, Bubba? Bubba dear? Bubba darlin'? You don't, do you?"

"You pretty lady. I don't want to hurt you."

"Then let me go."

"I can't do that."

"Yes, you can."

Eulalee was back, full of energy, ready to go.

"Now let's get the napkin back on her—the towels, we have to straighten the towels on her lap."

She was compulsive about things being lined up.

"There we are! Now we'll fill the cup again—and here we go! Hold tight, Bubba!"

I tried to knock the mug away.

"Hold her arms."

She was forcing my mouth open, holding my jaws where they hinged and forcing them open, a technique I'd used many times to get pills down my dogs. It hurt. Some of the stuff went into my mouth. I struggled, spitting it out, spitting and spitting and gagging and spitting and struggling—and suddenly I was standing. Free. And Eulalee was on the floor with

Bubba's garland wrapped around her neck and Bubba kneeling beside her and holding it there. Eulalee's face was dark, her eyes popping.

"Bubba! That's enough!" I tried to pull his hands away but they were tight on the garland. Eulalee went limp. Garotted by the prettiest garland you ever saw. "Bubba!"

"I did bad thing."

". . . I think she's dead."

"That's good thing."

"I have to call the police."

"Yes, ma'am."

"They'll put you in jail."

"Yes, ma'am. With other people. No chains."

He stood up.

I phoned 911.

We sat together and waited for the police.

"Sister do bad things. She hurt my bunny rabbit. Break his legs. He screaming. She hurt my kitten. Hold kitten in fire until it dead. Hurt Vicki bad. She make me do bad things. She don't like pretty lady—"

"Who's Vicki?"

"Pretty sister."

"You had another sister?"

"Pretty pretty—dead."

"How did she die?"

"Pretty pretty pretty. She like flowers, all kinds of flowers. Pretty pretty."

"You must tell the police. Tell them everything."

"Yes, ma'am."

"Did you hurt Miss Emily?"

"No, ma'am. Sister make her present. Lemon chutney. Hot pepper, mistletoe berries. She eat a lot. Whole jar."

"Did you hurt Miss Sammy Jo?"

"No, ma'am. Miss Sammy Jo too pretty. Sister say she too pretty. She make oleander tea."

"How about Elvira Lewis?"

"We d'int hurt Miss Elvira!"

"You tell the police that. Be sure and tell the police."

"Yes, ma'am. You help me?"

"I will."

I held his hand while we waited. He was perfectly calm and steady. I tried not to look at Eulalee on the floor with her tongue out and a neckful of leaves.

Then I heard Warren's truck.

Bubba dropped my hand.

Warren came into the house beaming. "Got something for you," he said, stepping over Eulalee. "I stopped at the post office on my way to the court and I started a game but then I thought why make her wait?" And he pulled thirty inches of ten and a half millimeter pearls out of his pocket. "You know that stock I thought was risky but it was so cheap? The biotech stock? Well, they're cloning fir trees with DNA to cure cancer and I sold not even half of it—for this—and we've got all the rest of it and it's going up every day." He had to step around Eulalee to fasten the pearls on my neck. "I could have gift wrapped them but I wanted you to know we've got *money* again." He was staring at Eulalee on the floor. "Holy shit!"

And then Sam Pollock and Joe Donovan were there and they called Beau Johnson to come get Eulalee. I asked about Vicki. Sam said, "Yeah, she was purty! She'd sit out on her po'ch swing and every boy and man in town was settin' on that railing. Some that shouldn't be there at all. Hard on Miss Eulalee, havin' a younger sister be the town beauty."

"How did Vicki die?"

"Eulalee and Vicki took Bubba out on the shoals for a picnic and Vicki must have fallen into the water and drowned. The whole town mourned Vicki. So pretty and she was about to be married the next month. Joe just about broke his heart. That's prob'ly why he turned aroun' and married Eulalee. But they weren't married too long when he up and shot hisself. Yes, Miss Eulalee had a right hard life."

"I do bad thing to pretty Vicki. Sister tell me."

Sam turned to Bubba and whipped out his notebook. "Now, Bubba, let's hear all about it. You can tell me."

He sat and took Bubba's statement in his usual calm and businesslike way, declining even a Pepsi. Then Beau Johnson collected Eulalee and Sam and Joe Donovan took Bubba away. I promised to come and see him. Poor man.

Chapter 28

♦

• That night, over our Greek salads, we discussed the possibility of returning to New York. Warren felt quite positive we'd have enough money. He said I'd been hankering to get back there for so long he was tired of it, and if we gave the tenants three months' notice, according to our lease, we could get our own place back. I'd forgotten about the cancellation clause. There had never been any reason to think about it. We'd been clinging to that rent check for dear life. Then he told me he'd sent the first hundred pages of the novel with an outline to a very good agent and he'd gotten a very enthusiastic reply. Warren likes to keep things to himself, good or bad. Close-mouthed.

We started calling our city friends. I was very hyper. Kept telling everyone our exile was over! The refugees were coming back to the homeland! They immediately started planning parties for us! I had to dig out our daybook, find the right month, start making dates. Lunches. Brunches. Dinners. Cocktails. Weekends. Very exciting. I looked at my hands. Ugh. Rubber-glove time. And my hair. Color and cut time. Have to call Mary Farr.

About ten o'clock, past my bedtime, I took Mathilda out for a little stroll. The night was very quiet. Not a soul on the streets. I let her walk without a leash. She was very good that way. I wondered how she'd readjust to the city. Without Jackie. With all that noise. And people. And filth in the streets.

That night in bed I asked Warren if we'd have enough money for clothes for me. "Unless they've taken to wearing jeans and sweats up there I'm going to need a whole new wardrobe. And little black dresses are about a thousand dollars give or take the tax."

"How many of those do you need?"

I mentioned my concern about Mathilda's adjusting to city life. Especially without Jackie to guide her and then started to cry at the thought of leaving Jackie behind.

Warren gave me his red bandana to cry into. "Listen," he said, "I've been thinking. This is the perfect place for me to finish the novel. I mean, we could go up there for a bit and see our friends and eat some great food, but then we could come back here again. How about that?"

"Ideal," I said.

"Go up there, see the agent, discuss the book, come back here and finish it."

"Totally ideal."

"We could spend winters here," he said. "New York winters are almost as bad as the Dakotas. When that wind blows along the streets from river to river."

"Everyone's away for the winter anyway."

"Summers when it gets too hot and touristy here we could charter a boat in Greece or Turkey—"

"Weekend in the Hamptons—"

"This would be our home base," he said. "Feels like home to me."

"Fine."

"Real people."

"Right."

"Legal residence. Tax base."

"Right."

* * *

This town. I swear you'd think *I* had personally strangled Eulalee myself! These people actually *resent* the murders being exposed! Not that there was any noise about it. Believe me, when they want to keep something to themselves here, they know all the ways to stifle a story. Nothing ever got out. I mean, it's not like the town got a bad reputation or anything, but they seem to feel *I* could have given Davis Landing a major black eye given half a chance! They resent *me*! Oh well, it's that clannish thing. Eulalee was one of their own, and although I'm a born Davis, I'm still considered a foreigner. And a troublemaker. Conversations tend to stop when I get within hearing. Superficially it's all smiles and "Good moanin's" as usual. But my feeling is that's pure facade. Warren is saying paranoia. But he's wrong. My intuition is telling me different. Well, maybe if we ever leave as planned they'll appreciate us when we come back. It's me, really. They have nothing against Warren. I bring poor Bubba a batch of oatmeal cookies and brownies about once a week. He's so grateful. Nobody else ever goes to see him. I bring flowers and dried leaves and berries (nonpoisonous), and I've given him watercolors and a couple of lessons in the technique and a lot of paper. That man is more peaceful and happier than he's ever been in his life.

We haven't given the tenants their three months' notice yet. Warren's agent told him that there was a better chance of selling the book if it were finished. And once my husband got so adorably expansive with that gorgeous string of pearls, biotech stocks dropped with a thud. So we are not yet able to afford living anywhere without that rent check. That new life out of this swamp hole and filled with luxuries is necessarily on hold.

Meanwhile I've decided to be just as two-faced as they are. If they can resent me bitterly and cover it all up with smiles and graciousness, well, I can be gracious and smiling, too. While resenting their attitude as deeply unfair. But they'll never know I know how they feel. Warren and I are closer than ever which makes me feel a little disloyal when I wear Zio

Roberto's pearl. I toyed with the idea of throwing it into the sea and dramatically renouncing all fooling around. But practical thinking intervened. I will not wear it, but I will not throw it away either. It's too valuable. However much, hundreds or thousands, it's worth something and can be useful if we need it. So I'm putting it in my little satin travel jewel case. That way, whenever I'm feeling depressed I can look at it and remember that I am a living, breathing, attractive woman.

The day of the Historic Homes Tour was a pretty day, the first day of almost springlike temperatures. Warren and I were in costume, standing on our front porch, smiling, telling strangers it was good of them to come barreling through our house, peering into corners.

We heard them as they left: the exit polls so to speak. "Fabulous bathroom! Where could they ever replace those fixtures today? The overhead flush? And all that wood? And the pump in the kitchen? It still works. I tried it!"

I smiled at Warren from under my mobcap. He leaned on his musket and winked at me.